287
009

Praise

ANGIE AMALFI Series

"A winner . . . Angie is a character
unlike any other found in the genre."
Santa Rosa Press Democrat

"Pence's tongue-in-cheek humor keeps us grinning."
San Francisco Chronicle

"A tasty treat for all mystery and suspense
lovers who like food for thought, murder,
and a stab at romance."
Armchair Detective

"This series just keeps getting better and better."
Literary Times

"Joanne Pence is a master chef."
Mystery Scene

"Deliciously wicked . . . Don't miss one tasty bite."
Jacqueline Girder

Other Angie Amalfi Mysteries by
Joanne Pence

TO CATCH A COOK

A COOK

AN ANGIE AMALFI MYSTERY

JOANNE PENCE

AVON BOOKS
An Imprint of HarperCollinsPublishers

AVON BOOKS
An Imprint of HarperCollins*Publishers*
10 East 53rd Street
New York, New York 10022-5299

Copyright © 2000 by Joanne Pence
ISBN: 0-06-103085-6
www.avonbooks.com

First Avon Books paperback printing: November 2000

Avon Trademark Reg. U.S. Pat. Off. and in Other Countries, Marca Registrada, Hecho en U.S.A.
HarperCollins® is a trademark of HarperCollins Publishers Inc.

Printed in the U.S.A.

OPM   10 9 8 7 6 5 4 3 2 1

ACKNOWLEDGMENTS

Many people generously gave their time, knowledge, and insight to help me pull together the elements of this book. First of all, thanks to everyone on Clues-N-News, particularly Jan Daugherty, a font of understandable medical knowledge, and to Amy Sikes Haskins (and her mother, Monti, who got us together), Joe Fernandez, Liz Jennings, Erika Lockhart, and Barbara Truax. Extra special thanks go to my agent, Sue Yuen, for her help, patience, and wonderful suggestions; to my editors, Carolyn Marino for believing in Angie and Paavo, and Jeffery McGraw for his infectious enthusiasm; and of course, to my husband, David, who's always there to help me get "unstuck."

Writing this book deepened my appreciation and admiration for those in my family who, as young people alone or with family members, crossed troubled seas searching for a better life in the United States. This book is dedicated to the memories of those adventurous voyagers: Francisco Lopez, Esperanza (Ida) Moldes, Guiseppe Addiego, and Michelina (Madeline) Lucchese.

Chapter 1

San Francisco Homicide Inspector Paavo Smith wrenched himself awake in the dark bedroom. He didn't move, but listened, searching for sounds that existed only in his head. When all remained quiet, he slowly collected himself, calmed his racing pulse, and reassembled himself into the now of his existence. He was a cop; he'd seen firsthand the living nightmares men foisted upon one another. There was no reason his imagination should bother him this way. For it to do so was unacceptable.

Abruptly he sat up in bed and ran a hand over his eyes, against his nose. A small ripple of cartilage marked where it had been broken. Most people assumed the break had come as a result of police work, but the first time he had broken it, he'd been wrestling with his older sister. She had raised her head just as he lowered his own, and the world exploded. For a couple of months his nose looked like it was heading leftward, while his eyes and mouth aimed straight ahead.

That Jessica came to mind now made sense. She'd been in his nightmare. It was an old dream, but recently he'd begun having it again—three

1

times in the past few weeks, each time more vivid than the last.

He stood up, his body slick with sweat. At the foot of the quilt-covered bed his yellow tabby, Hercules, lifted his head, twitched an ear, and yowled with annoyance at having his sleep disturbed. Paavo left the lights off and paced the room, rubbing his forehead, as if through physical force he could shove the alarming memories away.

The dream wouldn't bother him half so much if he could figure out what it meant. The nightmare placed him in a shoot-out. He had been in a few since joining the force, but had never experienced the stark terror that filled him in the dream. He was low on ammunition, trapped, with no way out, and the worst part was that Jessica was with him.

Yet when she died, he'd been only fourteen years old.

Most likely she'd been on his mind because of the brooch that had belonged to their mother, a cameo of a woman's profile in a gold setting. Jessica had never liked it and refused to wear it. She was into grunge before there was such a style. Brooches weren't "her thing."

At Christmas Paavo thought of the brooch while trying to come up with a meaningful gift for his girlfriend, Angie, who had enough money to buy herself anything she wanted twice over. Although it was only costume jewelry, the design was beautiful and delicate and elegant. Just like Angie. Its sentimental value, he knew, was something she would also appreciate.

Seeing it, holding it, must have stirred up recollections of his family, what little family he had. They then could have jumbled together in his head with current thoughts and blended his life as a police officer with memories of his sister. That was the only explanation he could think of. Guns had never entered his life as a child, he didn't think. And yet . . .

He wished whatever the hell was causing this nightmare to surface would stop. Now, with Angie in his life, he was happier than he had ever been. He didn't want to remember the past, the days of his childhood; he didn't even want to talk about them, and didn't.

Still, from the dream, an awful dread hovered over him, as if an omen of what was to come.

Angie Amalfi thrust a handful of money at the Yellow Cab driver. "Keep the change." In a waft of Quelques Fleurs and a mint-green Donna Karan silk suit, she dashed from the taxi to a small jewelry shop on California Street. Gold lettering over the shop proclaimed ROSE JEWELRY, LTD., and an OPEN sign dangled on the front door.

Inside, recessed lights shone onto walnut-framed glass counters set in a U shape along the back and side walls. Gold- and platinum-set stones and diamonds were tastefully displayed on black velvet. Atop each long counter was a rectangular mirror on a lacquered stand, while more mirrors discreetly hung from the paneled walls.

A white-haired man sat at a wooden desk behind the farthest counter. "Thank God you're here," Angie cried, hurrying toward him on dyed-to-match Giacomo Ferre stilettos.

He raised his head. Slowly pushing himself to his feet, he unhooked the jeweler's magnifier from his eyeglasses and placed it on the table. He was quite old, his back curved so badly that even standing upright, he seemed to be searching for something at his feet. He peered at her through bushy gray eyebrows, frowned, and shuffled closer.

"I hope you can help me." Anxiety made her voice shrill. "Mr. Warner at Tiffany's told me you were the only one he knew who did this kind of work."

His eyebrows lifted with interest at the name. Ralph Warner was the senior jeweler at the prestigious store. Shaking, gnarled hands rested on the glass countertop. "What kind of work is it?" His voice was deep and he spoke with an accent, mixing his *v*'s and *w*'s.

"I'll show you." She set down her tiny green Prada handbag and, from a black leather Coach tote, removed a small padded jewelry box. The hinged top opened like a clamshell. "My boyfriend gave me the brooch for Christmas. I was polishing it—the cameo had gotten some dust and dirt in it over the years—and the stone fell out of its setting. You've got to fix it for me!"

His gaze fixed on the brooch. "Oh, my," he murmured.

"It was his mother's," she continued, trying to keep the dejection and panic from her voice. "I can't tell him I broke it. This is so upsetting! I could just die!"

She waited for a word, a reaction, but he gave none. She stopped talking and watched his fascination with the piece. The cameo was oval, an elegant woman's profile carved on rose-hued agate against a black background.

He stared at the broken brooch a long time, then picked up the stone and laid it in the palm of his hand. Touching the stone, his hands had become sure and steady. Moving slowly, he carried the cameo to his desk, carefully placed it on a square of black velvet, and sat. He reattached his magnifying glass and studied the carving under a strong lamp. "Oh, my," he repeated.

"What's wrong?" Angie was practically stretched out across the top of the counter trying to see what he was doing. "Do you think you can fix it?"

Her words seemed to jar him out of his reverie. "Do you know where your friend got this?"

She didn't like the tone of that question. "It was in his family a great many years. That's all I know."

He shuffled back to the counter and used an eyepiece to study the cameo's setting. Surrounding the empty spot where the cameo had been was a gold border made of two rows of what Angie assumed were zircons with a frame of primrose yellow between them. At the top was a flower spray, also set with zircons in gold.

"I can see why your usual jeweler did not want to touch this brooch. It is not mere jewelry, but a work of art."

She was stunned. "It's just a cameo. I didn't think they were all that valuable."

"The perfection of the stone and the quality of the cut make all the difference. Although the diamonds are small, they are perfect, as is the guilloche between them."

Diamonds? Angie knew diamonds. She had beautiful earrings and a pendant necklace. The brooch had so many stones that she couldn't imagine they were anything but fake.

"Do not worry," he continued, studying her reaction. "I can fix the brooch for you. I am one of the few people in the country who can do it."

"Thank goodness!" She found her voice. "You don't know what a relief that is to me."

"Tell me, would you consider selling this piece?" he asked. "I am sure I could find some collectors of fine Russian jewelry who would be willing to pay quite handsomely for it. Work like this is almost impossible to find outside of museums these days."

"Russian? The piece is Russian?"

"Of course. The profile is most certainly that of the Tsarina Alexandra. It is . . . er . . . similar to jewelry exhibited at the Hermitage in Saint Petersburg."

"Really?" She was bewildered. How could Paavo's mother have come to own such a piece? Angie had always assumed his mother was an American. Was she wrong? Had the woman been Russian? "Well, no matter. I would never sell it—and since it belonged to his mother, I'm sure my boyfriend wouldn't want to sell it either."

"You might ask him. What is his family name, by the way?"

"Smith. Why?"

"I thought he might be Russian . . . that he might even be someone I know."

"No. I doubt he's Russian. His first name is Paavo, but he's probably not Finnish, either."

He glanced at her quickly, then turned back to the stone. "Finnish . . . I see."

"Excuse me?" Angie asked.

"Be sure to ask him if he's interested in selling. And if not . . ." He shrugged. "I'll give you a receipt for the brooch." He handed her a sales pad. "Please write down your name, address, and telephone number in case I need to reach you."

Angie jotted down the information.

He wrote "cameo brooch repair," signed with a scrawl, and gave her a copy. She looked at the identification printed at the top—*Rose Jewelry, Ltd., Gregor Rosinsky, Prop.* "I'll call you in a week, maybe more," he said.

"A week?" How was she going to explain to Paavo why she wasn't wearing the present he'd given her? She had worn it almost every time they'd been together over the past month since receiving it.

"Please call me if it's ready any sooner," she pleaded.

"Of course," he said. He turned his back on her as he again walked to his desk, then slowly, painfully, sat down. "Good-bye."

Gregor Rosinsky waited until the woman had gone. He read the name and address she had written, then picked up the telephone.

Chapter 2

The top of Russian Hill was the highest spot in the northern sector of San Francisco. From there, cable cars made a long descent to the Bay, Alcatraz in the distance. There, tourists massed and drove their cars down the "crookedest street in the world." And there, Angelina Amalfi lived in an elegant apartment on the top floor of a twelve-story building owned by her father.

Paavo had always thought of Angie's home as a quiet haven in a world of brutal madness. That was why he'd been so shaken by the call he'd received from her earlier that day—four hours earlier, in fact. Four guilt-laden hours.

He stepped off the elevator and hurried down the hall. Only two apartments were on each floor, one on each side of the hallway. Angie's door was wide-open. Paavo entered to find crime scene investigators combing the apartment. Closet doors and drawers were open, their contents strewn on the floor.

"Hey, Paavo!" Ben Chan greeted him while he hovered over a dusting of fingerprint powder. "We're just getting started."

"Good. I appreciate you coming by," Paavo said as he scanned the area for Angie, without success.

"Your girlfriend's right next door. She's fine."

"Thanks, Ben." Paavo crossed the hall and pounded on Stanfield Bonnette's door. Angie's neighbor was the last person he wanted to see just then. On the way to becoming a young bank executive solely through family influence, the guy was a choice piece of work. Paavo found him obnoxious and lazy. Angie seemed to like him.

Instead of Bonnette, Angie pulled open the door.

She was just a little woman, almost a foot shorter than his own six feet two inches. He often forgot how small she was since she loomed so large in his life. Her skin was creamy, with the slight olive cast of the Mediterranean. Her hair would have been chocolate brown, but she had added some red streaks to it—highlights, she called them. She said red hair was "in" these days. He liked her natural color better, but that was the sort of opinion he knew enough to keep to himself. Her eyes were big and brown, the skin beneath them and on her brow pinched and drawn with worry.

As she looked at him, her eyes calmed, and she smiled. "Thank God," she whispered.

Relief filled him and he opened his arms to her. "I'm sorry it took me so long. Are you all right?"

She took the comfort he offered. "It was a shock, that's all." Cupping the back of her head, he held her close. With all the grim experience of a homicide inspector, he knew what might have happened had she been home instead of out when the break-in occurred. The harsh world of the streets reminded him of how fragile she was, how easily and unexpectedly disaster could strike, and how tenuous happiness could be.

Whoever broke into the building had to know

how to get past the doorman, or how to sneak in through the garage, one of the service entrances, or an emergency exit without setting off alarms. Finally, they had to get past Angie's dead bolt lock. Professional tools would be needed to enter, not kid's stuff, although, for a pro, the security measures represented more of a minor inconvenience than a major obstacle.

Angie took a deep breath, then stepped back. Holding Paavo's hand, she led him into Bonnette's apartment and shut the door. "What did they steal?" he asked.

"Nothing as far as I could tell. Either something scared them, or they just didn't like my taste." She forced a smile, but her face was pale and her eyes appeared even larger than usual. "When I arrived home, I noticed the dead bolt wasn't on. I thought I might have forgotten to set it, but as soon as I saw the mess inside, I turned around and ran over here to Stan's."

Stan was lounging on a gray and blue plaid sofa, one arm dangling over the back. He wore a turquoise short-sleeved polo shirt, his light brown Hugh Grant hair flopping casually onto his brow. "I was sick today," he said by way of explanation for not being at work. The thirty-year-old had a problem with his job—he never went to it. "It was a lucky thing, too," he added, with a flick of his head that made his hair fly back off his face. "This way at least *someone* was with Angie in her hour of need."

Paavo frowned and slipped his arm around Angie's waist. As much as he'd wanted to come to her as soon as he learned that her apartment had been burglarized, he was in court waiting to testify in a murder case. He couldn't walk out.

The best he'd been able to do was to talk Ben

Chan and the crime scene technicians into checking out Angie's apartment.

Now her neighbor was rubbing salt in the wound. He shouldn't let Stan get to him, but the guy always did.

"Angie, I'm sorry I couldn't be here sooner," he said.

"It's okay," she said. "I understand."

"We were fine, Inspector," Stan said. "Just fine. When the cops arrived, I was right by Angie's side as she went through her apartment to see if anything was stolen. I made sure she was safe."

Paavo tried to ignore Bonnette's taunts. "Did you see anything odd or hear any noise from Angie's apartment while she was out?"

"No. As I said, I'd been sick. I was in bed with the TV on."

Paavo turned to Angie. "How long were you away?"

"Oh . . . a couple of hours. I went out to breakfast with my sister, Bianca. I came up with an idea for a business, and wanted to run it past her. Finding a great job or starting a new business is my number one New Year's resolution." Her eyes caught his and a light blush touched her cheeks. "Well, number two, actually, but who's counting? Anyway, Bianca didn't think gourmet dog biscuits were a great concept. So I came home, and found the break-in."

Paavo didn't comment on her business idea. He had to agree with Bianca, though—the market for gourmet dog biscuits seemed a bit narrow. "I'd better go talk to the crime scene techs," he said, hesitating to leave Angie so soon, particularly after Stan's jab. But she knew it had to be done and sent him on his way.

Now that he had seen for himself that she was safe, he was able to return to her apartment and feel some satisfaction that the technicians were there looking for clues to the break-in. So many home burglaries took place in this city that they rarely got more than the time of day from the police, especially if nothing had been stolen. Still, the victim was Angie. He wanted to catch and jail the lowlife responsible. He should get some benefit from his years as a cop.

"Thanks for helping here, Ben," he said.

"No problem, Paavo. Angie's a good woman, and as close to family as you can get without being family." Ben paused, then continued with weighted deliberation. "Of course, you can change that . . . if you know what I mean."

Paavo shot him an icy glance. Another cop playing matchmaker.

Ben chuckled. Everyone loved kidding Paavo about his nervousness at the thought of marriage. It was more than that, though. Much more; more than he wanted to explain.

When he turned, he saw Angie standing in the doorway, her arms folded and her eyes sad as she watched strangers going through her designer clothes and expensive knickknacks and antique furnishings. She loved good clothes, fine food, and beautiful artwork and music. She had the money to support those loves. Even standing there in cream-colored slacks and pink silk blouse with cream piping, to his mind she personified delicate and refined. The strangest thing about her was that for some reason she loved him. Who was it who said a woman was a contradiction wrapped in an enigma? That was Angie.

He tore his gaze from her and surveyed her apartment, room by room. A nervous prickle touched his spine. It didn't look like a burglary; it looked like a search.

He returned to the living room. Angie was no longer in the apartment. She must have gone back to Stan's.

"What do you think, Ben?" Paavo asked.

"I'd worry, Paavo." Ben Chan had spent years with the S.F.P.D robbery detail. "Between stereo and video equipment, a digital camcorder, a laptop computer, not to mention a Fort Knox worth of jewelry in her bedroom, something should have been taken. But it wasn't. It seems they were looking for something small, easy to hide. All the disruption was done in drawers and cabinets, and places like the top of her closet where she had boxes of souvenirs and the like."

Paavo hadn't wanted to hear a confirmation of his suspicion, but Ben's words rang true. This break-in wasn't random; it was personal. If whoever was behind it hadn't found what he was looking for, he'd be back. What could Angie have that was worth so much trouble? "Any evidence?"

"Nothing jumps out. We'll keep looking."

"I owe you, Ben," Paavo said.

"No problem."

Following the procedure he'd use if this were a homicide, Paavo canvassed the building, talking to neighbors and the doorman. No one had seen any strangers lurking about, or anything at all suspicious.

Finally he returned to Stan's apartment. Angie blanched when she saw his expression, and she stood up. He must not have been as good at hiding his emotions around her as he liked to think. "Why don't you stay at my place a few days?" He tried to sound casual. "Just until we're sure that whoever came here won't return."

What little color she had in her face disappeared completely. "You think they'll be back? But why? What can they possibly want?"

"Most likely they won't return, but I'll feel more comfortable if you aren't here alone in case they do."

She nodded and went to her place to pack. "One bag, Angie," Paavo called. "We can always come back for more later." He remembered the time they'd gone on a cruise. She'd brought so much luggage that if the ship had listed and sunk, she could have been held responsible.

Stan folded his arms. "She can always stay with me, Inspector. At least I'd be around to take care of her when she needs me."

"Bonnette, go f . . . fly a kite."

It was nearly midnight before Angie finished packing and picking up the mess in her apartment. Although she'd been shocked to arrive home and find it broken in to, that was hardly rare in city life. Nothing was stolen; no one was hurt. Life went on. On the other hand, if Paavo wanted to make a big deal out of it and have her stay with him a few days, she wasn't about to complain. Look for the silver lining, her mother always said. And moving in with Paavo for a while was pure gold.

She packed enough to make this a nice, long visit.

Paavo drove a tiny, very old Austin Healey. Her car was a white Ferrari with a tan leather interior. Using both, they could barely manage to fit all her luggage. Maybe it was time for a more practical car . . . perhaps even a family-oriented car. She wondered how she'd like driving an SUV.

Her Ferrari roared to a stop behind his convertible. He was standing on the sidewalk wrestling with a large Fendi suitcase, trying to pull it out of the passenger seat without having to lower the cloth top. The top was temperamental, and one of these days he'd get it down and not be able to put it back up again. She realized that he, more than she, needed to think about a bigger, more up-to-date vehicle.

She stepped up behind him, holding her laptop computer.

Earlier that evening he had loosened his gray and blue tie, and unbuttoned the collar of his white shirt. Because of the day's court appearance, he was wearing a charcoal-gray suit instead of his usual sport coat and dress slacks. Angie admired the view as he bent deeply into his car. He was a handsome man—tall, broad-shouldered, with a slim but physically powerful build. His cheekbones were high and pronounced, his hair dark brown, and dark brows and eyelashes surrounded the bluest eyes she'd ever seen. But there was also a world-weariness lining the corners of his eyes and in the set of his mouth that reminded her he was a man who had seen more than his share of suffering and sorrow.

A hard tug sprung the suitcase free from the tight space in which it had been wedged. "You really didn't have to pack so much stuff," he grumbled. "We're only across town from your apartment."

"I'd hate to discover I'd left something important at home. Besides"—she batted her eyes innocently—"who knows how long I'll need to stay? Anyway, my suitcases all have wheels."

Her gaze swiveled, following his, to the stairs that led up to his front door.

"Once I put things away, you'll hardly notice how much I've brought," she said.

"You'll have plenty of time tomorrow to figure out where to fit it all. I have to go in early. Yosh is on vacation and Rebecca Mayfield has been helping with some of his cases. She's still fairly new and needs a lot of guidance."

"Hmm, what a little helper bee." Angie knew all about Rebecca's crush on Paavo. She especially detested Rebecca's implications that only another cop could understand and be good for him—and that Rebecca was that cop.

He lugged the two big suitcases up the steps and set them on the stoop while fishing the house key from his pocket.

"Actually, I had assumed you wouldn't be home much," she said. This was a good time to show him just how understanding she could be about the demands of his job. "I know how hard you have to work, no matter what's happening in your personal life."

He glanced at her quizzically.

"One of those suitcases is filled with books for me to read while you're out," she said. "I wasn't sure which I'd be in the mood for, so I brought a bunch of them."

"Ah . . . that explains it." He pushed open the door and stepped aside to let her enter first. "I wondered why your clothes were so heavy."

Flicking on the lights, she stepped into the living room and abruptly halted. "Oh, my God." She backpedaled right into him.

One glance at her face and he hurried past her. Hand on his gun, he stopped in the doorway, then drew his 9 mm automatic and moved inside.

Ignoring his whispered demand to remain by the door, Angie followed close as he crossed from room to room. In the living room, books had been strewn onto the floor, sofa and chair cushions ripped open, and desk drawers overturned.

The bedroom had also been torn apart and the mattress slashed. This was far, far more frightening than what had happened to her own apartment. There was anger here, perhaps hatred.

"What is going on?" she cried. "Why would anyone destroy your things?"

"It looks like a search, followed by frustration."

As she wandered through the little house, she realized he was right. It wasn't random destruction as she had first thought, but where the search to her apartment had appeared slow and meticulous, here it was hurried and frenzied.

"Hercules!" he called. "Herc? Come on, boy, are you all right?"

Angie's breath caught. His cat . . . He loved that cat.

"Do you see him?" she asked, standing in the bedroom doorway.

"No. They better not have hurt my cat," he muttered, his jaw clenched. They looked under the bed, in the closets, and throughout the backyard.

She was afraid—and for Hercules, more afraid that they'd find the cat than that they wouldn't. If he had run and was hiding, scared, he should return home eventually, but if he was nearby, and unable to come when called . . .

They couldn't find him.

Finally, back in the living room, Paavo bleakly took in the damage, the ugliness before him. "Who's doing this, Angie, and why?"

Chapter 3

The bellboy wheeled in a cart with Angie's luggage and turned on lamps. Paavo put down his duffel bag and inspected their room at the Huntington, an elegant hotel at the top of Nob Hill. The walls were papered powder blue, and the cream-colored gilded furniture was imitation Louis XIV. The view overlooked Huntington Park and the exclusive Pacific Union Club, from Grace Cathedral to the Fairmont Hotel.

"Didn't I tell you this would be much nicer than sleeping on the floor at your place?" Angie asked, clearly pleased with her choice.

"This is much nicer than my whole house," Paavo remarked as he tipped the porter and locked the door.

"Very funny."

Now, in the hotel room, she looked exhausted. No wonder; it was nearly four o'clock in the morning. They'd spent hours waiting for the police to arrive. During that time, he'd packed a few things and changed out of his suit to Levi's, a maroon pullover, and a brown leather jacket.

"Tomorrow I'll contact my cousin Richie," she said, flopping into a chair. "He might have a house or apartment on the market we can use for a few weeks."

"Let's wait until we see what's going on." He unzipped his duffel bag. "Most people get new locks or a burglar alarm after a break-in, not a whole new place to live."

She watched him a moment, then walked to his side and touched his shoulder, stopping him as he unloaded underwear into a bureau drawer. He straightened, and she eased herself against his chest.

"I think it's wise to be prudent—just as you said when you suggested I stay with you for a while. Oh, maybe I didn't think it was necessary at first, but now I do. My house, then yours? It's bizarre."

Paavo's arms tightened protectively around her. "Tomorrow I'll talk to Ben Chan, get him to check out my place for fingerprints and signs of entry." *And I'll look for Hercules.*

She seemed to study him. "Once he knows it's safe, Hercules will come home," she said, making him wonder once again if she could read his mind or his expression. Most people called him stone-faced, but not Angie.

He brushed a lock of hair back from her forehead and ran his thumb lightly along her cheek, taking in the dark shadows under her eyes. She was so beautiful, so soft . . . and this hotel room was theirs to share . . .

"You'll be fine here," he said, setting her from him. "I'm going to take a shower, eat breakfast, and go to work. It'll be morning soon and I'll feel worse if I try to sleep for just an hour. This way, you can get some sleep."

She firmed her jaw and nodded. "All right." Her voice was a little too husky. She opened a suitcase and pulled out a satin nightgown when suddenly she threw it back into the case. "Just a minute!" Hands on hips, she marched toward him. "On second thought, it's not all right at all. Not at all. Someone broke into both our homes, made your furniture look like it'd been ground up by a Cuisinart, and you're going to work? You've got better things to do, like getting some sleep so you'll have enough energy to find the crook who did it and pulverize him."

"Angie—"

"Even if you're not worried about this, I am. Especially for you! What happened to your home, your things . . . I can't get it out of my head. If anything happens to you—"

He gripped her shoulders. "Take it easy." Moving his hands to her back, he drew her closer. "Nothing's going to happen to me, or you. I'm sure it's not that serious. We'll catch whoever's behind it soon. Heck, I needed new furniture anyway."

He kissed her once, twice, then more, wanting to kiss away her anxieties. He thought of how she'd gone to Stan when he wasn't able to be with her after the break-in. Was he really going to be such a jerk as to leave her alone again? "Maybe that stuff I was going to do at work can wait a few hours."

Her arms circled his neck and she held him tight, kissing him back while a fearful shudder rippled through her.

He led her to the king-size bed and lay down beside her. There was no way he could leave her now. Instead, he held her, loving her as dawn lit the sky. She fell asleep before he did. As his own eyes shut, he gathered her close, and tried to keep the nightmares from them both.

Even after thirty years, the view from his office window caused Harold Partridge's narrow chest to swell with pride. The world's cleverest engineers, computer scientists, and programmers strode briskly through the Silicon Valley complex, their minds ticking with the latest inventions and the next enhancements to the worldwide business that was Partridge Industries.

His private phone began to ring. *Finally!*

He held it to his ear. "Well?"

"Not yet."

"Not yet?" Skinny arms began to shake. "Impossible! You missed it! You cretins! Imbeciles!"

"We didn't—"

A pulsating pain crossed his brow. "Do you think I'm doing this just for fun? It's important, goddamn it!"

"We understand, Mr. Partridge."

The words, so cloyingly spoken from these sycophantic fools who couldn't follow simple instructions, made his overly acidic stomach curl. "Don't call me again until you are successful."

"That"—the caller coughed nervously—"that might require more than you said the first time."

"I don't care! Do whatever it takes!" He slammed down the phone but kept his gaze fixed on it as he nervously cracked his knuckles one by one. The time had come to do what he must, what he should have done immediately, much as he loathed the idea. Fighting the tremor in his body, he picked up the receiver again and began to dial.

Chapter 4

"You're going to get us thrown out, Angie." Connie Rogers leaned across the table and spoke in a loud whisper. Angie's best friend was in her early thirties, blond, divorced, the owner of a small gift shop, and a grudging accomplice in too many of Angie's screwball schemes. Like now.

The two of them, dressed to kill—Angie in a Rena Lange burgundy brocade embroidered jacket and matching skirt, and Connie in an emerald-green silk dress from a mall shop's fifty-percent-off rack—sat in Pisces, an elegant restaurant high on Nob Hill, newly opened and filled with a young and hip clientele. Angie was running her camcorder. So far, she'd taped a sweep of the restaurant, their table, the menu, and the wine list.

"If I walked in with a camera," Angie explained calmly, "no one would object. It's the same thing."

"People with cameras take pictures of each other, not the food, the tables, and the help."

"Look, restaurant reviews have to be made incognito." Angie placed the camcorder on the table. "If the reviewer is known, it defeats the whole purpose. So we're here pretending to be casual diners

22

who happen to have a camcorder. This way, instead of me taking notes and verbally describing everything I eat, we're simply discussing the meal as we go along, and I'm taping it."

"And then showing it to thousands of viewers on TV!" Connie scrunched her lips to the side like some gangster as an unsuspecting waiter sailed by.

"Shush! Not so loud." Angie looked from one side to the other. "What's the big deal? Taped TV restaurant reviews are a fabulous idea. They'll catch on in a big way—in other words, I'll make it big. The public will love them much more than bland old newspaper articles."

"We could be sued!"

"Don't worry. As I said, restaurant reviews are always written in secret, and all I'm taping is our dining experience, which is my right. You can also look at this as investigative reporting—photos and film are often used. Besides, I plan to only go to good restaurants with good food, ones that should appreciate the publicity. And if I do find something wrong, to sue because of a bad review would give a restaurant even more negative press. That's the last thing they'd want."

"Somehow, this seems wrong."

"It's fine. Quiet, now. Here comes our waiter." She snapped open the camcorder viewer and aimed it at him.

"What are you celebrating?" The waiter grimaced into the lens as he served a salad of arugula, shaved Parmesan, and sliced artichoke with olive oil and lemon to Angie. Connie's salad consisted of radicchio, scallions, and olives in a balsamic dressing.

"I'm going to buy a new car," Angie said promptly. It wasn't a lie. She had been thinking seriously about it ever since the problem of fitting her luggage into the Ferrari.

"Oh? Is that why you're taking movies in this restaurant?"

She chose not to answer. "Haven't you seen it done before?"

He peered down his nose. "No. I've never seen anyone do such a thing."

"Oh . . . in time, you will. Just like cell phones." She smiled. "Soon these will be all over the place. People talk on the phone everywhere, so why not film everything, too? You'll get used to it. This is a great little recorder. It's got sound and it's digital, so you just talk into it." She centered the viewer on him. "Tell me, do you enjoy working here?"

His eyes shifted left and right. "I'm sorry, but I'm afraid some of the other customers are bothered by your filming."

"They are?" Sure enough, everyone was staring at her.

"If you don't mind . . ." the waiter said.

With a weighty sigh, she shut off the camcorder and laid it beside her plate again. "Sorry," she mumbled.

The waiter sniffed, and then marched away.

"See what I mean?" Connie whispered.

"It's none of their business! Next time I'll be a little more subtle, that's all."

"Hah! You subtle? That's the day I'll become the next Mrs. Donald Trump! Anyway, why should there be a next time?"

"Because TV pays a lot more than newspapers."

Connie tasted her salad, and decided to add a bit more salt. Quick as a flash, Angie taped her salting the food. "Your point?" Connie asked. Now she was grimacing at the camcorder, too.

"When I realized I was actually *glad* my apartment had been broken into so I had an excuse to move in with Paavo, I knew it was time to do something about our living situation." Angie took a bite of salad, and chewed thoughtfully before continuing. "I want to be with him. Despite the break-ins, we had a great day yesterday—we saw his friends at the police department, contacted his insurance company, then shopped for a new bed for him. Of course, this morning when I woke up in a beautiful hotel room—romantic, room service, every convenience at the touch of a button—and I found a note beside me instead of a man, I gritted my teeth. I swear, he doesn't have a clue. Not a clue!"

"You don't sound very worried about those break-ins," Connie said as Angie rolled the camera on her salad and softly spoke into it about crispness and a slightly tinny flavor.

"In the clear light of day, I decided they were nothing," Angie said, the taping momentarily over. "I'm sure whoever broke in was searching for money, and something scared them away before they realized I don't keep money at home, and before they took any of my valuables. I'll bet they saw Paavo's name and address among my things. Maybe they thought we were together and figured since they'd been scared off from my place, they'd hit his. Who knows?"

"You're making a lot of assumptions, girlfriend."

"I'm sure the break-ins are no more than that. But if Paavo wants to worry about me, who am I to argue?" She winked conspiratorially.

Connie smiled back. "I get it."

"And that's where my TV restaurant reviews come in."

"Now I don't get it."

"It's simple. The two of us *need* a house. My clothes, and cookware, and antiques simply won't fit into his small place. And there's no way he'll live under my father's roof." She didn't have to tell Connie that Paavo and Salvatore Amalfi didn't exactly see eye to eye about Paavo's relationship with Angie. "Do you know how much houses cost in San Francisco these days? That's why I've got to get a TV job even if I have to hire a movie crew to film these restaurants!"

"All so you can buy a house?"

"Eventually."

Connie swallowed a big mouthful of radicchio. "Frankly, I really don't see how you can think about buying a house with a man when there's so much you don't know about him."

Angie stopped eating. "What do you mean?"

Connie shifted uncomfortably. "Well . . . you don't really know him."

"Don't *know* him? How can you say that after all Paavo and I have been through together?"

"That's what I mean. Things have happened to you both while you've been together, but how much of him do you know?"

"You sound like my father," Angie cried, waving her fork in exasperation.

"Think about it. He keeps so much hidden."

"Hidden? Nothing's hidden about Paavo!"

"How much has he told you about his past?"

"Connie, he had a hard life, especially as a kid. I can understand why he doesn't want to talk about it."

"Are you sure?"

Angie couldn't believe her friend was talking this way. "I thought you liked Paavo."

"I do, but you can't build a life together with too many unknowns—with hidden pasts. I know what I'm talking about—that's what killed my marriage. Along with my ex being a slime. But if I had known more about him, I would have known he was a slime before I married him. You've got to learn all you can about Paavo."

"I know about him!"

"Angie, you don't even know the man's real name."

She glared hard at Connie. "What are you talking about?"

"You told me he said his Finnish stepfather gave him the name Paavo." Connie jabbed the table with her forefinger to make her point. "Well, he didn't live with Aulis until he was four years old. What was he called before that?"

"Aulis might have given him the name when he was first born," Angie answered vehemently. "I don't know *when* Aulis came up with Paavo, and I don't care. I like the name!"

"Why didn't Paavo's own mother and father name him? Why some neighbor? Unless—" Connie gasped.

Angie felt a chill go through her. "Unless what?"

"Unless Aulis is really his father! Wow!"

"Connie, really!"

The waiter approached the table. Flustered, Angie started her camcorder rolling again, grateful for the interruption. She had no idea why Connie was talking to her this way. So what that she had wondered about some of it herself . . .

That was unfair. Whenever she asked, Paavo told her about his childhood. Maybe not all the particulars, but then, he didn't know much about them.

Still, Connie's questions bothered her.

The waiter smiled as he served Connie grilled Washington State salmon on spinach cream sauce, and scowled fiercely at Angie and the camcorder as he shoved a plate of steamed lobster medallions with saffron, tomatoes, basil, and thyme broth in front of her. Angie smoldered. He was probably afraid the camcorder would pick up some dandruff on his shoulders.

As soon as he left, Connie leaned closer to Angie and in a hushed voice said, "I'll confess that I never did give much credence to that story that Aulis simply took in Paavo and his older sister. I mean, being neighborly is one thing, but how many people raise their neighbor's kids? It just isn't done."

Connie's continuous harping moved beyond annoying. "Will you stop, already?"

"Angie, you're my friend—my best friend—and I think it's about time you learn exactly what's going on here," Connie insisted. "I mean, you're counting on him for your future, but you've got too many unanswered questions for you to do such a thing. It's foolish, Angie, and you're not a foolish person."

"I'm ready to stick a fork in my ear!"

"Damn it, woman, you are a certifiable wack job where Paavo Smith is concerned!" Connie cried.

Angie began to sputter, practically speechless for a moment. "Did you just call me a *wack* job?"

Connie put her palms on the table. "A short pier away from going over the edge!"

The two glared at each other.

Suddenly Angie grinned. "About to fall into the drink, eh?"

Connie chuckled. "Deep-sea-fishing time."

Angie laughed, then shook her head helplessly. "I wonder where I can find a diver's suit."

To Angie's amazement, Paavo was there when she returned to the hotel room. The day's court session at which he was to testify had been canceled, the CSU still hadn't found time to go to his place, and no new murders happened. He left work early to be with her.

The other inspectors must have gawked at him as if he'd sprouted wings.

They ordered room service for dinner. Dessert was memorable . . . and it wasn't even on the menu.

Chapter 5

Paavo strode briskly down Post Street, past porn shops and massage parlors, past doorways filled with wide-eyed Vietnamese children. In daylight, kids could be seen in the area, darting about, playing, or huddling in clusters and watching the goings-on. Once the sun went down, they disappeared, and San Francisco's version of the zombie class took over those streets— hookers, pimps, and addicts, plus a few lost tourists who didn't realize that edging close to the theater district lay this corner of despair.

Double-parked cop cars, their dome lights revolving, signaled which building the body had been found in. As a homicide inspector, Paavo worked to find out why people's lives were suddenly taken from them, even if that life had been lived in a hellhole like this.

A sheet from the afternoon *Examiner* blew toward him and stuck against his leg. He was careful to step over puddles of urine that stained the sidewalk next to buildings. The city had spent big bucks putting in fancy French-built portable toilets on sidewalks in tourist parts of the city—big enough for wheelchair access. Unfortunately, that meant they were big enough for other uses, too, like quick sex and drug deals. There were no Porta Pottis in this part of town.

A rank smell pervaded the building's entrance. Pale green paint covered the walls, a color that must have been given away by the barrel to tenements and jails. Lurid graffiti was scrawled over the paint.

"Two floors up, Inspector," the uniform at the door told him. "Elevator's not working."

They never were in places like this, Paavo thought, which was probably for the best because few owners of such buildings would pay for their proper maintenance anyway. Riding one could cause more chills, thrills, and spills than found at Disneyland.

At the top of the stairs more enlightening graffiti about the sexual habits of various residents filled a long, dark hallway. The debris and dirt on the floor crunched as he walked down the linoleum hall. With his partner on vacation this week, he wasn't supposed to be going to death scenes, but handling paperwork and court dates, and investigating cases he already had. This week's on-call team, Benson and Calderon, were mired down in a double homicide that involved a doctor and his wife who had been big-time contributors to the city's mayor. Rebecca Mayfield and her partner, Bill Never-Take-A-Chance Sutter, were the backup team, but they had already gone out on a homicide investigation when this third call came in. Paavo should have looked to see if the moon was full last night. If so, it would have explained a lot.

A patrol officer guarded the crime scene. Paavo signed the logbook, ducked under the yellow police tape, and stepped inside.

Before him was a typical tenement apartment— the walls a dingy yellow, the single window so

filthy little sunlight came through. A torn shade
covered the top half. The main room held an old
sofa, coffee table, chair, and TV, and a kitchenette in
one corner. Next to it was the bedroom, and beyond
it, the bathroom. Drawers had been pulled from
chests and upended. He was growing sick of that
sight.

Despite the drawers, he noticed that, unlike most
of these tenement apartments, the floor and furniture weren't covered with empty food containers
and other garbage.

A little girl sat on a tattered sofa. She had long
brown hair pulled back in a ponytail. Her bangs
were thick, and cut straight across, a millimeter
above blue eyeglass frames. The frames were the
defining feature on her face, which was pale and
plain. Her hands were folded on her lap, and brown
eyes stared at him through the thick glasses.

"Hello," he said.

"Hello." Her voice was firm and no tears showed
on her face. With her was a patrol officer Paavo
knew, George McNally.

"This is Jane Platt, Inspector," McNally said. "She
was the one who called nine-one-one when she
found her grandfather." McNally pointed toward
the open door. "Jacob Platt is in the bedroom."

Paavo was surprised at the news that the calm-
looking little girl had found the body. He'd seen
adults fall apart over such discoveries. He didn't
remark on it, but gazed at her and nodded his
approval. Her eyes held his a moment, then lowered.

After a quick perusal of the living room, he carefully entered the bedroom. "Did you or anyone else
touch anything, McNally?" he asked.

"Didn't need to," McNally said.

McNally certainly had no need to question the

fact of the man's death. The floor was covered with blood, and in the middle of it, Jacob Platt lay, shot point-blank in the forehead. The entry hole was small, with powder burns surrounding it. The way Platt had fallen made it possible to see that the entire back of his skull had been blown off. Paavo couldn't help but think about the young girl finding this.

The bedroom held a twin bed, a small, rickety dresser, the contents of it spilled onto the floor, and two enormous tables, standing side by side. Two high-intensity lamps stood on one table, plus some strange equipment. He recognized the soldering iron, wire cutters, fine-nosed implements, Bunsen burner, and microscope. The RS Mizar tester was a mystery, as was something called a Ceres Secure Moissanite Tester. Things started to make a little sense with the Raytech-Shaw faceter, the Diamond Jem cabbing machine, a centrifugal magnetic finisher, and finally, a magnetic polisher. Jewelry-making equipment.

No jewelry, metals, or gems were found, and he wondered if Platt had been killed for them. Judging from the equipment, Platt could have had a lucrative business—and judging from its location, it was probably illegal, or at best questionable.

Officer McNally talked with the girl while Paavo continued to sketch and survey the scene. He had no sooner finished when the CSU arrived. He went over to the young girl and sat down beside her. She wore jeans and a gray zippered sweatshirt over a red T-shirt. "How are you doing, Jane?" he asked.

"I'm all right." Her voice was soft, and she looked more shy than tearful. Wide-eyed, she watched the crime scene investigators enter the apartment.

"How old are you?"

She lifted blue-eyeglass-framed eyes to his. "Nine."

He flashed onto his nightmare. Even staying with Angie in that beautiful hotel—an indulgence he would have to give up as he seemed to have exaggerated the danger she was in—the nightmare haunted his sleep.

In the dream, his sister was the age of this girl. Nine. Why had he dreamed of her being only age nine? She'd been *nineteen* when she died, not nine. He tried to dismiss the memory. "Do you live here?"

"Yes."

"Just the two of you?"

She nodded.

"When you came home, was there anyone in the apartment besides your grandfather?" he asked.

She shook her head. "I called hello, and when he didn't answer I looked for him." She shuddered. "Then I phoned nine-one-one."

Jane's eyes grew even rounder when Assistant Coroner Evelyn Ramirez walked into the apartment carrying a medical bag. She waved at Paavo, but one look at the young girl's face, and instead of making her usual ghoulish comments, she went straight into the bedroom. Two med technicians followed. Paavo noticed that the child's breathing had grown heavy. She was a good actress, but apparently not nearly as unmoved by her grisly find as she pretended to be.

He placed his hand on her narrow shoulder. "Where can we reach your mother or father?"

"They aren't here," she said.

They aren't here. That was how Jessica used to answer whenever kids at school or teachers or others would ask about their mother or father. Older, and tough, and protective of her little brother, Jessie would never say, "They've gone away," or "They abandoned us," or what he knew she really wanted to reply to the busybodies who questioned them, to shake her fist and cry out, "We don't know who the hell our fathers are, and we don't give a goddamn about our mothers anymore, so what's it to you, asshole?" Instead, she'd politely reply, "They aren't here."

"Do you have any relatives or friends to stay with?"

"I have an aunt," she said in her matter-of-fact manner.

"I called her already, Inspector," McNally said. "She's on her way."

"Okay, good." Paavo's gaze swept over the apartment. There was a limit to how long a kid could sit in a room permeated with the smell of her grandfather's death, and this little girl had gone way past that point. "Want to go outside to wait for your aunt?"

"Yes." Her face filled with gratitude and she stood. On the floor was her book bag. She picked it up and hitched it to her shoulders.

As they left the apartment, his gaze caught the equipment-laden table in the bedroom. "Do you know what your grandfather did in there?"

"He made jewelry." She reached under her collar and pulled out a pendant on a gold chain.

Paavo stared in disbelief. The necklace was beautiful. It looked like something Angie might have owned—a large ruby with a small diamond on each side.

"It's just a fake," the girl said. "It has a flaw in it. That's why Grandpa gave it to me to play with."

"I really don't think this is going to work, Angie," Connie whispered, crouching behind a row of industrial-size garbage cans.

Angie, also stooping low, said, "Once, just once, I'd like to hear a bit of encouragement from you."

"Maybe I'd feel more encouraging if my knees weren't getting so stiff I'm afraid they might never straighten," Connie whined. "I don't relish spending my life looking like Groucho Marx."

Earlier that evening, when Paavo called to say he'd be working late, the idea for the perfect addition to her video restaurant review popped into Angie's head. She decided to act.

Now, both dressed in black jeans, black turtleneck sweaters, and black boots, she and Connie huddled in the alley behind the Pisces restaurant where they'd eaten the day before.

Angie checked and doubled-checked her new palm-sized video camcorder. "Just relax," she said to her fidgeting friend. "I'm trying to figure this out. I think that window looks in on the kitchen, but it's too high off the ground for me to see into. I'm going to have to get up on something."

"Forget it. Let's go home."

Ignoring her suggestion, Angie tugged Connie along in a half crouch, half crawl. "We need to move one of these big garbage cans to a spot under the window."

They found a can that was fairly empty, though reeking nonetheless. Each took a handle and carried it where Angie indicated.

"That can isn't very steady." Connie nudged it and watched it rock.

"You worry more than Little Red Riding Hood facing the wolf!" Angie tried to hoist herself up onto the flat, round lid, but couldn't do it. The top reached to her armpit. "I need a boost."

"This is dangerous, Angie," Connie grumbled, bending over and clasping her hands so Angie could use them as a step.

"It's fine."

Angie stepped as Connie held firm and lifted.

With a wobbly clatter Angie was atop the garbage can on her knees, and turned to look at Connie. "Connie?"

"Down here." She sat on the ground rubbing her hands.

"Are you okay?"

"Only if you call being used as a ladder and tumbling on your butt okay."

"You're okay." Angie stood up on the groaning lid to look in the restaurant's window.

"What do you see?" Connie asked, rising to her feet.

"This is so cool! I'm looking into the kitchen!" Her plan was working.

"Fantastic!"

"Unfortunately, there's a rack in front of this window. It's loaded with pans and blocks most of the view. I'm going to have to go to the next window to the left. That one should work better."

"Come down, then," Connie urged.

"Look, this can wasn't very heavy. Why don't you just drag another one over here? Then I'll just step from this can to the next one."

"We're on a hill, Angie. The cans are too unsteady for that."

"They're huge and half-full of garbage. They aren't going anywhere."

"Since when have I become Connie-the-garbage-woman?"

There were times, Angie knew, when silence was golden.

Connie wrestled another can into place. Angie gingerly stepped onto it. "Much better." She raised her camera. "Testing. One, two—oops!" She ducked down.

"What is it?" Instinctively Connie ducked, too. Her fierce whisper floated up to Angie.

"Someone's coming. Shush!"

Angie slowly raised herself up to peer over the windowsill. The heavyset chef she'd seen earlier stood with his back to the window, chopping chicken. She had to get this on film. She put the camera up to her face, hoping against hope it was working.

The man's backside filled the lens. It was not a pretty sight.

"What are you doing?" Connie tugged faintly at her ankle. "Come down before someone sees you!"

"Quiet," Angie whispered back. "I need another can over there." She pointed to her left.

"Angie, I don't think—"

"Hurry, Connie! This is a great shot!"

She waited until she heard Connie say, "Okay." Keeping her eye on the camera, she lifted a foot through the air, then toed the garbage can that Connie had put into place.

"The can has a little problem . . ." Connie warned.

Angie squared her foot on the new can.

"The lid doesn't fit very well."

As she shifted her weight, the garbage can cover gave way. The part she was standing on plunged downward while the other half soared straight up. Angie dropped like a stone. Connie ducked as the lid became airborne, whizzing by like a B-movie UFO to land with a ringing clatter on the street.

When Connie looked up again, Angie was gone. She clutched the lip of the can and looked down at Angie sitting in the soupy muck. "Get out of there! Someone might have heard you screech as you dropped."

"This is so disgusting!" Angie stood. She wanted to wipe her hands, but she had nowhere to wipe them. Finally she gave up, grabbed the lip of the can, and tried to hoist herself up. The gunk she was standing in and the sides of the can were so greasy she felt like she was trying to climb straight up an oil slick. "I need some help."

"Ah, I know what to do." Connie circled the garbage can to the uphill side. "Lean against the downhill side of the can."

Angie grasped the lip opposite Connie. "Why?"

"Now, duck!" Connie yelled, pushing with all her might. The can began to tip.

"Noooo!" Angie's world tilted. As the sidewalk rushed up at her, she bobbed down. Garbage sloshed over her like a great, smelly tidal wave.

On its side, free from the confines of the other cans, Angie's had room to roll. And it did.

A high, slightly gurgling wail filled the night air.

Connie watched in mute horror as the can bounced down the hill, accelerating with each roll like some great planet spinning madly on its axis. Scraps of garbage whirled out onto the pavement, tracing a trail down the alley.

Connie ran down the hill after it, waving her arms. "Angie! Stop!"

The wail grew higher and louder.

Finally the can smacked into a lamppost and, with a small, dying teeter, came to rest.

Connie dropped to her knees beside it, afraid to look inside. "Angie?" she squeaked. She gave it a little tap. "Angie? Are you still alive? Can you talk to me?"

Slowly, painfully, Angie crawled onto the street.

Suddenly a male laugh erupted, then cut off as quickly as it began, followed by the sound of running footsteps.

"The nerve of some people," Angie said, wiping from her face and hair coffee grounds, eggshells, all manner of once-green vegetables, and what looked like inner parts of a crab.

"Is there anything I can do?" Connie blubbered, wringing her hands.

"One thing." Angie sat woefully on the sidewalk. "Next time I ask you to help me . . ."

"Yes?"

"Refuse."

Chapter 6

Monday morning, Paavo sat in Lieutenant Ralph Hollins's office on the fourth floor of the Hall of Justice. Although the room was minuscule, tucked in a corner of the fourth-floor Homicide bureau, the Hall itself was massive, ugly, and overlooked a freeway. It was not your high-class real estate. By comparison, the new city jail built behind it looked like Kubla Khan's pleasure dome.

He told Hollins about the break-ins at his and Angie's homes. "I can't figure out what they want, what they were looking for, or why they tore up my place after giving Angie's the kid-glove treatment. It's like they were pissed off, or irritated that they couldn't find what they wanted. Whatever it was."

Ben Chan finally had found time to check Paavo's house, but so far had nothing to report. The only good news was that his cat had come home.

"It sounds weird," Hollins said. In his fifties, with gray hair and a protruding stomach, he was in charge of Homicide, which gave him a close acquaintance with Rolaids. "Take the time you need and keep me posted. I don't believe in coincidence either." An unlit cigar was held firmly between his lips. He couldn't light it—not with San Francisco's no-smoking policy—but he could pretend. "Any leads yet on Friday's Tenderloin murder?"

"No leads, but I found something interesting," Paavo said. "The vic had a record. Served time for armed robbery, burglaries, was even accused of some killings, but they were never proven."

"Killings? Plural? You talking organized crime?"

"Not sure. He seems like a loner—a guy who, now and then, got in over his head. We were told his name was Jacob Platt, but it's really Platnikov. Jakob-with-a-K Platnikov. He was born in Russia, came over here in the sixties. I haven't heard that there were Russian gangsters in this country back then."

Hollins quietly watched cars zip by on the freeway. "These Russian mafias are fairly recent, but there's always been a criminal element. He could have been part of it. Hell, I've heard their black market worked better than the Communist party. That's why it survived while the party went to hell."

"We're trying to find out what Platnikov was involved in, if anything. Based on something his granddaughter said, he might have been making forgeries of good jewelry. Whoever killed him might have been looking for the good stuff. We found no jewelry—real or fake—in the apartment, so my guess is that they found what they were looking for."

Hollins took the cigar from his mouth. "Jewelry? Have you talked to Mayfield about her new case?"

Rebecca Mayfield . . . the one Angie called the "little helper bee." "Not yet. Why?"

"She's got a dead jeweler on her hands. A well-known and respected jeweler. The jeweler's name was Gregor Rosinsky—another Russian."

* * *

As much as Angie welcomed living with Paavo for a few days, staying at a hotel was extravagant.

Especially when he walked out and left her alone each morning. There was duty, and then there was suffering from being enjoyment-challenged.

She was walking a little slowly this morning; the bumps and bruises she'd gotten rolling around in garbage had stiffened over night. She took a couple of Advil, then made an appointment for a locksmith to meet her at her apartment. New, maximum-security locks would make it safe for her and Paavo to simply stay at her place until his new bed was delivered. A couple of days under Sal Amalfi's roof shouldn't bother him too much.

As she approached her apartment building, her nerves jangled, and her mind replayed Paavo's reaction to the break-ins. He was usually pretty sanguine about things, but this robbery attempt seemed to shake him up. That troubled her.

When she reached her block, she scrutinized the sidewalks, the doorways, the parked cars. Being this close to home, she'd expected her uneasiness to dissipate, but it didn't. Driving slowly, she continued past her building. Around the corner, situated with a view of the main entrance to the apartments and the garage, two men sat in a dark blue Mercury. One raised a newspaper higher as she drove by.

Was it to cover his face?

What kind of people sat in their cars to read newspapers in a residential neighborhood? She didn't think she wanted to know.

As she circled the block, she called Stan on her cell phone.

"Look out your window," she said when he

answered. "Two men are sitting in a dark blue sedan at the corner. Do you see them? Do you know if they've been there long?"

"Gee, Angie, I don't make it a habit to sit at my window and ogle parked cars." She heard him moving about. "I see the car. So what? Where are you?"

"I'm a couple blocks away. I'm just being a little paranoid, okay? I want to be sure those guys aren't waiting for me."

"A *little* paranoid? You've hung out with that cop too long. This is not normal behavior. I know you had a break-in, but—"

"Humor me. I'm going to park and walk slowly toward the building. If you see those guys get out of the car, tell me, and I'll run back to my car and get away."

"That's ridiculous! Why don't you park in the building's garage like you always do? It's secure."

"Not secure enough. If anyone is after me, I'm not entering some dark, creepy garage. Now, will you just watch, please?"

"All right. I'm watching. If I were you, I'd just put more locks on my door."

The only open parking space was a half block from her apartment. She took it, then unclipped the keyless-entry remote and left the key in the ignition. She might have to make a fast getaway.

"You still there, Stan?" she asked as she neared the building.

"I'm here. I see you. I can't see the guys in the car, but I see the car."

She froze. *"What do you mean, you can't see the guys in the car?"*

"Not from this angle. But if they get out, I'll see the doors open."

"Oh. Okay." She slowly began walking again. "So far nothing?"

"Nothing."

She was just two doors from her building, with each step feeling more self-conscious and foolish for having asked Stan to help.

"Angie, *stop!*" Stan's voice was hushed, urgent.

Her feet felt glued to the pavement. "What?"

"I moved to the bedroom to look. The blue car is empty. Of course, it could mean nothing."

Or it could mean . . . She bit her lip, clutching the phone. How paranoid was she? They could be anybody. Two men looking for an apartment to rent, checking the want ads. Or . . .

Oh, hell! She could meet the locksmith another day when her nerves weren't as wound up as a Slinky toy.

She turned back toward her car.

"Angie, run!" Stan yelled.

Aches and bruises forgotten, she didn't even stop to look back, but hurled herself at her car, jumped inside, and slammed down the door locks. All she could think of was to turn the key, throw the transmission into drive, and stomp on the gas.

Heart pounding, she glanced in her rearview mirror and saw the backs of the men's heads as they hurried toward their car.

Her Ferrari left them in her dust for the moment, but she wasn't sure how long it would be before they caught up with her.

"Hello? Hello?" Stan yelled.

Her hands were too tight on the wheel to pick up the cell phone. She careened wildly down Russian Hill, tearing across level intersections and then feeling the car become airborne as the pavement dropped steeply after each cross street. The jarring as the wheels bounded onto the roadway made her wince, both for her car's body and her own. She felt like a stunt driver in a Hollywood action film.

"Angie? Angie? Where are you? Can you hear me?" Stan was sounding desperate.

She glanced again in the rearview mirror. No dark car followed. With shaking fingers, she lifted the phone from the floor where it had fallen. "I'm here." She was breathless. "Did you see them follow me?"

"No. They went back to their car, sat awhile, and then drove off."

"Thank God!"

"I tell you, you made a faster getaway than Bonnie and Clyde."

Homicide Inspector Rebecca Mayfield walked into the detail and sat at her desk.

Hangdog eyes that always made Paavo slightly uncomfortable peered up at him as he approached her. If it hadn't been for Angie coming into his life, the two of them probably would have been a bureau item. She was the type of woman who had attracted him in the past, the type everyone who knew him believed was right for him. On some gut level, he knew Rebecca and the bureau matchmakers had a point.

The way things were, though, this was one bureau romance that was never going to happen. He couldn't see past Angie—outwardly wrong for him in every way. His colleagues in Homicide knew that, too. For all their apparent incompatibility, he felt more alive when with her than at any other time in his day. He trusted in that.

Rebecca gave Paavo the files he'd requested on Gregor Rosinsky, the jeweler whose murder she and Never-Take-A-Chance Sutter had been investigating. Their too polite and all too professional discussion denied Rebecca the conversation she really wanted.

Back at his desk, Paavo began to read.

Rosinsky was seventy-two when he was killed. He'd been in the U.S. fifty years. After World War II, he had left the USSR by way of China, working his way to Japan and finally to California.

He seemed to spend his early years in the U.S. walking a fine line between legality and crime. His rap sheet showed several arrests, but he had spent less than a week in jail, and that was at the county level for passing bad checks. He probably would have been given a suspended sentence for the crime, except that he'd been allowed so many chances in the past.

Then his arrest record suddenly stopped. That meant he had gone straight or had found protection.

Rosinsky was married, with two sons and a daughter. His wife didn't work; all three children were married. The daughter had moved to Phoenix and was a realtor, one son lived in Los Angeles where he worked as a cameraman at Warner Bros., and the other, the oldest, was still in San Francisco, now calling himself "Rosin" and working as an attorney.

Twenty years ago, Rosinsky had opened Rose Jewelry, Ltd. Small and exclusive, it had earned a reputation for quality jewelry and fine workmanship.

Nothing in the file indicated why Rosinsky ended up on the wrong end of a bullet.

His death occurred at approximately eight o'clock in the evening. The store was closed, and he apparently had stayed to do paperwork. Rosinsky's wife had called her son late that night, worried when she couldn't contact her husband. She'd been particularly anxious because three nights earlier, someone had broken into the store. They must have been scared off because nothing had been stolen.

This time, strangely, there were no signs of a break-in. Rosinsky's body had been found in back of the shop. Whoever killed him may have entered from the back door, but if so, Rosinsky must have opened it for him. Paavo couldn't see a jeweler opening any door after hours unless he knew and trusted the caller. Rosinsky had known his killer.

If whoever killed him had stolen some of the jewels, the crime would have made more sense. That, at least, would have been a red herring and thrown the police off on motive. Right now it looked like an execution.

Paavo read through the crime lab reports. A lot of fingerprints had been lifted in the back area. He doubted anything conclusive would show up, though. Since he knew no one had whacked Rosinsky as part of a conventional robbery, it couldn't be investigated as that kind of a case. Paavo's instincts told him that this had been a professional job. Someone had wanted the jeweler dead.

Paavo read through Mayfield and Sutter's reports on talks with friends, neighbors, and associates of the victim, but nothing there was helpful. Something niggled at him as he read, and he turned back to the beginning of Rebecca's write-up.

Then he saw it. Rosinsky's wife had said the store was broken into three nights before he was killed. Angie's and his homes were burglarized the very next day. It was an interesting coincidence, but nothing more, he was sure.

Chapter 7

While Angie directed, Paavo drove her Ferrari nearly to the top of Telegraph Hill, and parked on Montgomery Street near Filbert. While most of the hill sloped gently down from Coit Tower to Fisherman's Wharf and North Beach, the east side dropped steeply to the Embarcadero. Streets were no more than footpaths and stairways, and ended abruptly at retaining walls, hillsides, or parapets. Sections of unpaved landscaping and terraced, private gardens made the area green and lush.

Angie could have danced with excitement, but kept mum about where they were going or why. After telling Paavo about the two men watching her apartment building, she knew she wouldn't be returning there until this situation was settled. He seemed to assume she'd move in with her parents for a while. She had a better idea.

The block of Filbert they walked down had no paved roadway. Instead, wooden stairs and walkways zigzagged along the hillside, surrounded by trees, vines, ferns, and a lush central garden.

About a third of the way down, she opened a small wooden gate and stepped onto a stone walkway through a tiny fern garden to a white cottage. Paavo wore a bemused but curious expression. Many of the homes on this hill had been miners' shacks when first built, but had withstood the big earthquake and fire of 1906, and by way of age and location, were now worth nearly as much as one of the mines might have been.

As she pulled a key from her purse and dangled it in front of him, he murmured, "Home sweet home."

"You figured it out!" Wearing a big smile, she unlocked the door and stepped inside.

"I don't believe this," he said.

In almost no time, she showed him the little foursquare house. The front door opened to a pleasant parlor, with casement windows overlooking the Filbert gardens, and a brick fireplace on the right-hand wall. Beyond the living room an archway led to a dining area with French doors that opened to a deck. The kitchen was to the left of the dining area. The sole bedroom was to the left of the front door. Like the living room, it also looked out onto the Filbert steps and central gardens. A bathroom had been built off the bedroom, probably as an afterthought many years ago.

Angie could have put two of these cottages into her apartment.

"My cousin Richie, who's in real estate, owes my father a favor," she said. "When I told him what happened to me, he gave me the place for a month. Two if we want it."

"You've never talked to me about your cousin Richie before."

She shrugged. If she were to tell him about all her relatives, they wouldn't have time for anything else.

Paavo didn't pursue it. "So where is he going to live?"

"He doesn't *live* here. It's one of his rentals. It's vacant now, that's all." She couldn't explain why the place was nicely furnished and stocked with food. Some things were best not to question.

"I don't know about this," Paavo muttered. Despite his uncertainty, he seemed to find the little house appealing. It invited comfort and relaxation. As he peered out the window at the Filbert steps and the lush, green garden that gave it a secure, almost tropical feeling, she thought he was weakening. "This is nice, but it would make more sense for you to leave the city and stay at your parents' house."

Her gaze gripped his. "Is that really what you want?"

"No," he admitted.

She smiled with relief. "It's settled, then. We'll stay here, safe and comfortable, while you find out what's going on." Taking his hand, she led him through the French doors to a postage-stamp-size deck filled with containers of flowers. The hillside dropped away beneath it. "Look at how pretty the geraniums and impatiens are, even at this time of year. It's like a touch of springtime, right in the heart of the city. This place will be good for us."

"To find out how incompatible we really are?" he asked.

Her arm circled his waist. "We know that already. Siskel and Ebert had nothing on us."

She's right about that, Paavo thought. He draped an arm over her shoulders. "It sounds like you've made up your mind." He knew a steamroller when one hit him—even if only a hundred ten pounder. He had to admit the thought of living here with Angie on a trial basis appealed to him. He even had to admit that living with Angie on a permanent basis was something he dwelled on at length.

"We're here. Let's enjoy ourselves." She faced him, her back against the railing. "I stopped at the grocery. How do grilled strip steaks with olive and oregano relish, pine nut and basil rice, steamed zucchini, and a romaine salad with Parmesan dressing sound to you? I thought it would be nice to stay home for dinner."

Home . . . He liked the sound of that. He placed his hands on her small waist.

"And after dinner we can go to your place and pick up Hercules," she added.

"Can I trust you not to spoil that cat, Angie?"

"Nope." She grinned wickedly. "And I'll spoil his master, too, if given half a chance." He moved closer, very much liking the gleam in her eye, and quite ready to let himself be spoiled any way she wanted.

Her cell phone began to ring. Her voluminous tote was on the pine table in the dining area. She dug around in it until she found the phone. After listening for a minute, her face paled, she murmured, "Okay," and handed the call to Paavo. "It's Yosh. I thought he was still on vacation. Your phone is switched off or the battery's dead. That's why he tried me. He says it's urgent."

Paavo took the phone, a thousand questions going through his head at the word his partner used. *Urgent* in police lingo meant very bad news.

"Yosh, what's up?" he asked.

"It seems there was a break-in," Yosh replied. "At your stepfather's." A long moment went by before Yosh added, "He was shot."

Seventy miles south of Tucson, US Highway 19 crossed the Arizona border into Mexico at Nogales. Other Arizona crossings were smaller, like the mountain pass from Douglas to Agua Prieta about a hundred miles east, or the blistering, barren desert crossing at Sonoita, over a hundred miles to the west. Around Nogales, the land consisted of rough desert, parched ranchland, a few paved roads, and lots of footpaths for illegal crossings.

On an expanse of land on the Mexican side, thirty miles southeast of the border checkpoint, in an area so remote and desolate not even illegals dotted the landscape by night, stood a two-room adobe. The house and garden were ringed by a four-foot adobe wall with a flat overhanging stone along the top, and a solid wooden gate. Such a wall helped keep down the number of snakes, scorpions, and tarantulas that made it into the house.

A woman walked out of the gate and shut it firmly behind her. Her tooled leather boots crunched on the umber-colored rock and gritty sand as she continued along the well-worn path from the gate to the nearest saguaro. She was tall and angular, her muscles toned from a daily routine of weights and running. Her gray hair was clipped short. Her eyes were also gray, but tinged with green—the color of the cholla and Mexican sage that dotted the Sonora Desert she had learned to call home.

She didn't know if she could ever learn to truly love the desert. She'd grown up along the eastern seaboard, Maryland as a child, then to Massachusetts while a teenager, until she moved south again. She missed the greenery of that area, the thick foliage of the trees and bushes in spring and summer, the bright colors of autumn, and the peacefulness after a fresh snow. But most of all, she missed the water. Beautiful, blue, cool water. She missed the streams and ponds, lakes and rivers, of her childhood.

She had learned to respect the desert in all its

craggy intensity, its harshness, and its desolation. It constantly tested, and had made her stronger. The desert, more than anything she had ever known, taught her to abide.

A square metallic target holder hung from an arm of the cactus. She attached a new paper target to it. Then, just for the hell of it, she reached into the yellow straw pouch she carried, and lined up five tin cans in a row on the ground beneath the target.

The day before, she'd made her weekly jaunt across the border to the main Tucson post office to pick up copies of the *San Francisco Chronicle* and *Examiner*. The papers had no routine delivery to any location in southern Arizona, and having them mailed directly to a small town closer to home would have caused too much local curiosity. For that reason, she subscribed to them as "Jennifer MacGraw"—as good a name as any. Tucson was big enough, and so full of sun-seeking out-of-towners, that such mail deliveries received little notice there. And if anyone was sufficiently curious, let them try to find Jennifer MacGraw with her shoulder-length platinum-blond hair and heavy makeup.

Last evening, after a simple dinner of refried frijoles, chorizo, and tortillas, she'd settled down to read the news. For years now, she'd found nothing of importance in the papers, and never expected last night to be any different. Force of habit kept her at it. With some shock she noted the murder of a jeweler during a robbery. It wasn't an unexpected occurrence, she realized, even if the jeweler was Gregor Rosinsky.

Ironically, she'd almost overlooked the tiny article tucked deep in the *Examiner*, near the obituary page, about the murder of another old man—Jacob Platt.

Only as she read about that second murder did

her heart begin to drum and her nerves turn raw and tight.

She wondered if the authorities had found out yet that the victim's name was really Jakob Platnikov. And if they had, did they realize what it meant?

She paced off exactly twenty steps from the target. Keeping her back to it, she placed her gear on the ground and picked up each item in turn. She first put on the polycarbonate wraparound safety glasses, then fitted the shooting muffs over her ears and slung her magazine pouch over her shoulder. Last, she removed the Glock 19 from her shoulder holster, dropped the half-used magazine, and slapped in a new ten-rounder. The 9 mm compact was less than seven inches long and five in width. It fit easily into her handbag, and was comfortable in her hand. She knew it intimately, knew every nuance of its high-impact-resistant polymer grasp. She'd used it to practice with on numerous occasions. Soon she would use it for more than practice.

She breathed deeply, head bowed slightly, feet wide apart, clearing her mind of the distractions of the day. A blue-black buzzard circled overhead. Near a dry creek bed, two cottontails scampered. She saw none of it, saw only the real target, not her phony paper one.

In one fluid motion, she spun to face the target, formed the isosceles position, and fired ten rounds. The completed magazine dropped out and she slammed a new one into place, then began moving leftward. As she did, she fired another ten rounds, then ten more as she worked her way back to her starting place.

Twenty-five of the shots were bull's-eyes, the other five missing by scarcely an inch.

Last of all, she straightened, one arm extended, eye on the sight. She shot the five cans, watching with satisfaction as they *pinged* and flew up into the air, dropping down to land on the ground like so many dead men.

Gray-green eyes, cold and hard, swept the barren landscape. She shoved another magazine into the Glock. She knew what she must do.

Cops were easy to find.

So were dead men.

She had waited long enough. It was time to act.

Chapter 8

Angie hurried alongside Paavo from the parking lot to San Francisco General Hospital, a massive complex of old brick and modern cement-gray buildings. Her chest ached with fear. Aulis was the only family he had left.

Apparently a neighbor had found his stepfather and called for an ambulance. The police were contacted, and the responding officer knew Paavo. When he couldn't reach him directly, he phoned Yosh. The blue brotherhood in action, she thought, not wanting Paavo to find out about Aulis from some stranger.

The hospital was chaotic. Most of the city's emergency and trauma cases arrived there, hundreds each day, plus over a thousand scheduled patients. To simply get the desk nurse to direct them to the proper waiting room presented a challenge.

Seated on an aluminum and blue plastic chair in the bright yellow room, Paavo leaned forward, elbows on thighs, hands folded, and stared silently at the gray linoleum floor.

"Aulis will be all right," Angie said gently. She sat beside him, her hand lightly rubbing circles on his back.

His complexion had a sallow cast to it, his eyes filled with sadness. "Not many eighty-year-olds can survive a gunshot wound."

She had no words to ease his pain and blinked back tears. "I'm so sorry, Paavo."

His hands clenched. "Damn it! I should have thought of Aulis when they hit your place, then mine!"

"Don't! You can't blame yourself for this. Any connection between you and me makes some sense. Or between you and Aulis. But you and me and Aulis? There isn't any. It's got to be chance coming up all wrong—one of those horrible, random things, so much a part of city life, that end up touching all of us."

"I've worried about him living alone at his age."

She rested her hand atop his. "He's surrounded by friends and longtime neighbors, as he's told you whenever you've brought the subject up. He's happy in his home. This isn't your fault!"

He pulled his hand away and clenched it. "I'll know if that's true, once I know what caused this to happen to him."

"He's going to be all right." She tried desperately to give her voice conviction, but she failed. Like Paavo, she knew Aulis's age was against him. A head wound . . . She shuddered.

Needing to do something more than sit helplessly and wait in the excruciating silence of the waiting room, she went in search of coffee. Near the waiting room, a canteen area held a coffee machine. On the first floor was a large, busy cafeteria. The coffee tasted weak and oily in both.

Paavo was talking on his cell phone when she returned. He soon hung up and eyed the Starbucks

label on the paper cup she handed him. "I was wondering where you'd gone off to."

She offered some lemon tarts and almond bear-
claws, but he shook his head.

"Has the doctor talked to you yet?" she asked, sitting in a plastic chair beside him.

"No one has," he said bitterly, "except to say the
doctors are with him. I tracked down the patrolman
who took the call to go to Aulis's place. He said the
apartment had been pretty well trashed, and that
Aulis had lost a lot of blood."

Angie's outrage nearly spilled over, but she
forced it in check. Paavo had always been her
Gibraltar. She was the one who got emotional, and
he would rationally calm her down. Now he was
the one hurting, and she had to help him. She
wasn't sure what to say or do, so she placed her arm
across his broad back and silently held him.

After a while, a buxom, middle-aged nurse
entered the waiting room and walked toward them.
Paavo's face paled. He slowly stood.

"You're Mr. Kokkonen's son?"

"Yes."

"I understand no one has given you much information yet. I'm sorry."

He nodded quickly.

"Fortunately, the bullet did not enter Mr. Kokkonen's brain. But it did graze the skull and caused
some bone damage and considerable swelling from
the impact. We will have to see how much trauma
the brain suffered. He's in a coma. With his age, and
this type of wound, I'm afraid the situation is
extremely critical. You need to prepare yourself for
that."

He nodded again, not answering. Angie watched
his hopes fall when the nurse said there was swelling.

"The doctor will probably be with him another hour or so. You might want to grab a bite to eat, then come back later when we'll be able to tell you something more substantial."

"I see," Paavo murmured.

"Also, we'll need Mr. Kokkonen's insurance papers. Medicare will cover some of the expenses, but you might want to know all that he's entitled to and what it will cost. I suggest you bring his policy into the hospital as soon as possible so that our billings staff can go over your options with you." She shoved a set of papers as thick as the city's phone book into his hands. He just stared at them as she walked away.

"Christ almighty!" Paavo collapsed into the chair again, then slapped the papers onto the empty seat beside him. "He might be dying and she wants me to worry about insurance forms."

"The world is going crazy." Angie reached over, grabbed the papers, and stuffed them into her tote bag.

"You go and eat," Paavo said. "I'm not hungry."

She gazed at the doors the nurse went through. Aulis was back there, alone and hurt, fighting for his life, and Paavo here, his heart aching.

"We'll wait." She took his hand.

"You, then me, now Aulis," he whispered, his hand tightening painfully on hers. "Why, Angie? It doesn't make any sense. What could we have that would make anyone interested in us, and why in hell would anyone want to hurt a sweet old man like Aulis?"

There were no words she could say. They sat in silence, Paavo's hand in hers, and she hoped the connection brought some comfort beyond his dark, lonely thoughts.

* * *

"Rosinsky and Platnikov are dead!" Harold Partridge screamed into the phone, his voice growing shriller with each word. "Do you realize what this means? Do you?"

"We're sorry, sir."

"Sorry? That doesn't begin to say what you'll be!" He had a strangle hold on the phone and wished it were their necks. "I still don't have the brooch. It's got to be with the woman."

"She seems to be hiding. She hasn't returned to her apartment."

"I'm surrounded by complete, utter morons! Do I have to do everything myself? Her boyfriend's a cop, goddamn it! A homicide cop. Find her through him!" Partridge's voice was raw from yelling. It was good his office was soundproof.

"I guess we can try to find him and put a tail on him."

"Hell, if you can't find him any other way, you can always *kill* someone, then wait while he shows up to investigate!" He hung up, his heart beating so hard and fast he feared for his blood pressure.

Rosinsky and Platnikov. He took off his glasses and shut his eyes, fear and dread drenching him with sweat.

He wasn't about to let it start again; he would stop it, one way or the other.

Chapter 9

Paavo parked in the driveway of Aulis's apartment building. As he and Angie got out of the car, the area seemed eerily quiet. Usually neighbors milled about on the street chatting with each other, children played, dogs barked, and low-rider cars generated a pulsating *thump-tha-thump* from bass speakers as they cruised by.

They were about a block from Mission Dolores, built by Spanish padres with Ohlone Indian labor at the same time as the Revolutionary War was erupting on the other side of the continent. This part of the city was a touch of Mexico in the heart of the city, filled with *los restaurantes y las abarroterías*.

Aulis's apartment was located on the ground level of a three-story building, at the end of a long, flowerpot-lined path behind the garage. Paavo unlocked the front door and walked in, leaving the door wide for Angie to follow if she wished. He wouldn't blame her if she preferred to remain outside. Being here, knowing Aulis lay hospitalized and close to death, chilled him to the bone.

Three steps inside the door a dark pool of blood stained the beige carpet. His breath caught.

Yesterday, investigators had swept through the crime scene. He was glad he had asked the CSU to go over Angie's apartment after the break-in there, as well as the one in his own home. Now the crime lab could look for similarities between the three. There had to be some.

Yesterday, too, he and Angie had spent the entire day and most of the night at the hospital. Aulis remained in a coma in intensive care, and was allowed no visitors. His condition had not changed this morning.

The only joy in the past twenty-four hours came from bringing Hercules back to the little cottage. He was so ecstatic to be with Paavo again that every time Paavo sat down, all eighteen pounds of cat bounded onto his lap. Angie immediately treated the big tabby to a plate of fresh salmon. Paavo found himself barely acknowledging the happy cat, though. His thoughts were elsewhere.

Now he forced his eyes from the carpet stain to the rest of the apartment. The destruction so much resembled what had been done to his own home, for a moment he was unable to move. Sofa and chair pillows were slashed, drawers pulled out, books and magazines opened and strewn all over. A throbbing in his temples beat dully in synch with the heavy beat of his heart.

A quick walk-through left him ready to explode in rage and frustration. Nothing, it seemed, had been stolen. He would talk to Aulis's neighbors, find out what they saw and heard.

Once he found out who was behind this, there'd be no stopping him. The bastard would pay in blood.

When he returned to the living room, Angie moved toward him. "What would you like me to do?" she asked.

"Nothing! Don't touch a thing."

He was immediately ashamed of his tone with her, especially when she gazed at him with quiet understanding. "I'll look for his address book," she said. "You'll need to make some phone calls, Paavo, to let his close friends know what's happened."

He hadn't thought of that. He stood again unmoving as a moment of excruciating silence went by. God, how was he going to get through this? He turned toward the bedroom.

In the top drawer of the pine highboy, Aulis kept important papers. Paavo and his sister had been taught to never go near that drawer if they valued their skins. Aulis had a "system" and if the system was in any way disrupted, it meant he might not pay bills on time or find important papers, and the stability of the world order would fall into disarray.

It was heartrending to see that most crucial drawer on its side, the contents littering the floor. Grimly he righted the drawer, knelt down, and began to stack the papers.

He didn't have to dig too deeply through old tax filings, Social Security notices, property tax billings, and other such documents before coming across the medical policy. Along with Medicare, Aulis had good coverage and should be well taken care of.

As he gathered up the rest of the papers and envelopes to return to the drawer, an envelope from the Ford Motor Company caught his eye. He added it to the stack. It was odd, though. Aulis had never owned a car. Didn't even like cars, Paavo thought. Had Aulis harbored some secret passion for a Mustang GT? Curious, Paavo pulled it out of the pile and opened it.

Inside was a photograph and another, smaller envelope. He pulled out the photo, and his blood ran cold.

Three people stared at the camera. One of them,

looking very young and very innocent, was his mother.

He knew her immediately, even though he had seen only one other picture of her. That other picture, one of his most valued possessions, showed him standing on her lap, leaning across a table and staring intently at a birthday cake with two candles. His hair was blond and wispy—it hadn't turned dark brown until his teens—and he wore canary-yellow short pants with matching suspenders over a white shirt. His cheeks were puffed out and he seemed to be blowing hard. His mother was holding him at the waist and laughing.

She was a pretty woman, her face fine-boned, with white, almost translucent skin. He couldn't tell the color of her eyes—they were Kodak-flash red in the photo—but her hair was auburn, shoulder length, and parted on the side. Her head was cocked and her hair swung free and easy except for a strand of it tucked behind one ear.

His only vivid memories of his mother were seeing her laugh in that picture, and hearing her cry as if her heart had broken.

In this newly found photo, she looked very serious. Her eyes squinted against the sun, causing her brow to furrow, and her lips were set firmly. Her hair was cut in an over-the-ear bob, the bangs so short they only covered the very top of her forehead. Her pink dress was big and boxy, with a high-necked Peter Pan collar. She held a black-haired baby in her arms in a way that showed off the baby's frilly matching pink dress and booties. The baby had to be Jessica. She had a knockout smile even at that young age.

The woman in this picture didn't mesh at all with the image he had of his mother. She was taller than he'd imagined, and bore herself in a stiff, cautious manner. Clipped to the waistband of her dress was an identification badge of some kind.

Beside her stood a hard-featured older man. He wore a similar badge clipped to the lapel of his suit jacket. His face was heavily lined and shades darker than the woman's. His eyes were thin slits from squinting, his mouth turned down at the edges, and his brows crossed. His short hair, Paavo saw, was as black as Jessica's had been.

Jessie had never known who her father was. It was hard to imagine this dour-looking man being him, but the resemblance showed in the dimpled chin and in the widow's peak. How odd that Aulis hadn't given her this picture. But then, Paavo didn't know his own father either—only that he wasn't the same as Jessica's.

He'd always assumed that meant his mother was "just that kind of a gal." Love 'em and leave 'em Mary Smith. She walked out on men, on her own kids. She was a real winner. Good old Mom.

Sitting cross-legged on the floor, he reached again for the Ford envelope and shook it, dropping out the smaller white one still inside. On its face, in a cursive, feminine hand, Aulis's name had been written.

Inside were two sheets of paper. The first was a simple statement.

> *I hereby grant Aulis Kokkonen full authority to care for my children, Jessica Ann and Paavo Smith, until my return. This includes the right to authorize any medical care necessary.*
>
> *Mary Smith*

He snorted, surprised his mother had bothered with such legal niceties. Maybe she'd run off and left them with Aulis more than once, and the last time hadn't returned.

He put the sheet aside. The one under it was a letter, written in the same hand as the statement had been. As he read, his throat began closing, tightening, until he could scarcely breathe.

> Aulis,
>
> I'm a dead woman. I've failed. Take care of my children, dear friend. Enclosed are the documents you will need. Tell them nothing about me—absolutely nothing. It's the only way they will be safe. Kiss Jessie and Paavo good-bye for me. Please destroy this letter.
>
> Cecily

He stared at the letter, unable to believe its contents. Reading it again, he was hurled back in time and place. The old pain, the loneliness, the question *why*—all those feelings he had sworn he would never again allow himself about his mother or his past—washed over him. He was back at the age when he told himself that strong boys don't cry, the age he had taught himself not to do so any longer.

He dropped his head forward, his eyes squeezed tight. *Kiss Jessie and Paavo good-bye for me.*

It hurt his heart to see those words.

Cecily. Why had his mother signed her name Cecily? Her name was Mary. Mary Smith . . . so common a name he'd almost, *almost* believed it was false. But then if someone were choosing a fake name, he'd convinced himself, she would certainly pick something less blatantly phony than Mary Smith.

Over the years he told himself he was being too suspicious thinking her name was false, being too much the cop. Now he wondered if he'd been right. Strangely, the name Cecily resonated with him. He had no idea why, but seeing it written there, hearing it in his head, made the hair on the back of his neck stand on end.

His fingers smoothed the folds of the letter. It was undated. What did she mean about keeping her children safe? Aulis had never given any indication of them having been in danger, but that would explain why he had taken them to L.A. shortly after their mother had abandoned them . . . not that Paavo remembered being there. He was so young it didn't much register on him which city he was in, but Jessica had told him about it. All he did remember was that Aulis seemed to move around quite a bit, taking him and Jessie from city to city, one small apartment to another, until they all became a blur to him. Eventually they returned to San Francisco.

He didn't understand what any of this meant, but he did know that Aulis had kept his part of the bargain. He had told Paavo nothing about his mother.

Chapter 10

"I didn't know what to do or say, Bianca." Angie was fighting tears. It was early morning, and she sat in the kitchen of her sister's house, telling her about Paavo finding the strange letter from his mother. "First the shock of Aulis's attack, and then that awful letter!"

"There's not much you could have said. You were there for him, that's what matters." Bianca was the oldest of her four sisters, the one she went to when she was troubled. She was little, like Angie, but outweighed her by about fifteen pounds. Where Angie's hair was short and wavy with auburn highlights, Bianca's was straight, chin-length, and dark brown.

"Hercules is *there* for him. The man is hurting and confused. I've seen Paavo upset about his cases and—maybe once or twice—even about me, but nothing like this. You know how quiet he gets when he's upset; well, it was silent-movie time at our place last night. I kept waiting for a piano player to show up."

Bianca had just taken a blueberry strudel from the oven, and cut a piece for Angie and one for herself.

"When Aulis gets better, Paavo can ask him about his past."

"And if he doesn't get better?" The two sisters looked at each other sadly. "If Cecily's letter—*if* that's what her name really is—is to be believed, Paavo's whole life, his whole childhood, is based on a lie. It was such a strange, frightening letter. She gave Aulis her kids! I just don't get it. How could any mother do that?"

"It's hard to imagine that such a story could have been kept quiet all these years," Bianca said, pouring hot coffee and then sitting across from Angie. "People know about such things—and talk."

For the first time that morning, Angie smiled. "That's right, they do. They'll know. Neighbors will know. Anyone around at the time will know!"

"Slow down! This happened thirty years ago."

"I'm not saying it'll be easy. But we aren't talking Harry Houdini here, either. She was just a woman with two kids, and no husband. Maybe she was heavily in debt, or . . . or owed money to some drug dealers. Who knows? That would be a reason to leave town!"

"Poor Paavo," Bianca murmured. "What a thing to discover."

"It's got to have been really bad or she wouldn't have left those kids, I just know it." Angie sipped some coffee, lost in thought. "I wonder if he should be the one to find out. It could be potentially devastating for him. Aulis kept the past hidden for a reason. At the same time, it's important. It's the . . . the prelude, so to speak . . . of the good man he's become. I'm afraid for him, Bianca. Maybe I should see what I can find out."

Bianca was lifting a piece of strudel to her mouth, but put it down at Angie's words. "Aren't you supposed to be hiding until the police catch whoever has been lurking around you, or your apartment, or whatever?"

Angie pushed her piece of strudel aside, her appetite gone. "Oh, the more I think about it, those two guys might have been salesmen, or Jehovah's Witnesses, or even Mormons. I might have made a mountain out of something completely innocent."

"And Aulis's shooting?" Bianca asked, with a worried frown.

"Well..." Angie didn't even try to answer. Instead of mountains and molehills, she was clutching at straws.

"Ah, here you are," Ray Faldo said as Paavo walked into the photo laboratory on the second floor of the Hall of Justice. "I'm just about ready to print. Give me a couple more minutes."

Faldo was the best lab man in the department. He could work wonders with the equipment they owned, making it perform almost as well as top-of-the-line merchandise. That was why Paavo had gone to him for help. Faldo stared into the scope of a photo enlarger, slowly adjusting dials. "I made a negative of the photo," he said, "and now I'm trying to see how large I can get it and keep it in focus."

Paavo sat on a stool at the end of the counter where Faldo worked.

"Who are these people, anyway?" Faldo turned the magnification knob.

"I found the photo at a crime scene," Paavo said. "It might be important."

Faldo made a few final adjustments to the focus. "The woman's quite a dish. A little flat-chested for my taste—"

"It's the badges I'm interested in," Paavo said, interrupting.

Faldo gave him an odd look, then he placed an

eight-by-ten piece of low-contrast resin-coated paper under the enlarger, set the timer, and flipped it on. "Badges? Oh, yeah. Those that she and the guy are wearing. Christ, is he her husband? Looks old enough to be her father. Homely bastard, isn't he? They made a cute kid, though." When the exposure was complete, he moved the paper into the developer tray, and after a short while turned it faceup. The enlarged photo began to appear.

"How's your dad doing?" he asked as he used tongs to move the print into the stop bath.

Paavo shrugged, tamping down his impatience. "Same. Still in intensive care."

"Well, he's hanging in there. Good for him. I've been working with Ben on the CSU materials from the break-ins. Nothing. I hate to say it, Paav, but the guys who did it were pros. Keep your girlfriend out of their way."

"She's found a place to stay until this is settled."

"Good." Faldo washed the print in plain water, squeegeed it, and hung it on an easel. "Here you go."

As Faldo turned on the fluorescent overhead lights, Paavo walked up to the photo. He could see some kind of symbols on the badges, but they were angled in a way that made them hard to read, and were still a little blurry. "Can anything be done with these to make them clearer? I'd like to know what they say."

"I doubt it, but I'll give it a try. If you're just curious about the badges, I can tell you about them. I used to wear one of those myself, years ago, before I decided I'd much rather live here in foggy and damp San Francisco than in hot and humid Washington."

Paavo eyed Faldo with surprise. "You know what these badges are?"

"Sure." Faldo grabbed a sponge and wiped up some spilled developer solution. "And if I didn't, the building would be a dead giveaway for old-timers like me. It's the Old Post Office Building in Washington, D.C.—Twelfth Street and Pennsylvania Avenue. Years back, when the post office moved out, other federal agencies moved in, including the FBI's metropolitan office. The badges they're wearing are picture IDs. Employees had to wear them to get inside. The blue background on the guy's meant he was a special agent. She isn't, of course, given the time. But it's pretty darn certain both of them worked for the FBI."

Angie unlocked the door to Aulis's apartment. As she entered, she shuddered, finding being here as eerie this time as the last. An unearthly chill hung in the air, along with a musty smell.

The investigators had finished their work, so the cleaning service she'd hired would be coming by in about an hour.

Today, when she'd first arrived in the neighborhood, she'd knocked on doors and asked people if they'd seen anything strange—particularly a dark blue Mercury—before or since Aulis's attack. As casually as she could slide it in, she also asked if they knew his old friend Cecily. To both questions, everyone's answer was the same—no.

Paavo had told her that Aulis had lived in the small apartment for only the past fifteen years or so, but he had lived in the area for most of his life.

Her earlier phone calls to several of Aulis's old friends—Paavo left the address book at their house after making calls about Aulis being hospitalized—had given the same results. The people she'd spoken with were all quite elderly, and sounded confused and anxious about her questions. She felt bad about upsetting them, and stopped calling. For the moment, at least.

So far, her Ferrari had received more notice and interest from the neighbors than either her or her questions.

Now, walking around the ugly bloodstain inside the apartment, she rubbed the goose bumps on her arms. Something despicable was going on here. She wanted to scream, "Stop! Leave us alone!" and to explain that there was nothing that she or Paavo or Aulis owned that anyone might want. But what good would it do to shout at the walls?

She'd brought in the mail and flipped through the bills and advertisements before placing them on the coffee table with other mail accumulated since the attack. Paavo would need to take care of the bills, plus any others unpaid. She should try to find them while they were on her mind.

Suddenly, outside the apartment, car wheels screeched, followed by a loud thud. She ran out to find a man lying on the street near her car. His head was bathed in blood.

Neighbors poured onto the street. "A dark blue car hit him!" a little boy informed anyone who would listen. "I saw it!"

A man dropped on his knees to the hit-and-run victim. Angie understood when he used the word *muerta*. The man was dead.

Chapter 11

Since 1974, FBI headquarters has been housed in the J. Edgar Hoover Building, a two-and-a-half-million-square-foot monstrosity located on Pennsylvania Avenue between Ninth and Tenth streets in Washington, D.C. It stands seven stories tall in the front, but the rear rises to eleven stories. Of the more than seven thousand employees in the building, fewer than a thousand are special agents. Most employees work on maintaining files, running the Uniform Crime Reporting Program, indexing and confirming fingerprints, and handling freedom-of-information requests.

Special Agent Nelson Bradley stood at the third-floor window by his cubicle and watched a turbaned Sikh and a woman in a bright-hued sari emerge from a cab. His thoughts weren't on the couple, who meant nothing to him, but on the message slip in his pudgy fingers. He didn't like the way his fingers had gotten fat, or the way the rest of him had as well, or the way his hair had thinned, and the years wore heavy on his face.

Simply reading Paavo Smith's name on the message slip had made his hip begin to throb, adding to

the generally aging and decrepit sentiment he had
about himself. He hadn't heard from Smith in years,
not since San Francisco happened. That was how he
thought of it—*San Francisco happened.*

He went back into his cubicle. The blue burlap-
covered partitions that divided the agents' desks
made him feel like a rat in a maze. A Northern Tele-
com multibuttoned telephone set, filled with features he didn't understand or care to use, waited
silently for him. He hated his desk-bound job, but it
was all he could handle ever since going out to
Frisco on a special assignment with a gang task
force. Several Vietnamese families working in computer hardware manufacturing had been victims of
home invasions. The FBI found an informant within
the Vietnamese community and set up a sting operation. Bradley was a part of it, and when the sting
went south, he was nearly killed. A couple of homicide cops, Smith and his partner, Kowalski, happened to be in the neighborhood investigating the
latest home-invasion murders when bullets started
to fly. Kowalski had called for reinforcements as
Smith went into the house with the agents to see if
he could help. Smith found Bradley with his leg and
hip torn up and bleeding badly. He pulled Bradley
out of the back door and toward an ambulance that
answered Kowalski's call. Seconds after Bradley
was clear of it, the house went up in a firebomb. The
two other agents had been killed.

Bradley had heard that Kowalski, too, had been
killed a while back. It was too bad. He'd been one of
the good guys.

Bradley owed his life to Smith. He didn't like
being in debt to anyone. He liked it even less than
he liked being stuck here at a desk job in headquarters when he'd always been a field agent. No wonder he'd put on so many pounds. But at least they

hadn't been able to retire him on disability like they had wanted to do. He had fought them. Leave it to the Bureau to turn against you when you had given your all, he thought bitterly.

Always on his mind were the two guys who never had a chance for disability, Harris and Lane. They'd only been dead two weeks, he'd heard, when two new special agents were given their desks. Nobody cared, it seemed. Just him.

He returned Smith's call, and was given a strange request. Smith wanted to know if, some thirty-five to forty years ago, anyone working for the FBI in Washington had been named "Cecily." That was it, just the one name.

He told Smith it would take a while. For him to act on such a request without higher-up authorization was strictly illegal. He'd have to access employee records, which were protected from routine searches by anyone other than the personnel department.

He'd manage. Once he hacked into the database, he'd have plenty of time to manipulate it until he found what he needed. In fact, he had time for a lot of stuff these days. The work the Bureau gave him was garbage, something to keep him from twiddling his increasingly pudgy thumbs all day long. They wanted to insult him, to force him to ask for disability retirement, to somehow get rid of him.

No way. He'd stick around just to needle them. It was fun. It was payback.

"He's been moved out of intensive care," the nurse, a slim, blond woman in a crisp white uniform, said as she led Angie through a maze of corridors to Aulis's new private room.

"That's wonderful!" Angie cried. She felt as if her prayers had been answered. "He's awake, then?" she asked.

"Not yet. He's still in a coma," the nurse said. "But it's a light one. He can breathe on his own, his vital signs are strong, so he doesn't need the special equipment in intensive care. He's just not awake. We nurses call it a twilight sleep. The doctor will give you all the medical details, I'm sure."

"But overall, this means he's getting better?" Angie urged, trying hard to find some positive news.

"Let's just say, it's a good sign. Now, we have to wait and see how he is when he wakes up."

"You're saying he *will* wake up."

As if jarred by the question, the nurse stopped and glanced sympathetically at Angie. "At his age . . . the doctor will be able to tell you more."

Their gait was slower this time. "What has your experience been?" Angie asked.

"In my experience"—the nurse seemed hesitant—"in my experience, it's pneumonia, not the coma, that you have to be worried about. For older people, having to lie on their backs, being unable to move, fluid collects in their lungs, and sometimes there isn't a thing we can do about it."

"I see." The graveness of it was all but overwhelming. The two continued on in silence.

In the hallway, two nuns stood talking. They both wore traditional, cream-colored habits.

"Here we are." The nurse turned in to the private room right where the nuns were standing. Their proximity gave Angie a chill, as if Aulis might be closer to death than anyone had been led to believe.

The nurse bustled about the room, quickly checking Aulis and scanning his chart. "I'll leave Mr. Kokkonen in your hands," she said, then was gone in a flurry of white.

Angie went to Aulis's side and held his hand as she greeted him. She told him that she and Paavo were well, and looked forward to him getting better and going home. She said a few more words, then stepped back, saddened that she could see no change, no reaction at all in the old man. She covered her face in her hands.

"Are you all right, dear?"

Angie glanced up to see one of the nuns in the doorway. She was an older woman, heavyset, with a round face. Her hands were folded, her expression curious but serene.

"Yes," Angie said. "It's just that I'm so worried."

The nun entered the room. "I'm Sister Ignatius. I visit our Catholic patients here, along with Sister Agnes. But I'm afraid I don't know this man."

Angie placed her hand on Aulis's. "His name is Aulis Kokkonen. He's Lutheran, but I'm sure he wouldn't mind your visits or your prayers."

The nun smiled. "Well, thank you. I'll be sure to stop by, then, on my rounds. Is he a relative?"

"No . . . not yet. I'm dating his son."

"Ah, I see," the nun said warmly. She studied the bandages on Aulis's head. "What happened to him?"

"He . . . he was shot."

"Oh, my!"

"It was a robbery, we think, at his apartment." As Angie began to explain what had happened, the thought that niggled at the back of her mind sprang forth and her eyes filled with tears. "First my apartment was burglarized, then Paavo's—that's my boyfriend—and a few days later, Mr. Kokkonen's. I'm so scared that the three might be related . . . and if so, it all started with me." She took a Kleenex from the bedside table and wiped away her tears.

"Why you?"

"I don't know! That's the problem. If it was me, why? I don't understand the connection between

Paavo and Aulis and me with these robbers. Yet they struck my apartment first."

Through her rimless eyeglasses, the nun's warm brown eyes were calming. "It's not your fault, dear. You can't know what would possess someone to go after another person."

"Thank you, Sister," Angie intoned, the nun's words making her feel a little better. She even felt a twinge of good old Catholic guilt over her initial reaction to the two nuns in the hall.

"It does sound as if you and your friend need to be careful, however," the nun cautioned.

"We're trying to be," Angie replied.

"Good. I'm glad." She glanced at the clock on the wall. "Oh, gracious! I must go now. I'm sure Sister Agnes must be ready to leave without me. We can't be late for evening prayers."

"I'm glad to have met you, Sister," Angie said. "My name is Angelina Amalfi, by the way. People call me Angie."

"I'm sorry for your friend," the nun said, and then she was gone.

The room felt emptier and colder. As Angie watched over Aulis, she said a few prayers as well, for Aulis, for herself, and especially for Paavo.

Paavo glanced at the clock on the once-white, now-in-need-of-paint wall in the Homicide bureau. Nine o'clock. At night.

The detail was empty, everyone gone but him. Mayfield and Sutter had been here until about ten minutes ago when a new case landed in their laps, a domestic dispute gone bad. Neighbors called the cops, but by the time the uniforms got there, all was quiet. They found the wife dead in the kitchen, the husband missing.

Nelson Bradley had phoned earlier and told

Paavo he'd best be able to access the personnel info when only the night-shift people were around. They were the forgotten people. There weren't many of them, and no one bothered, at that time, to peer over anyone else's shoulders to check on the validity of their "need to know" the data they were accessing.

A friend in Personnel had given Bradley the password and access codes to get into those files without raising red flags in the Integrity Branch. One disaffected employee helping another, Paavo thought. He guessed it was some sort of bureaucratic sense of justice.

Now he awaited Bradley's call.

The evening quiet gave him a chance to make a few phone calls to speed up the identification of the hit-and-run victim outside Aulis's apartment. Paavo didn't like the preliminary findings, that the victim—slim, late thirties, no distinguishing characteristics—had no identification on him, and no fingerprints on file. He was a John Doe, and unless something dramatic turned up, he'd continue to be one.

The only interesting information came from a med tech at the scene, who had noticed the victim's teeth. Several were missing, and the ones still in his mouth were decayed. In Paavo's experience, most people with bad teeth ended up in a dentist's chair at some point. The only ones he'd seen who hadn't were generally from poor, third-world countries.

Witnesses couldn't agree on whether John Doe was heading toward Angie's car, or even scarier, Aulis's apartment, when struck by a dark blue car with no license plates. Something in the features caused everyone to believe the driver was a woman with short hair. Just what it was about the features couldn't be agreed upon, and the consensus was

that the car sped by too quickly for anyone to get a
good enough look at the driver to attempt a com-
posite drawing.

A few people also noticed another car, a black . . .
or brown . . . or dark blue one, leave the scene
immediately after the accident, going in the opposite direction from the hit-and-run driver. No
details could be given about that driver, either.

The phone rang shrilly, and Paavo started.
"Smith, Homicide."

"It's me."

Paavo's spine stiffened. "Any luck?"

"I searched the personnel files going back from
thirty to forty years ago searching for the name
Cecily," Bradley said. "Thank God it isn't that common a name. Anyway, there were three. I think I've
got a good idea which one you want."

"Tell me."

"Well, first, let me ask you about the one who
worked the longest for the Bureau. She was in her
forties during that time—Cecily Drury. She was a
typist for thirty years, and retired at age fifty-five."

"Not her."

"Then I've got a sixty-year-old librarian, Cecily
Reiner, who spent a year reassigned from DOJ to
put our library in order."

"No."

"This is it, then. Cecily Hampton Campbell, a
young woman, only in her twenties, married to a
special agent, Lawrence Campbell. She was hired to
work in Ident—that was the old fingerprint identification section. It used to be a big paper operation
with thousands of people, most of them women. It
was like an assembly line. Anyway, she left Washington and was transferred to the San Francisco
Field Office. Her record shows deceased. So does
his. She died over thirty years ago."

Paavo's hand tightened on the receiver. That was her. The woman he'd spent a lifetime wondering about. To learn her name, hear of her marriage . . . her death . . . hit him a lot harder than he would have imagined. Cecily Hampton Campbell. "You were right. That's the one. Would you send me her file? His, too."

"I'll need another day or so," Bradley said. "Files this old are in storage. It could take a while to get them. Of course, you know I shouldn't send them. This is confidential information."

"I don't think so." Paavo's voice was harsh, jagged. "There's no privacy act for the dead."

As soon as he hung up the phone, he searched California and then national death records for Cecily Hampton Campbell.

No record existed.

Chapter 12

Angie constantly monitored the answering machine in her apartment for messages, especially on the lookout for those from her mother since Serefina knew nothing about her and Paavo living together in cousin Richie's house, but also from the Russian jeweler. He hadn't yet tried to contact her, or at least, hadn't left a message. She called him, but the phone simply rang and rang. She wanted her brooch back.

Since she was going out anyway to take some video shots of a new downtown restaurant with the unappetizing name of Les Chats, she decided to swing by Rose Jewelry and find out what was going on.

As she drove slowly by the shop, searching for a parking space, she saw a CLOSED sign hanging on the front door. Taped below it was a note. She left her car double-parked and ran up to the note. It gave a telephone number in case of emergency. Back in her car, she punched in the number on her cell phone as she drove.

"Lyons, Bernstein, and Rosin," the receptionist's voice said.

"Hello. My name is Angie Amalfi. I'm a customer

of Rose Jewelry, Mr. Gregor Rosinsky's shop, and it's closed. A sign in the window says to call this number. Do you know what's going on?"

"I'm sorry to tell you, Mr. Rosinsky passed away," the nasally voice said. "His son, Martin Rosin, is handling business matters. Would you like to speak with him?"

"He died? How awful. Had he been sick?"

"Not at all. His shop was broken into. The robber killed him."

"My God!" Angie was shocked. How hadn't she heard? But then, with so much going on, she hadn't read a newspaper in days.

"It was a terrible tragedy." The woman spoke with all the emotion of announcing the weather. "I'll put Mr. Rosin on the line for you."

When Rosin answered, Angie offered her condolences before telling him about the brooch she had left for repair.

The son had a list of all the jewelry that was awaiting customer pickup, but after looking it over, didn't see her name.

A description of the brooch was no help. Rosin hadn't seen a cameo in the entire collection. Not only was there none among the jewelry that was being repaired, there was none for sale, either.

"That's impossible!" Angie cried in a panic, trying to remember what she had done with Rosinsky's receipt. How was she going to tell Paavo she had lost his present on top of everything? "I was given a receipt."

"Would you read the number to me?" Rosin said. "I have all my father's business papers here. I've been getting calls for days from customers."

Her tote bag! "Just a second, I think it's right here." One hand on the steering wheel, the phone crammed in the crook of her neck, she rummaged through the bottomless carryall, her car only occasionally crossing the double yellow line as she pulled out grocery and things-to-do lists. A red light allowed her to search two-handed and find the receipt safely tucked in her checkbook. "Got it!" she whooped, just a little while after the light turned green again. She read out the information he needed. The driver behind her seemed to be having some kind of fit—his face looked contorted and his arms waved spastically. She zipped away from him quickly.

Rosin put her on hold to check for her receipt's numbers. After a long wait, he came back on. "The store's copy with that number is missing," he said with undisguised surprise. "I have the one before and the one after, but that page was removed from the sales book."

She was first stricken, then furious. Her car weaved from one lane to the other as she screamed into the phone. "Removed? What do you mean, *removed*? Where is my brooch? It's important to me!"

"I'm sure it is—"

"It's a family heirloom!" She pounded the wheel instead of steering with it. "It was given to me by my—"

"Miss Amalfi, calm down! Give me your phone number," Rosin said soothingly. "I'm sure we'll find it. I'll contact you as soon as we do."

"I just don't understand how it can be missing," Angie protested, unsuccessfully trying to calm herself. "I heard your father was killed in a robbery. My brooch must have been among the things stolen! God, oh, God, how will I ever get it back?" She stamped her feet, and the Ferrari lurched and jerked and nearly sideswiped a startled pedestrian crossing the street.

"Nothing was stolen, miss," he declared, his

voice increasingly obstinate. "Perhaps my father took the brooch home to work on. I'll search. Now, you say you didn't pick it up, but might someone else have done it for you? After all, the store's work request is missing."

"Someone else? No! No one even knew the cameo was broken"—then she remembered mentioning it to Connie—"except a girlfriend, and she wouldn't have gotten it."

"Did you check with her?"

Apoplexy threatened and she nearly ran a red light. "Of course I didn't! The repair work wasn't even paid for. *No one picked up my brooch!*"

"I'll call you." He hung up.

She slammed her phone shut, dropped it in her tote, and looked up to find honking cars and cursing pedestrians all around her.

Just stepping inside the little house soothed Angie's overheated emotions. Not only had Rosin sounded like a pompous blowhard talking down to her, but at Les Chats, the food looked and tasted like something Roto-Rooter flushed out of a clogged drain.

Rosin would find her brooch or discover what it was like to meet a master nagger. A crazed pit bull was wishy-washy by comparison.

She brought a raspberry tea Snapple out onto the deck and sat. It was a perfect place to calm down. She loved living here—and knew she loved it because Paavo was with her. She realized, too, that she was merely playing house with him.

But playing it was better than not living with him at all, especially during this time when he was so upset about Aulis and, much as he didn't want to admit it, his past. He tossed and turned each night, and at times seemed to dread going to sleep. She had never known him to be afraid of anything, until he told her about his recurring nightmare. Mixing his sister and his current job—the past and the present—would be troubling for him.

To her surprise, she, too, had fears about the outcome of his discoveries about his parents. Before he reached his journey's end, the path he was taking could lead to overwhelming or disturbing places, psychologically, if not physically. Somehow, she needed to help him through it.

As she sipped her tea, her mind turned to poor Gregor Rosinsky. She could scarcely believe he had been murdered. He had seemed like an interesting old man. Robberies were so common—too common—in this city. Heck, everywhere. That was a reason she liked this little house. Since it was on a street too steep for cars, if anyone came here to rob, they'd have to lug the stolen goods up or down the stairs to a getaway car. Not very likely. But then, she always used to feel safe in her own twelfth-floor apartment, and look what happened. There, she'd been specifically targeted. She was sure of it. Just as Paavo had been, and Aulis.

And Rosinsky? Why was his copy of her receipt missing?

All of Paavo's warnings to her came back again. She nervously raced through the house checking the locks on doors and windows, and then double-checked the gun Paavo had put in the nightstand for her if anyone tried to force his way in while she was home alone.

After locking the French doors to the deck, she lounged on the sofa and tried to read the latest issue of *Vanity Fair*. The umpteenth article on Gwyneth Paltrow and a fashion layout from Milan had all the staying power of cheap lipstick. Feeling cold and lonely, she snuggled into an afghan and waited.

When her tall detective walked in the house, his blue eyes found her and he smiled, and the world became right again. She ran to him with a hug and kiss. After Rosinsky, she didn't want to hear any more about death and sadness. At times she wondered how he stayed sane in his job.

So she chattered brightly about books and movies and TV shows, phone conversations she'd had with her mother and her oldest sister, her visit to Les Chats, and her video restaurant reviews. The first one was finished. All she needed was a television program to show it on. She had sent letters, E-mails, faxes, and phone calls to all the local TV stations. So far, no one had replied.

Not until dinner was over and they were nestled side by side on the sofa did Angie bring up her troubling discoveries.

"I have a confession to make," she began, pulling nervously at a loose thread on a needlepoint pillow.

He looked startled. "A confession?"

"It has to do with my Christmas present."

"I noticed you stopped wearing it." His voice was soft, his eyes resigned. "You decided you don't like it after all?"

"No, that's not it." The thread was getting longer and longer.

"It was a silly present. I should have gotten you something new." He sounded embarrassed.

"Paavo—"

"Stupid of me. I'm never sentimental—"

She tossed the pillow aside and grabbed his shoulders. "Will you listen? I love the brooch. The only reason I stopped wearing it is because the cameo popped out of the setting. I brought it to a Russian jeweler to have it fixed. Did you know it's an old, rare Russian piece?" He looked incredulous.

"Anyway, when I went to get it back, I learned the Russian jeweler had been murdered."

He frowned at that news. "Rebecca Mayfield is investigating a Russian jeweler—Rose Jewelry."

"That's it! Gregor Rosinsky was the owner."

"Where did you get this information?" he asked, brows furrowed.

She told him all about her conversation with Martin Rosin.

"Tell me again what you heard about the brooch being Russian," he said.

"The cameo is a profile of Alexandra, the last Tsarina—you know, Nicholas and Alexandra? Their daughter was Anastasia. Anyway, I first brought the brooch to my regular jeweler, and he sent me to Rosinsky. Rosinsky all but drooled over it. The little clear stones around the cameo are real diamonds—perfect diamonds, he said. He asked if I'd be interested in selling it. I told him absolutely not. He implied I shouldn't keep it—that it was museum quality."

"Museum quality?"

"Yes." Angie looked at him hard. "What is it?"

"I'm not sure." He stood and silently refilled their coffee cups, lost in thought. Only when he sat again did he speak. "Another man with a connection to jewelry was recently murdered. He, however, was on the other side of the line—he was a forger."

"A forger? A criminal? I don't see the connection."

"He was also old, and of Russian descent."

"Old and Russian . . . It sounds like my brooch!"

Blue eyes met hers. "I know."

"You think there's a connection?"

"Gregor Rosinsky's shop was broken into the night before your place and mine were hit."

"A jeweler and a forger, my brooch, then you, me,

and Aulis," she said. "We can't all be connected, can we?"

When he made no reply, a chill went through her. Of the people she'd just mentioned, two were already dead, and the third might be dying.

Chapter 13

Leave it to Angie to have set up a printer and a fax machine in temporary living quarters, Paavo thought with a small smile. When Nelson Bradley called him on his cell phone at seven A.M., and said he had the requested files, Paavo was in the house getting ready for work. Not that he had slept in. He had hardly slept at all, but kept reworking the strange information about Angie's brooch.

He gave Bradley the fax number and asked Angie to turn on the machine.

The phone rang, the fax took over, and in a matter of seconds, the first page began to spill out. *It can't be*, kept running through Paavo's head. All these years he had carried an image of his mother, and her being a government bureaucrat, married to an FBI agent, just didn't fit it. Didn't fit it at all.

But then, Bradley's words that Cecily Campbell was dead didn't fit his image of her either.

It was peculiar, but even though she had walked out on him and his sister, even though she had made it clear she didn't care about them, and didn't want them in her life, he always felt that someday . . . somehow . . . he would meet her. And then he could ask her, *why?*

When Jessica died, he'd been positive their mother would show up for the funeral. He remembered standing beside Aulis, trying to keep his face stiff, not letting anybody see how hurt he was, or how angry. At the same time, he wanted to look around, to see if a strange woman was in attendance. He wondered if he'd recognize her, if she'd look like Jessica, although he couldn't imagine anyone else being so pretty.

Jessie had been beautiful and fun. She was one of the few people outside of Angie he'd ever known who could get him to make an out-and-out belly laugh. And make him angry. Yes, he was furious at her. Furious at the type of people she'd decided to hang out with, the type who'd caused her to overdose at age nineteen. Furious at her for dying.

He shut his eyes, trying to tamp down the emptiness from losing her that would never go away. His mother hadn't shown up that day. That was when he knew she was never coming back. He hadn't cried about her since he was a little boy, but alone in his room, on the night of Jessie's funeral, he had cried for the loss of them both. After that, he'd toughened, and never shed a tear for either one again.

He took the information from the fax machine, folded it in half, and walked out onto the deck to sit.

Angie, in a satin nightgown and pink robe, placed a hot mug of coffee beside him, her eyes heavy with concern, then she went into the house, leaving the French door partially open.

He took a sip of coffee and unfolded the papers.

Their words were too cold, too mechanical, to be about a parent. They had a bureaucratic, impersonal ring—true government files, all dates and facts, about a stranger.

At age twenty-two, Cecily Jean Hampton, both parents deceased, took a job as a clerk-typist with the FBI. Six months later, she married Lawrence Campbell, and a year after that, Jessica Ann was born.

He stopped there for a moment. Jessica Ann Campbell. How odd that he'd never known that. She never let on. She'd been nine years old when Cecily walked out. A nine-year-old understands a lot, and recognizes when it is necessary to hide, and to create a false identity. The realization of all that Jessie must have known and kept hidden from him was staggering.

He continued reading. When Cecily was twenty-four, her marital status changed to widowed. Three years later, at twenty-seven, she transferred to the San Francisco Field Office. Nothing appeared in the file for six years, until the annotation "deceased" was entered. That was it. No explanation, no embellishment.

No nothing.

He turned to Lawrence's file. Campbell had been an agent, twenty-three years older than Cecily. The file showed his parents' names—Jessica's grandparents. Paavo wondered if they had still been alive when Jessica was a child, and if so, why they had never contacted their granddaughter, never sent her a Christmas present or birthday card. He could look up information about them; a lot of personal data was available to him in his position, but some things were better not knowing about. Some could do nothing but open old wounds and cause more heartache.

Lawrence Campbell had died of a brain aneurysm at age forty-seven. Until the time of his death, he'd apparently been a healthy, active man. Survivor benefits had been paid to his daughter, Jessica, until she was age nine, when the folder was annotated "Suspend benefits until new address received. Checks returned. Unable to locate."

Paavo stared at that a moment.

Cecily had walked away from her children thirty-one years ago, leaving that strange letter with Aulis, and the change in name to Mary Smith.

What had happened that made the FBI think she'd died, and was it true or not? Why was Jessica's name changed, and her whereabouts hidden, so she no longer even received survivor's benefits from her father's account?

Paavo searched for answers in Cecily Campbell's file. He worked his way through tedious reports on her progress as an employee, but found nothing of note. She was rated as competent and hardworking, a team player, not one to take risks, and she followed protocol. Generally, the reviews were uninspired, unhelpful. Her supervisor in San Francisco was shown as Eldridge Sawyer, and his reports were second-signed by Tucker Bond.

Paavo went back inside. As he tapped into his cell phone's address book, he caught Angie's anxious expression from the living room and motioned her to join him.

"FBI," a woman's voice answered.

"I'm trying to reach an agent named Eldridge Sawyer," he said.

"Thank you." After a short wait the operator came back on the line. "I'm sorry. No one by that name is here."

"I see. What about Tucker Bond?"

Her response was immediate. "One moment, I'll connect you."

A second pleasant female voice came on the line. "Mr. Bond's office."

"This is Inspector Smith from the San Francisco

Police Department. I'd like to meet with Mr. Bond
as soon as possible."

"Can I tell him what this is concerning?"

"A former employee, Cecily Campbell."

"Let me check his calendar." She put him on hold.
About two minutes went by before she came on the
phone again. "He has a few minutes available today
at twelve-thirty."

"That's fine. Can you tell me what Mr. Bond's
exact title is?"

"Certainly. He's the Special Agent in Charge."

"Thank you." Paavo hung up the phone. The
SAC was the head of the San Francisco office. So
Bond had moved up in the world over the past
thirty years. He wondered what had become of
Cecily's boss, Eldridge Sawyer.

Angie was bursting with questions by the time he
hung up. "Did you find out anything?"

They went out to the deck and he handed her the
FBI files. "There isn't a lot here."

She scanned them quickly. "I wonder where she
lived. No address is shown."

"So I noticed. There are names, though. I'm starting with one of her bosses. I wonder how much
he'll remember about her."

Angie's eyebrows rose. "Judging from the pictures I've seen of her, whether he admits it or not,
he'll remember a lot."

Chapter 14

Although the FBI files didn't show Cecily's address, Angie had a good idea how to find out where the woman had lived, or darn close to it. Despite the many lies Paavo had been told about her, Angie was fairly confident that Cecily and Aulis had been neighbors. What else could a young widowed FBI employee and a middle-aged Finn have in common? Hmm, Angie decided not to pursue that, especially in view of Connie's brainstorm about the two of them.

The cleaning service had done a nice job on Aulis's apartment. Still, being here made Angie's hair stand on end big time. And the fact that the last time she was here, a man standing beside her car ended up wearing a toe tag only added to her nervousness.

She dashed into the bedroom and flipped through papers and old envelopes until her eye fell on one postmarked thirty-three years earlier from the Pacific Gas and Electric Company with stock certificates.

The address showed Liberty Street in the city. She had no idea where that was. Several more recent envelopes had different addresses, even some in

Los Angeles and Bakersfield, but Liberty Street was in the correct time frame.

Not until she was back in her car, doors locked, did she breathe again. In the glove compartment, a Thomas Bros. map of the city gave her the information she needed. Liberty Street wasn't far at all.

What the map didn't tell her was that she couldn't reach it by the most direct route, along Sanchez Street. An imposing cement wall, with stairways on both sides, blocked the way. She had to circle around and approach from the opposite side.

The street was quiet and narrow, high on a steep hill, with a barrier at the far end to prevent cars from going any further. Most of the homes were elegant Victorians, some badly weathered, and others "gentrified." A couple of modern houses looked overbearing and sadly out of place. Near the end of the block, she found Aulis's old address in a two-story Victorian. A long staircase with an ornately carved wooden banister led up to a covered front porch with four doors. An overhang on the porch mirrored the ornate carvings of the banister. As with many older buildings in the city, the house most likely had once been an elegant single-family home that was divided into four apartments. Such apartments used to be inexpensive places to live. No more, though.

Getting out of her car, she lifted her tote bag to the shoulder of her plum-colored, tweed Ellen Tracy suit, and picked up her camcorder and purse. Nobody would slam the door on a stranger wearing a sophisticated Ellen Tracy.

She knocked on the door to Aulis's old apartment. A barefoot young woman in jeans and a T-shirt, a toddler on her hip, opened it.

"Hello, there!" Angie said brightly. "My name is Angie Amalfi." She thrust a business card into the woman's hand. One good thing about not having a set business, her cards were generic. "I'm working on a special feature for *San Francisco* magazine on people who have lived in neighborhoods for many, many years. Like, say, thirty years."

"Oh?" The woman stuffed the card in her pocket and pushed a strand of brown hair back off her face. The butterfly clip high on the back of her head wasn't doing its job. "That's not me."

"We're giving away a year of the magazine to everyone who helps us put the article together. Do you happen to know any neighbors who have been here a long time?"

The woman looked blankly at her. "We just moved in last year." She put her little girl down inside the house and stood blocking the doorway so the child couldn't get out. "I've never heard of that magazine."

"You haven't? It's quite wonderful. Can you tell me about the other people in this building? Have they been here long?"

The woman rolled her eyes upward as if the answer might be printed on the underside of the porch roof. This was no candidate for Mensa. "Well, I live upstairs in back. The guy below has been here a few years, but he's only twenty-eight. A gay couple lives in front. They've been here five years at most. I guess the oldest is Terry, above them. Her and her old man bought the building ten years ago, or something like that."

"Have any of them ever mentioned some Finnish people living around here?"

"Finnish people? What do they look like?"

Angie was getting desperate. "What about neighbors? Can you at least tell me if any of them are *old*?"

"What are you, pimping for AARP or something?" the woman asked.

Angie tried hard to be nice. "I'm just trying to do my job. *San Francisco* magazine wants that article."

"I don't know any old neighbors, and even if I did, I wouldn't tell you." She cast a sneering, albeit envious, glare from Angie's suit to matching high-heeled Ferragamos to the Ferrari parked in front of the house. "I don't want your old magazine, anyway."

Angie stared at the door that had just slammed shut in her face. She could scarcely believe it.

Maybe she needed a better cover story. She drove around the neighborhood until she found a Valu-Mart.

Two hours later, she was heading for home with ten of the fifteen boxes of chocolate mint patties she had bought to introduce herself as the neighborhood's new Avon lady. Most people weren't home, and of those who were—all young—few would take the candy or even listen to her spiel. You'd have thought they were afraid she wanted to poison them or squirt them with cologne or something.

The public could be so rude!

Up ahead, a sign on a building caused her to slam on the brakes.

Paavo entered the Federal Building at 450 Golden Gate Avenue. It was a plain, boxy-shaped, beige building, the width of the entire block, protected by a concrete barrier and cyclone fence that reached into the street so that no cars—or Ryder trucks—could park nearby. The FBI offices were on the eighth floor. Bond's secretary motioned him to sit in a well-appointed reception area.

Within three minutes, he was ushered into a corner office with windows facing a State of California office building across the street, and introduced.

Tucker Bond had just taken the lid off a small cottage cheese container, and had two packets of soda crackers, four crackers in all, side by side on his desk. He put down the lid, fastidiously wiped his fingertips on a napkin, and stood with his hand outstretched.

Paavo's first impression of Bond was that the man didn't look at all like the FBI agents he usually dealt with. They tended to be broad shouldered and thick chested, with close-cropped hair and the inevitable black or dark gray suit.

Bond looked like a hawk, gaunt, with prominent cheekbones, a thin, beaklike nose, and wavy gray hair. His navy-blue suit fit like an off-the-rack special offer. A white shirt and a light gray and navy striped tie completed the ensemble. Compared to him, Paavo felt almost fashionable in his gray herringbone Nordstrom's jacket and black slacks.

Bond's grip was strong, and as Paavo regarded the steely nature of his eyes, he realized the gauntness was the sort he'd often seen on long-distance runners, practitioners of exercise and dietary asceticism. He seemed to be all sinew and muscle, fastidious restraint and monklike intensity. Just as Paavo studied Bond, the man scrutinized him in return.

"I took the liberty of finding out which department you worked in, Inspector Smith, after receiving your request to meet." Bond's voice was surprisingly mellow. "Homicide. I was quite intrigued."

"I'm here about an employee you had many years ago."

"Yes, Cecily Campbell." Bond picked up a white plastic spoon. "I hope you don't mind that I'm eating my lunch? This was the only time I had free today."

"Go right ahead."

"I remember Cecily." Bond stopped talking as he ate two heaping spoonfuls of cottage cheese, then grasped the red cellophane tear strip on the crackers. "I haven't thought about her in . . . God, twenty-five years or so. What does she have to do with Homicide now?"

"Perhaps nothing, although there may be some connection between her and a case I'm working on."

Bond's mouth compressed. "Your superiors weren't aware of any such connection."

Paavo tensed at Bond showing his muscle with the higher-ups so quickly. "My superiors don't work my cases. I do."

Bond gave a slight nod as if to grant him a touché. "So, Inspector, does this mysterious case of yours involve the Bureau?"

"No."

"Given that, I don't see how I can help you." He shoveled more cottage cheese into his mouth. At this rate, the container was almost empty.

"Tell me what you remember about Cecily Campbell."

"It's been a long time. One thing, however, I remember well. She died. It was tragic. Very tragic." Bond ate a cracker in two bites. Paavo's mouth was feeling dry just watching him.

"How did she die?"

Bond scraped the last bites from his cottage cheese container, then tossed it into his wastebasket. "An auto accident."

"There's no death certificate on file."

"Impossible. It must be lost—some bureaucratic screwup. Her husband had been a special agent. When he died, she requested a transfer out here." He ate another cracker, and then threw away the cellophane wrapper. After dropping the unopened packet into a desk drawer, using his napkin, he meticulously brushed the cracker crumbs into his hand, being sure not one escaped his notice. He tossed both the crumbs and napkin into the waste-basket. Desktop tidy once again, he faced Paavo. "She worked as a research clerk. We have a lot of them."

"And so," Paavo said slowly, "she transferred here, worked for you, then died. That's all you remember?"

"She didn't work directly for me. Did you know that?"

"I understand her direct boss was Eldridge Sawyer," he said. "I'd like to speak with him as well."

"Mr. Sawyer is no longer with the Bureau." Bond's voice was clipped. Obviously the SAC did not like how much information Paavo had obtained.

"Do you know where I can find him?"

"As a matter of fact, I don't. Sawyer quit the Bureau some number of years ago. We lost track of him after that. If you find him, do let me know. I'd like to see him again."

"Why did he quit?"

"Nothing serious—he just became a little . . . trou-bled. There's a lot of stress in this job. It happens."

"What about the others?" Paavo asked. "Are there other people still working here who knew her?"

"A couple, perhaps, although by now most had the good sense to retire, I'm sure. I'll have the records reviewed, and if I find any employees who worked with her, I'll have my secretary contact you with their names."

"I'd appreciate it."

Bond stared off into space a moment, then said, almost gratuitously, "She was an excellent employee."

The bland words, the blasé tone, sliced into Paavo like a razor. Here he finally met someone who knew and worked with his mother, and the guy acted as if she was nothing. Perhaps he had expected too much, hoped for too much. After all, it'd been so long, and as Bond said, the Bureau had dozens and dozens of clerks.

Against his better judgment, he asked, "Do you remember anything at all about Cecily Campbell? Her character? Her personality?"

Bond stared at him as if trying to decide how to respond. "She was young and impressionable." He paused a moment. "And a bit on the emotional side." He stood. "I'm sorry, but I have a meeting to attend now."

Paavo handed him his card. "Thank you for your time."

From his desk, Paavo faxed a list of clerks and supervisors named in Cecily's file to Nelson Bradley at FBIHQ. It would take Bradley little time to let him know if Bond was telling the truth about few of them still working for the Bureau.

While waiting for Bradley's response, he searched for addresses and phone numbers of any who had retired and still lived nearby.

Eustacia Florian, who had been Eldridge Sawyer's secretary, was listed on Noriega Street. A woman with a young-sounding voice answered his phone call. He introduced himself and asked to speak to Mrs. Florian.

"The police?" The woman sounded frightened. "What's wrong? I'm her daughter."

"Nothing's wrong," Paavo said. "I have some questions regarding a case I'm working on."

"My mother's involved in a case?" She sounded incredulous.

"It concerned her former employment. If you could tell me when I might reach her?"

"Now I understand. What a relief—for me, anyway. I'm sorry, but I doubt she'll be able to help you."

"Why's that?" he asked.

"My mother's in a nursing home. She has Alzheimer's."

Chapter 15

Angie followed the matronly woman down the dark hallway to a sunny room at the back of the small house. A man sat by the window, eyes closed, a blue blanket over his shoulders and a green plaid covering his lap. His frame was slight and his hair billowed like tufts of white cotton.

"Henry!" Mrs. Eschenbach shouted. "Henry, are you awake?"

The old man's body jerked from the aural assault. "Huh?"

"The young woman who phoned is here to talk to you." The woman bellowed like a foghorn.

"Okay, okay." Sharp blue eyes turned toward Angie. "Come over here where I can see you."

Angie hurried across the room to a chair facing him. "Thank you so much for allowing me to come by, Pastor Eschenbach."

"It's no problem. My days aren't very busy anymore. I'm glad to hear Pastor Meier remembered me. It's been years since I was well enough to minister."

"He spoke wonderfully of you," Angie said. It was true, too. When she'd spotted a Lutheran church not far from Liberty Street, she entered and spoke with the current pastor. He'd directed her to Pastor Eschenbach, who led the congregation from the 1950s to the early 1980s. "He thought you could tell me about a Finnish man who used to attend your church, Aulis Kokkonen." She waited a moment, and when she got no reaction, she added, "He used to live on Liberty—"

"I remember Aulis," Eschenbach said. "A nice fellow. I haven't seen him in many years. I'd complain that he stopped going to church, but then I did, too!" He leaned toward her and whispered, "The fire-breathing dragon who showed you here says I'm too old."

Angie thought it prudent not to comment. "Did you . . . did you know any of Aulis's friends?"

"Oh, yes. There were some other Finns, younger than Aulis, I believe, but they were all good friends. Once in a while—not often, in the ways of young men—they would all show up for service. Aulis attended regularly, and he always brought his two children."

Angie's heart leaped. "You knew his children?"

"But of course! We—"

"Henry!" Mrs. Eschenbach's voice was stern. He glanced up at her. Angie hadn't noticed her hovering in the doorway.

"What is it?" Angie asked, looking from one to the other.

"Let me think," the old man said. "It seems they were his sister's children. Yes, that's right. She died, and he raised them. They were very well mannered."

Well mannered? There was a lot more than the kids' manners being remembered here. She was quite sure that wasn't what he nearly said before his wife interrupted. "So you must have known Cecily?" she asked.

"Cecily?" He glanced at his wife.

"Mary, I mean," Angie said.

"We didn't know Mr. Kokkonen's sister, if that's what you're asking." Mrs. Eschenbach moved into the room. "Why are you asking these questions?"

More than ever, the sense they were withholding something filled Angie. "I'm asking because Aulis is in the hospital. He's not doing well, and he seems to want to talk to some of his old friends. I don't know how to find them, so I'm trying this way."

"Why don't you look in his address book, or at old cards and letters?" Mrs. Eschenbach gazed at her disparagingly.

"He doesn't keep them," Angie replied sweetly.

"Neither do I," the pastor said. "My wife takes care of all that."

As the couple seemed to communicate wordlessly, Angie hoped they would open up to her.

"It's quite sad," the wife said, "but we don't have the information you seek."

"I will pray for my old friend." Pastor Eschenbach's gaze was warm.

Standing to leave, she took his hand. "Please, if you think of anything at all that might help, call and let me know. I would appreciate it so very much." She placed her card by his side.

Mrs. Eschenbach walked her through the house. "Miss Amalfi," she said, holding the door open for Angie to leave, "my husband is old and sick. You are not welcome here. I suggest you stop asking questions and stay away from us."

The good news was that Tucker Bond hadn't lied. The bad news was that, of the people named in

Cecily's personnel folder, four were dead, two were clerks who merely processed paperwork, one was so high up the clerks used a rubber stamp for his signature, Eustacia Florian was in a nursing home, and he couldn't find Eldridge Sawyer in any directories, DMV files, or, for that matter, death records. Thinking back on Bond's strange request, he wondered if the FBI had also tried to find Sawyer and failed.

Paavo had hoped to use those people as leads to Cecily's peers—the ones who best knew her and could tell him what was going on in her life that made her run away and change identity. There were two possible scenarios. One, since there was no death record on her, despite how frightened and desperate her note to Aulis had sounded, she had survived the ordeal and chose not to contact her children. Ever. Or, if Bond was right, she was dead. Either way, end of story.

There was no logical reason for him to pursue this one step further.

On his desk was a ballistics report on the bullet that killed Jacob Platt. He focused his attention on it, and then compared it to the one removed from Gregor Rosinsky. Both were 9 mm 147-grain hollow-points, but not fired from the same gun.

He left Homicide for some street work on Platt's investigation, and ended up within a few blocks of Eustacia Florian's nursing home. Her daughter had indicated she still had a few lucid moments now and then. If he caught her at such a time . . .

Even as he explained to the home's supervisor who he was and why he wanted to speak with Mrs. Florian, he cautioned himself against getting his hopes up. Not even his caveat prepared him for how bad it would be.

Eustacia Florian, a Filipina, had a face crisscrossed with wrinkles and hair cut so short her scalp showed in patches. She sat atop the bed, fully dressed in black slacks and a yellow top, wearing green slippers instead of shoes. As he entered the room, black eyes bored into him.

"Mrs. Florian." He approached her slowly and showed his badge. "I'm Inspector Smith. Nothing is wrong. I'd just like to talk with you a few minutes if I may?"

A thin hand reached out and snatched the badge from him, turning it upside down and over before giving it back. "Do I know you?"

"No, we've never met. I spoke with one of your old bosses, Tucker Bond."

"Mr. Bond? Do you know Mr. Bond? He's very smart. Very smart." Her eyes sparkled. "He's a little sweet on me, you know. He always gives me the biggest bouquet of flowers on Secretary's Day."

"That's very nice," Paavo said, sitting on a chair near the foot of the bed. "I'd like to talk to you about someone who worked for your boss, Eldridge Sawyer, years ago. Her name was Cecily Campbell."

"They tried to kill Gerald Ford, you know. President Ford. Right there, under our very noses! Mr. Bond, all of us, were there watching." She punched the air. "We stopped the bastards, we did!"

He wondered if he should continue. "Do you remember Eldridge Sawyer? Or Cecily Campbell?"

She gazed at him. "Do I know you? I met Mr. Hoover once, you know." She sat up tall. "He came to San Francisco. We had to scrub the office until it shined. He came right up to me and said, 'Hello, Eustacia. Good job. We'll make you a special agent soon.'" She beamed. "Do you know Mr. Hoover, too?"

Paavo stood. This was a good idea, but wasn't working. "Good-bye, Mrs. Florian."

"Cecily was just a clerk, you know," Eustacia said, clasping her hands. "She wasn't an agent. Mr. Bond liked to give me special jobs."

He sat down again. "Do you remember Cecily?"

"I complained to Mr. Sawyer, but he told me to keep my mouth shut! I hate him!"

Paavo couldn't follow her rambling. "Tell me about Mr. Sawyer."

"Mr. Sawyer left. He ran away." She put her finger to her mouth. "Shush!"

Sawyer seemed to be his best bet to learn about Cecily. Paavo leaned toward her, keeping his voice low and modulated. "Where did Mr. Sawyer run to, Mrs. Florian? Do you know where he is?"

"He's with . . . he's with . . ." Her eyes darted down, then to the side, then up, and around again.

He leaned forward. "With who?"

"I need my planner. Where's my planner?" She jumped off the bed, opened a drawer, and began to toss her underwear, piece by piece, onto the floor. "*Where's my planner?* WHERE'S MY PLANNER!!!"

He backed out of the room. "Nurse!"

Angie met Paavo at San Francisco General. He'd managed to talk the S.F.P.D. into posting a guard outside Aulis's door for a few days, at least. After sitting with Aulis and meeting with his doctor, they returned to the little cottage, making a slight detour through Chinatown for some food to go. There was no news yet on the break-ins—no fingerprints, no witnesses—and so far, the only hard evidence was the slug that grazed Aulis, another 9 mm, same as the slugs found in the two Russians, although again, the markings showed different guns were used.

Paavo was putting out plates for their dinner when Angie handed him a glass of Chablis. "First let's take a minute to relax," she said, "and you can tell me what you learned from the FBI today."

Standing in the kitchen, sipping the wine, he gave her a brief recap of his visits with Bond and Mrs. Florian. "Cecily Campbell was a clerk," he concluded. "It's a dead end, not worth pursuing. What happened thirty years ago doesn't mean anything now, anyway."

Despite his words, his disappointment was obvious. "You don't know that yet." She tried to be encouraging. "Her old boss might remember. Did you try to find him?"

"I did, with no success. Bond said the guy's 'troubled.' He could be anywhere—new name and everything."

"Hmm, he sounds like Cecily," Angie observed. "What if she ran off with him?"

"I would imagine Bond would remember a scandal like that. He's convinced Cecily's dead. He's probably right."

"It sounds like Mrs. Florian thinks Sawyer's whereabouts are shown in her planner. You should find him."

"It doesn't matter. Cecily left. Why should I care what the reason was?" Paavo's voice turned hushed. "I never should have started this wild-goose chase."

Angie turned her back on him as she put on water for tea. His conflict between wanting to know his past and dreading it was clear. "I also did a little . . . checking . . . myself." She glanced back at him. Sure enough, a dour expression was on his face.

"You did what?"

"I went to the apartment Aulis lived in when

Cecily was a neighbor. Unfortunately, no one there remembered him, let alone her."

"You saw the old house?"

"It was pretty, an area with lots of steps instead of sidewalks." Their eyes met. Could that have anything to do with the quick, obvious appeal this neighborhood had for Paavo? Some harkening back to his childhood?

The tea was soon ready. Over mu shu pork, bok choy with beef, chicken chow mein, and Hunan-style prawns, Angie told about her visit with the Eschenbachs, and the wife's strange warning. "He said Aulis had several young Finnish friends. Do you know about them?"

"The only Finnish friend I know is Joonas Mäki, but he lives a few hours away, up the coast in Gualala."

"Well, there were more."

Together they cleared off the table. Then, as Paavo put on after-dinner coffee, Angie hooked up her camcorder to the VCR so she could watch her restaurant videos on the thirty-one-inch TV.

"Maybe I should try to track down Sawyer," he said, joining her in the living room. The coffee maker hissed and gurgled as it brewed. She simply loved how domestic Paavo was becoming.

"It couldn't hurt," she said.

"What's that?" He stood behind her, watching the TV.

"I wanted a behind-the-scene shot of a restaurant's kitchen. That's the chef's butt—"

"Gross."

"Like bread dough that rose too far. This part is a little shaky because I was moving to another can to see better."

"Another can?"

"Don't ask. This is—Hey, wait!" She hit Rewind.

He moved closer. "Did I see what I thought?"

Her heart was pounding. "I think so." She played the tape again, then hit Pause at the key frame.

As she had struggled to keep her balance and still take a video of the kitchen, the camera swung wildly in her hands, capturing the surrounding alleyway on tape. A man stood in a doorway watching her, with light from a streetlamp illuminating his features. He must have been the man she'd heard laugh and run away.

He was also the man who had been killed outside Aulis's apartment, right next to her Ferrari.

With horror, she now had proof of being watched . . . followed. And she had no idea why.

Chapter 16

"Here it is, Inspector." Mrs. Florian's daughter handed Paavo her mother's planner. He sat in the living room of the modest home.

"It's more than a calendar," Jill Florian said. She was attractive, with a small, upturned nose, pouty mouth, and large brown eyes. Her long, black hair hung free and reached nearly to her waist. "My mother used to carry it back and forth to work every day. She would write notes and reminders, and often said if she ever lost it, she may as well shoot herself." The daughter's eyes filled with tears. "No wonder she was so agitated when she couldn't find it."

"I'm sorry," he said.

"It wasn't your fault."

The planner was one of those five-by-eight multi-ringed binder types with lots of tabs that sort your life into a variety of categories—appointments, priorities, projects, finances, and one for addresses and phone numbers. He turned to the calendar section. It was dated 1994. "Is this when she retired?"

"No. She retired in eighty-four. She bought replacements for ten years, but as you can see, there wasn't much to fill them with."

He flipped to the address portion. The pages were yellowed with age, and the ink for the top entries on each page had faded into browns and purples, while those near the bottom were darker. The planner looked like it might have been used for a good portion of Mrs. Florian's career.

The *S* section was several pages long, with crossouts and additions, asterisks and arrows from names to addresses and annotations. A short way down the first page the name "Sawyer, Eldridge" was shown, with a South San Francisco address and phone number. He copied down the information, then hunted for a more recent entry for the man. There was none.

He thumbed through the pages until he found the *C* section. Near the top of the page was Cecily Campbell. The whole entry had a diagonal line over it. He wondered if Mrs. Florian did that after Cecily died.

The first address shown was on Ocean Avenue. It had been X'd out and an address on Liberty Street added below it. That must have been where Angie went. He wrote it down.

Cecily's name had an asterisk beside it. At the bottom of the page was the referral "*C's friend, Finland expert—Prof. Susan White," and a San Francisco phone number. He copied them down as well. *C's friend . . .*

If Cecily had been a research clerk, and it was her job to contact professors and such, why was only this one noted in the planner? On the other hand, she must have had a lot of contacts, so why was *any* such contact noted?

He looked through other addresses, finding lots of names and companies and experts and cryptic notes. An entire career's worth of contacts existed here, carefully noted by a secretary with dreams of becoming one of Mr. Hoover's special agents.

Paavo took a long detour back to Homicide, all the way to South San Francisco and Eldridge Sawyer's house.

Except for color, the small, plain house perfectly matched every third one on the block. The elderly owners had bought it from Sawyer nearly thirty years earlier. It hadn't been an easy purchase, they told him. Sawyer demanded he be paid in cash, and he had refused to allow his Social Security number or driver's license number to be added to any of the documents. "The guy was unhinged," the homeowner stated bluntly.

Back in Homicide, Paavo ran more checks on Sawyer, but still came up blank.

Then he did the same with Professor Susan White.

To his surprise, she had a rap sheet. There was nothing recent, but in the late sixties she had managed to get herself arrested on three occasions. Twice in Vietnam War protests, and once outside the Soviet consulate.

The Soviet consulate. A Russian brooch. Two dead Russian men. No—his mind was finding connections that couldn't possibly exist.

Could they?

Paavo's shoes echoed in the empty hallway as he searched for room 308C, the office of Professor Susan White. It had been surprisingly easy to find her. When her old phone number didn't work, he called San Francisco State College, the University of San Francisco, and finally U.C. Berkeley, where she was listed as a tenured professor in the History Department. Her specialty was twentieth-century Soviet and Eastern European history.

She agreed to meet him after her last class ended. The heavy Bay Bridge traffic made him late. He knocked on the frosted glass door.

"Come in."

A woman in her sixties sat at a large desk, a computer behind her. She wore light makeup and her blond hair pulled up in a loose knot. She had the well-toned look of a woman who pays close attention to her body and her diet.

"Inspector Smith, S.F.P.D." He held out his hand to her. "Thank you for waiting."

She removed her reading glasses and studied him with such absorption, it took a moment before she noticed his hand. "Inspector, you weren't one of my students, were you? You look familiar."

"I'm afraid not." He explained that he was trying to find out about someone she may have known long ago, Cecily Campbell.

"Cecily?" Her hazel eyes caught his. "I remember her well. We used to meet all the time at the library at SF State."

"At the library?"

"Yes. She was a law clerk, and I was a new professor at my first job."

He was confused. "A law clerk? I thought she worked for the FBI."

White's eyebrows rose. "Good God, I don't think so. She was as opposed to government policies as the rest of us back then. She didn't work for them."

"I must be wrong. What can you tell me about her?"

The professor's intelligent gaze assessed him a moment before she responded. "She was about my age. That's what started us talking. Most of the professors were 'old, white guys,' and the students much younger. I learned she was widowed with a young daughter, new to the area, and I was divorced. She was fascinated by politics and European history—my specialties."

"Finland, right?"

She cocked her head. "Yes. Why do you ask?"

"What else can you tell me about her?"

"Probably not much. She was bright and witty, I know that. Over time, after I took the job here in Berkeley, I lost contact with her. I heard she died a few years later."

"Do you know how she died?" he asked.

"An accident, I assumed."

"In the Bay Area?"

Large, questioning eyes captured his. "I don't really know."

It was a long shot, but he had to ask. "Did you know Aulis Kokkonen?"

She pursed her lips. "The name sounds familiar. I'll ask again—why?"

"Just trying to tie up some loose ends."

She leaned back in the chair. "It was a long time ago. I'm sorry, but I don't think I can remember anything more."

"It's important, if you can help—"

"I'm sorry."

He stood, not even sure why he had come here. What had he expected to learn? He handed her his card. "If you remember anything, call me."

She read it. "Paavo?" Her head jerked up. The tone of her voice stopped him at the door. An eternity passed as the two regarded each other and slowly the furrows on her brow smoothed. She tapped the card against the desktop a moment, as if unsure how to begin. "You came all the way to Berkeley for a reason. Now, why don't you sit back down, please, and tell me what this is *really* all about?"

The tautness of her posture, the intensity of her

gaze, made him decide to tell her the truth. He sat and faced her squarely. "I've recently learned that Cecily . . . Cecily was my mother. I'm curious about her. I heard you were her friend."

"Oh, my," she whispered. "You don't know anything about her?"

He shook his head. "What I thought I knew seems to be a far cry from the truth."

"Yours is possibly the strangest request of my career." She pressed her fingers to her cheek a moment. "I don't know how much I can help you, but let me start at the beginning."

He sat stiffly, scarcely breathing.

"As I mentioned, Cecily shared my interest in the Soviet Union," Professor White began. "A number of us on campus sympathized with the dissidents there and in the Eastern European satellite nations who wanted to be free. Cecily joined us. She particularly talked about Finland and its sub-rosa dissident movement. I knew some Finnish students, well, former students by the time she met them. It turned out there was a vacancy in the building where two of them lived, and she needed a bigger place, so I brought her along to see the apartment and meet them. She fell in love with both."

Her expression silently questioned if this was the kind of information he sought. He nodded.

"Where was the building?" he asked.

"In a nice area up near the top of Sanchez. A small street."

"Liberty?"

"Yes! That's it. This all took place so long ago. . . ."

"Please continue."

Her hands folded atop the desk. They were strong, capable hands, without rings. "Aulis Kokkonen—since you mentioned his name, I do remember him—lived in one of the apartments, but he was older, not caught up in helping the dissidents. The *samizdat* movement was going on at that time. Do you know what that was?"

He shook his head.

"I *am* a professor, so now here comes a lecture— I'll be quick." She smiled. "It simply means 'self-published.' Essays and newspapers against the government were being illegally copied in Russia so the dissident movement there could grow. To get equipment to make the copies—keep in mind, Inspector, that typewriters, let alone mimeograph machines and small printing presses, were nearly impossible for common people to own in that country—the dissidents looked to sympathizers in the West for help."

"And the Finns were such sympathizers?" Paavo asked.

"Correct. They believed that only by undermining the Soviet government itself would Finland and Communist bloc countries become free. As history proved, they were right."

Paavo nodded, absorbing the information. "Who were the Finns?"

"I'm trying to remember their names. There were four of them, thick as thieves. Let's see. Of the four, one Americanized his name—Sam? Yes, I'm sure that was it—he was quite the live wire. One was quiet, a little guy. One was tall and thin and had thick eyebrows that went straight across his face. He was a little older than my former students— although not as old as Aulis."

"Joonas Mäki?" Paavo asked, his voice hushed.

"Joonas. That sounds right. Then there was the fourth man." She gazed at Paavo with a strange smile. "My God, when he and Cecily met—I remember that evening—I think it was love at first

sight. The two had eyes only for each other. Me and
Sam and the little guy kept jabbing each other in the
ribs, watching the two of them stare at one another,
yet scarcely saying a word." She chuckled. "They
never even noticed us."

"What was this fourth man's name?"

She pressed her fingers to her brow, her eyes shut,
trying to dredge it up. After a while, she dropped
her hands in exasperation. "It'll come to me in time.
I know it will."

"Can you describe him, or tell me what he looked
like?"

A touch of sympathy, then resignation, came into
her eyes, and she reached for her purse. After rum-
maging around inside it, she took out a small mirror
and handed it to him. "Look." Her voice was gentle.
"Now I know why you're so familiar to me."

Chapter 17

"I can't tell you how much I appreciate your seeing me," Angie said as she walked into the elegant Pacific Heights home of retired de Young Museum curator Donald Porter. Her jeweler at Tiffany's, the man who'd suggested she bring her brooch to Gregor Rosinsky, had contacted Porter on her behalf after she told him the brooch was now missing. Porter had a particular interest in Russian artwork.

He led her into a living room crammed with antique furniture and nineteenth-century paintings. She paused in the doorway to catch her breath at the opulence before her.

"May I offer you some sherry?" he asked, crossing the Sarouk carpet to an ornate mahogany liquor cabinet.

"No, thank you." She sat on a Chippendale armchair and handed him an enlarged sketch of her brooch, annotated with its dimensions. "I wish I were a better artist," she said. "I added as much detail as I could remember. Gregor Rosinsky was quite surprised to see it and seemed to think it was very valuable."

"I knew Gregor well," Porter remarked, studying

123

the drawing. He stood tall, with a thick head of pure white hair. "It was a great tragedy that he was killed. He did fine work. You said he had this brooch, and it's now gone?"

"I believe it was the only thing taken in the robbery," she said.

He, too, sat. "Well, if this is authentic—and if Gregor said it was, I'd imagine he was correct—the thieves made off with something that could easily be valued at upwards of a half million dollars."

"You're kidding me!" she cried.

"I never joke about art."

"How could something so valuable end up in"— how should she put this?—"private hands? I mean, it was a gift to me from someone who had no idea of its value."

"I must confess, you have me intrigued, as well, about the brooch's history. I'll go to my sources to see what I can find out. I will say, if it was in a Russian museum, they've been rather thoroughly looted over the past half century, as have many churches and private estates. Smuggling is a huge business in Russia, as it was in the former USSR."

"I've heard a little about some *samizdat* movement," she added tentatively, recalling Paavo's words.

"Oh yes, many of the dissidents stole artwork and had it smuggled to the West to get money for their activities. That was quite common."

"Do you think this could have been smuggled out in that way?"

He gave her a toothy smile. "That's as good an explanation as any."

"I remembered!" The woman's excited voice all but sang over the phone. "This is Professor White."

Sitting at his desk in Homicide in the morning,

Paavo felt his heart begin to pound, and his hand tightened on the receiver. "Yes?"

"I was watching Leno on TV last night and a commercial came on for Formula One racing. One of the drivers is Mika Häkkinen. That jarred my memory."

She pronounced the name MEE-kah HAH-ki-nen.

He waited, holding his breath.

"His name was also Mika. Mika Turunen." Then she said words that Paavo never imagined he would hear. "I remembered something else. I'm almost certain I was told that Cecily married him."

At San Francisco's Hall of Records, Paavo resolutely filled out a form to request a search for a marriage certificate. He would see if there was any actual proof to the professor's story. Cecily's FBI files made no mention of any marriage. It might have been another of his mother's stories—like being a law clerk—one that she told people just to look good.

A bored clerk gestured him to the seats in the hallway with an even more bored assurance that he'd be called. While waiting for the marriage records, he decided to fill out another form. Why not be even more of a fool?

After turning in the second request, he sat back down on the wooden chair to wait.

A Mexican woman with three children stood at the table filling out papers while her children tugged at her arm, pulled the hem of her dress, dangled from the table, and ran along the polished tile hallway, then dropped to their knees and butts to see how far they could slide. An old man stood at another table, his hands shaking as he slowly, carefully checked his application.

Three other people sat nearby, expressions of varying tedium on their faces. All three glanced at

the tall, stern-looking detective, then quickly lowered their eyes. Did he look so much the cop? he
wondered.

The clerk called one person, after a while another,
and then the third. Paavo's assumptions that they
were pretty much on a roll proved wrong when he
had a long wait before finally hearing his name.

Prepared to be told simply that no record existed,
he was momentarily at a loss when the clerk thrust
a sheet with an embossed seal into his hand.

He walked back to his chair before looking at it.

It was a marriage certificate between Cecily Hampton Campbell and Mika Turunen, dated thirty-six
years ago. Much to his surprise, he found himself
doing a quick mental calculation between his birth
date and the date of the marriage. Eleven months.
His breathing grew shallow and fast.

As if from far off, he heard his name being called
again. He looked up. The clerk was glaring at him
as if he'd been saying his name for some time.

In his hand he waved another piece of paper.

Mechanically Paavo retrieved the result of his
second request. His ears were ringing, his temples
pounding, as he headed straight out of the building
and over to the Civic Center plaza in front of City
Hall, scarcely looking at anything around him.

He sat on the bench and stared a moment at the
pigeons. Earlier, someone must have scattered
bread crumbs, because the birds were still bustling
and bobbing to find a few morsels here and there.
He didn't think anyone had time for things like
feeding birds anymore. When he was a boy, sometimes he'd go to the park with Aulis and toss them
tiny bits of dried bread. Other times, Aulis would
bring him to the Palace of Fine Arts and he'd feed
bread to the ducks.

When did he last take the time to watch ducks or pigeons, let alone feed them?

His hands began to shake from the tight grip he had on the papers he held. The marriage certificate was on top. He moved it aside, exposing the sheet below, and began to read.

Certificate of Live Birth. Full Name of Child: Paavo Hampton Turunen. Maiden Name of Mother: Hampton. Place of Birth: San Francisco, California. Name of Hospital or Institution: Saint Francis Hospital.

His eye skipped down the document, past the address of the hospital, his birth weight, sex, and so on, to the next section, and then stopped.

Father of Child: Mika Turunen, age 26. Occupation: computer programmer.

Mother of Child: Cecily Jean Hampton, age 29. Occupation: housewife.

Pressure built behind his eyes and he quickly folded the papers in half, then in half again so they would fit into his breast pocket. This was what he had spent a lifetime wanting to know. The birth certificate Aulis had given him showed his mother as Mary Smith, his father as "Unknown."

Paavo Unknown, that was who he had been.

But suddenly he had a name, parents, a history. He stood, his legs strangely rubbery as he started to walk away from the Civic Center, toward the Hall of Justice, toward the life he knew. Yet, even as he walked the familiar streets, his emotions roiled and he couldn't stop a dark, hollow sense from filling him, a sense that he himself had become a stranger.

Angie paced from the living room through the dining area to the kitchen and back, sure she was wearing a groove through the plank flooring. With each turn, she checked the time, but the clock scarcely moved.

She didn't like calling Homicide to ask Paavo where he was, how he was doing, and when he'd be home. His job caused him to work long hours. If he was in pursuit of a murderer, he couldn't simply drop it because his girlfriend expected him to go home when it got late. She'd vowed not to hassle him about his hours, ever.

That didn't make it any easier to handle when he didn't call. He usually did phone her sometime in the afternoon or early evening to check in, make sure everything was okay, give her some idea of his schedule, and to find out about hers.

Tonight he hadn't done any of that.

After her visit with Donald Porter, she'd gone to the de Young and then to some smaller museums to look at Russian art and curios, trying to develop a sense of its aesthetics—an interesting mixture of Europe and Asia. The museum shops had books that would help, and she'd bought several. She tried concentrating on them, but all she could think about was her brooch and Paavo.

When Paavo told her about his visit with the professor yesterday, she realized she'd made an important mistake in her assessment of what was going on. She had thought of the two Russians, *her* brooch, and then her, Paavo, and Aulis. She should have thought of the two Russian, *Cecily's* brooch, and the three of them. In the past, there had been a clear connection—and political animosity—between Cecily, the Finns, and the Soviets. Why, though, should that be an issue today? The brooch was the key, but the key to what?

The slowly ticking clock brought her back to the moment. She went to the window and looked out. How strange it was to be in the city and not see a busy street with an endless stream of cars. The quiet here was unnerving.

She turned again to a book about Fabergé and other Russian artisans and their work.

Only when she heard the front door open did she realize she'd fallen asleep on the sofa. "Paavo," she murmured, and sat up.

He paused in the darkness of the doorway. "I lost track of time," he said, his voice subdued. He took off his sport coat and hooked it on the closet doorknob.

She stretched and got to her feet. "It's all right." She approached him, placing her hands on his shoulders, then down along his chest, feeling his warmth through the blue and white striped cotton shirt. "I'm making one of your favorite dishes tonight—pasta with prosciutto and sun-dried tomatoes." As she lifted her face to his, the bleakness of his expression struck her like a physical force and she reared back. "What is it?"

"Nothing." He kissed her lightly, then headed for the kitchen. "Is there any Scotch in the house?"

"Cousin Richie stocked this place quite well. Soda, too." She showed him where the liquor was stored, then twisted an ice tray to pop out a couple of cubes for him. "Did you go see Aulis?"

"Yes. He hasn't changed at all, and his doctor says there's still hope for a full recovery." He reached for the glasses. "Would you like a drink, too?"

She shook her head, and he poured himself one before continuing. "A couple of his friends stopped by, guys he used to work with at the bank, and even a nun was there—she said you asked her to pray for him 'even though he's Lutheran.' "

Angie shrugged. "Why not?"

His smile didn't reach his eyes. He sipped his Scotch, and looked even more desolate.

"Tell me what happened today," she said, watching him intently as they moved into the living room. She sat down on the sofa and expected him to join her.

Instead, he went to his coat and pulled some papers out of the pocket. "The lady professor phoned." He chuckled derisively. "It's a good thing she watches commercials—some Finnish race car driver helped her remember the name of my father."

"Oh, my." She stood again. He'd been shaken enough by yesterday's conversation with her. Today, to have been given a name . . . "Oh, Paavo."

He handed her the papers. As she read the marriage and birth certificates, the full impact of what this meant to him washed over her and tears filled her eyes. She carefully folded them again. "I'm glad you finally know," she said huskily.

He finished his Scotch, then opened the French doors and stepped onto the deck. The sky was overcast and drizzly. He sat on a chair, leaning forward, arms on thighs, and stared into the blackness.

She stood in the doorway. There were times, like this, when the past he'd tried to bury came through, and she could see the child who grew up an orphan, whose troubled sister met an early death, and who still had an empty, dark place deep inside him because of it.

Usually so glib, her mind had emptied of words to say. She had never thought she could ache so much for him.

A world of information was at his fingertips at work, and she wondered if he'd made further discoveries today. She was almost afraid to ask, but she had to. Her voice was scarcely above a whisper. "Did you find out what happened to them?"

After a long silence, he spoke. "I couldn't, Angie.

I thought about it, and typed their names to search the database more than once, but I couldn't hit the Send command. I wanted to think of them alive, for one night, at least."

She squeezed her eyes shut a moment, then stepped behind his chair and wrapped her arms around his neck, bending forward to kiss the side of his face, to press her cheek to his. "I know," she whispered, her throat so thick she had to force the words out. "I know." He interlaced his fingers with hers, pressing them to his chest. She could have cried aloud, and ranted and raged with fury at the hurt this was causing him. Why had they done it to him—all of them, Aulis, Cecily, Jessica, and maybe even this Mika Turunen? She would blame each one for not telling a small boy who he was, and blame his parents for walking out and leaving him all alone.

"I need to find out what happened to them, Angie. Why did Cecily write to Aulis the way she did? I've gone this far. I want the truth."

"We'll find out." She moved around the chair to face him, and crouched at his knee. "Give it time. Give yourself time."

"I thought I'd put it behind me, and now . . ." He bowed his head and she reached her arms around his back, just as he clutched her tight. She needed to make this right for him.

Somehow, she would find a way.

The woman shut down her laptop, then stood and paced. Her "security" work served her well now. She was able to find out all about the players— Angelina Amalfi and Paavo Smith in their cute little not-so-well-hidden hideaway. She smirked. Plus a cameo brooch worth hundreds of thousands of dollars.

That was a big part of this, certainly, but it wasn't everything. Not by a long shot.

There was more, and as soon as she found it, all hell would break loose.

Chapter 18

When Serefina Amalfi opened the front door the next morning, Angie threw her arms around her and hugged her hard. Angie's mother was short and heavy, her black hair pulled straight back into a bun.

"Angelina, *che fai?*" The startled woman asked.

"Nothing, Mamma," Angie said. "I'm just happy to see you."

"Come inside. It's that burglary, isn't it?" Serefina asked. Angie followed the dancing red polka dots of her mother's rayon dress through the house to the family room. "It has you nervous. That's why you're never at home when I call."

Angie still hadn't told her mother she was staying in one of Cousin Richie's houses, and definitely not that Paavo was staying with her. Her parents would worry if they knew about the break-ins at Paavo's and Aulis's homes, and if they heard Aulis had been shot besides, they'd insist Angie move in with them. "I'm not nervous," she said. She'd passed nervous days ago and was hurtling toward frantic. "Anyway, a locksmith put great new locks on the door. It's just that I've been busy with my video restaurant reviews."

Serefina sat down at a new computer. "I'm on-line. Can you stay for lunch?"

Angie's eyebrows popped up high to see her old-fashioned, won't-program-a-VCR mother sitting in front of a high-powered Pentium. "I've got a reservation for lunch at a new Basque restaurant for another video review. Bianca's joining me. Would you like to come, too?"

"You know I don't like restaurant food," Serefina said, staring at the screen.

Angie knew it. She also knew her mother would have been insulted to death if she hadn't invited her. Angie had failed to once, and the fallout, which the family dubbed Restaurant-gate, had had more whispering, hurt feelings, and innuendo than any political scandal. "What is this?" she asked, glad to change the subject. "I didn't know you owned a computer."

Serefina pushed a few keys. "Caterina brought it over. You know your sister thinks everyone needs the latest of everything. She says everybody shops this way now. You push the button and things you want show up at your door. No work at all."

Angie sat down and watched her mother study the screens and navigate her way through a Neiman-Marcus site.

"Hah! Look at that! *Dio!*" Serefina threw up her arms, then reached under the desk and yanked out the plug. The monitor went black and the computer made a whirring death rattle.

"That's not how to turn it off." Angie gasped. "You've got to shut it down step by step."

"*Basta!* I don't care." Serefina stood up and glared at the expensive system. "What nerve! I'm not going to use it again."

"What happened?"

"I've heard how people steal things off these

computers, and that once you put some information in, it's there forever. No way am I going to tell them what size dress I wear! *Ma che schifo!*" She smoothed her hands over her round waist and hips. "And anyway, I'm on a diet, so I won't be this size much longer."

Angie suppressed a smile. Serefina was always on a diet. "I don't think anyone cares—"

"I care!" As Serefina lumbered toward the kitchen, she called out, "Let's have some coffee. Your cousin Gina sent some of her biscotti. *Buonissimo!* Like butter, they are!"

A short while later, Angie sat in the sunroom across from Serefina, munching cookies and talking the way they had done, time and again, over the years. She couldn't imagine not having this warmth in her life, not having this security and place to come home to. Thoughts of all Paavo had missed swept over her—the mother's and father's hugs never given, tears of joy and pride never shed, hands never clasped doing something as simple as helping a child to cross a street.

"Why are you looking so gloomy all of a sudden, Angelina?" her mother asked.

"I was just thinking of someone who isn't as lucky as I am."

"Lucky?"

"To have you and Papá, and to know that you both love me, no matter what I've done."

An eyebrow arched. "How much money do you need?"

Angie was taken aback. "No, really. I was just thinking of my childhood, with all the family around, with Frannie to play with, and our older sisters to look up to. I was very happy."

"You used to torment Frannie. She was so sweet natured and you were such a little devil!"

"Mamma! I'm trying to tell you how much I love you!"

Serefina studied her a long moment. "Angelina, are you pregnant?"

Paavo waited until the lull after most inspectors headed for home around five-thirty to pull the files out of his drawer and set them on his desk. They'd been on his mind all day, even as he attended an autopsy for a drowning victim whose death investigation he'd been assigned, even as he testified at a prelim for a murder case he'd investigated.

When he'd first arrived at work that morning, he'd done what he should have done yesterday—he'd looked for records on Mika Turunen and Cecily Campbell Turunen. He'd found death certificates for both of them. Cecily had died in a car accident one week after Mika's death.

Mika had been murdered. He'd died of gunshot wounds.

So now he knew, and the knowing left him drained and empty.

When he'd requested the homicide book on Mika, he found an annotation on the system to the investigation of Sam Vanse. Sam . . . Professor White had mentioned someone named Sam. He'd called for that book as well. Several hours passed before Archives contacted him to say the files were ready for pickup.

The casebooks were old and dusty, and the clerk at Records had handed them to Paavo with all the reverence of giving him the Holy Grail. He pulled out Vanse's file. He wasn't yet ready to look at a report on his own father's death.

The reports were, for the most part, in chronological order. Paavo read quickly through the Preliminary Report. Vanse had been found in his car in the parking lot of San Francisco General Hospital, dead from a bullet wound to the back of the head. He had a second, nonlethal wound to his shoulder. The second wound had been inflicted some minutes before the first.

Vanse had been pulled to the driver's side of his car in an unsuccessful attempt to make it look like he had driven himself to the hospital. His condition and blood on the passenger seat showed this was not the case. Fingerprints found on the steering wheel and elsewhere belonged to Mika Turunen.

Mika Turunen was murdered the day after Vanse's death. The two men were friends and co-workers at the Omega Computing Corporation.

A number of people were interrogated—Paavo saw an Okko Heikkila, Joonas Mäki, and Aulis Kokkonen among them, but no leads developed, and although there were references made to Vanse's activism in anti-Soviet groups, no conclusions as to why he was killed were made.

Reading between the lines—the type of questions asked, the cross-reference to Turunen's folder—gave the appearance the investigators were speculating that Turunen killed Vanse, and then, in retaliation, was himself killed. The case remained open pending further developments.

Paavo's skin was chilled. Could his own father have been a murderer?

If so, why the two gunshot wounds, and why had Mika driven Sam to a hospital? The investigation gave no answers to those questions.

Paavo turned to photographs of the death scene. The body had moldered in the parking lot for almost two days before being discovered. Paavo knew that lot well, because of Aulis. It was enormous, with cars coming and going twenty-four hours a day, and a number of them remaining for several days.

He shut the folder, not wanting to look at any more photos or the autopsy report.

Slowly, tentatively, he reached for the next binder, the file on the investigation of Mika Turunen's death.

He had handled plenty of old homicide investigation case binders, but this was not any old case. This was . . . this man had been his father. As he touched the black cover, his hands trembled and his chest felt as if a tight band were around it, constricting the air from his lungs.

He cracked open the faded and stiff cover, and then skipped over the yellow, dusty pages of the Chronological Report and Preliminary Report, preferring to form his own conclusions from the base material. He turned to the first report and began to read.

The report had been filed by the patrol officers called to the scene by a motel owner. It began:

Victim, Mika Turunen, age 30, found Room 8, Cypress Motel, 6321 Bayshore Boulevard, at 0717. DOA multiple gunshot wounds.

Next came the Death Investigation Report. The motel owner, Victor Duggin, provided most of the information. Mrs. Turunen was in the office checking the family out, and the children were making him nervous playing with the ice machine outside. He wanted to get the family on its way, but he was having trouble accessing a phone line to verify the credit card.

Suddenly he heard a barrage of gunshots so loud he ducked behind the counter. Mrs. Turunen ran outside. He assumed she went to her children.

When the shooting stopped, Duggin lifted his

head to see a black Cadillac tearing out of the lot. He didn't see the faces—only that two men were inside. The door to Room 8 stood open, and some of the other motel guests were peeking from their rooms. The man from Room 5 ran into the office to tell him the guy in 8 was dead.

Duggin phoned the police and then searched for Mrs. Turunen and her children, but he never saw them again. She never even came back to pick up her credit card.

Under next of kin, the investigators had written:

Spouse—Cecily Turunen, age 33
Stepdaughter—Jessica Campbell, age 9
Son—Paavo Turunen, age 4

Paavo turned to the supplemental reports. The motel guests were all interviewed. No one saw the shooters. One person thought he saw the victim's wife and children outside the motel room after the shooters left, but he wasn't sure.

Twenty rounds of 160-grain hollow-points had been fired into the room; five hit the victim's chest— heart, lungs, and stomach penetrated, death instantaneous. The remaining shots were fired into the closet and bathroom, as if in search of anyone hiding there and killing them as well. Several shots penetrated the walls into Room 7.

Paavo leafed through reports investigating the victim himself. There were essentially two sets of reports—one immediately after Mika's murder, and another set after Sam's body was found with Mika's fingerprints in his car.

Turunen was on a work visa, and had nothing negative at all on his record. Co-workers gave him high marks for job knowledge and productivity. Reference was made to Mika being part of a group of Finns working to help anti-Communists in Finland and the USSR. Speculation centered around a falling-out between members of this group, since Vanse was also implicated in it, but no proof could be found. Joonas Mäki and Okko Heikkila were interrogated, but both had good alibis.

Cecily and her children abandoned their apartment and disappeared after the murder. None of the neighbors, including Aulis Kokkonen, had any idea where they had gone. No one mentioned Cecily's job with the FBI.

Suspicion immediately turned to Turunen's wife, even speculation that the deaths were the result of a romantic triangle—that Cecily could have ordered a hit on Mika after he killed her lover.

The next page in the file caused him to sit up abruptly. A week after the murder, Cecily Turunen's car was found, upside down, in the Pacific just below Devil's Slide in San Mateo County—not S.F.P.D jurisdiction. No body was retrieved.

The investigation basically ended there, although more questions were asked and more leads followed, but nothing new turned up, and the case remained officially open.

Twice in the following year the case had been picked up and reworked without consequence. Since the victim's children were still missing and the wife's body had never been recovered, the unsubstantiated conclusion within Homicide was that after having her husband killed, she faked her death and ran, taking her children with her.

FBI help to find Cecily Turunen and her children was sought, but they, too, failed. Eldridge Sawyer had worked as the prime contact for the S.F.P.D. on the case.

Mika's autopsy report came next. Paavo skimmed it, not wanting the details. Even flipping through the thick report, though, his head felt a little light.

Included in the binder was a brown envelope, ten by twelve. He knew what it contained—the crime scene and autopsy photos. He couldn't look, and set it aside.

Next in the file was an inventory of the evidence. Fingerprints lifted from the crime scene and their CSI IDs; lists of slugs and their CSI numbers; the clothes Mika wore, and clothes and belongings left behind in the motel room by the family.

No clear prints other than the family's and motel employees' were found. If it had been a professional hit—no matter who ordered it—they wouldn't have touched anything. Probably kicked the door open, or knocked on the door with some innocuous request, stepped inside, and started shooting.

Paavo closed the file and ran his hands over his mouth, nose, and eyes. As much as he'd tried to read the file purely as a cop, at times the enormity of what he was learning after a lifetime of questions shook him to the core.

He took the stairs back down to Archives, glad for the chance to move, and searched for the San Mateo County's investigation of Cecily's death. Often, complete files were copied and stored in cases clearly connected like this; if not, he would have to contact San Mateo.

He was in luck; a copy existed.

Back at his desk, he read through it. It was small and incomplete by big-city standards, but he could see that the police who took the case had been thorough with their contacts and their questions. They simply weren't given good answers.

Passersby had spotted Cecily's car at low tide and reported it. Her seat belt had not been fastened and

the driver- and passenger-side windows were both
open. It was assumed the tides had washed the
body out of the car and out to sea. Some strands of
the victim's hair had snagged onto the window, and
tests showed blood on the windshield consistent
with a face or head injury to a driver.

Tide currents showed that the body should have
washed up within a couple of weeks just north of
the Golden Gate. It did not.

When the connection between the missing victim
and San Francisco's two murders was discovered,
the case was basically turned over to the S.F.P.D.,
who added little to it.

He shut Cecily's folder, his mind filled with more
questions than the reports answered.

The envelope with photos of Mika's autopsy still
sat, unopened, on his desk.

Homicide remained empty. He hadn't even
noticed that three hours had passed. A couple of
guys would be dropping in soon. Some of the
skanks they dealt with could only be found after
the sun went down. Much later, eleven or midnight,
the on-call inspectors would probably show up
because that was when most of the city's murders
happened.

As if he were moving in slow motion, he lifted the
envelope, bent the metal clasps forward, opened the
flap, and slid out the photos.

A black-and-white eight-by-ten showed a man
lying on his back, on a carpeted floor, his plaid-
shirt-and-jeans-clad body riddled with bullet holes.

He'd seen plenty of photos like this one before,
but never had bile risen in his throat. He kept his
eyes riveted to the photo. Despite the carnage, the
thing that struck him the hardest was that the victim looked so very young. He was a thin man. His
long hair, almost black in the photo, had spilled

thickly around his head onto the carpet. His eyes were shut. No bullet marred the narrow, high-cheekboned face with a broad brow and high, straight nose. His eyebrows were dark, not particularly thick, and arched. He wore a mustache and a short, trimmed beard. Except for the last, it was Paavo's own face.

The photo blurred. His hand shook as he lowered it. Mika, in death, was younger than Paavo was now. He didn't feel like he was looking at a father—more like he should be a brother, or even a son.

The shock, the grief, gradually faded, leaving emptiness inside him. Although the office was well heated, he was filled with an incredible cold. Then he remembered the feel of Angie's arms circling his neck last night as he sat out on the chilly deck, remembered her warmth and sunniness, her compassion. He drew in a deep breath, and continued.

He quickly leafed through other crime scene shots, all taken from different angles. Lamps, the headboard, the walls, the bed, the closet, and the dead man.

He stopped when he reached the first autopsy photo. He didn't want to look at those. He didn't think he ever could. As he gathered the photos together to put them back into the envelope, he saw a five-by-eight white envelope.

He knew what was in it—a photo of the victim in life. Homicide inspectors often used them to talk to people when they tried to find out more about a victim. It was too unsettling for people to be asked what they knew about a person and to be handed a photo from the morgue, or even worse, the scene of the crime. Only police should ever have to see victims in such poses.

So here was the photo the homicide inspectors thirty years ago had used to ask people if they remembered Mika Turunen. Paavo opened the envelope and removed the photo.

If homicide inspectors had asked him their question, he would have answered, "Yes. I remember him."

They weren't precise memories, not sharp or definitive, but more of a blur. Yet, he *knew*.

Suddenly he had an odd sense of vertigo, of being lifted high in the air by sure but gentle hands, and looking down into the big, blue eyes of the man in the photo. Echoes of laughter, adult and child, wafted in his ears. Another fuzzy memory came of a zoo, the strong musky scent of animals in his nostrils, and climbing onto a railing to look down into a pit where Siberian tigers were kept, and the feel of someone's large hand on his shoulder, holding him, ready to grab him if he started to tumble over. He couldn't quite remember the face that went with those hands . . . maybe not even the hands, exactly. Yet it wasn't an unfamiliar touch. It was one he'd known. One he'd felt safe with.

Then it was gone, and he never felt safe that way again.

How could he have forgotten? And why hadn't Jessica and Aulis talked about him?

The vague sense of knowing his father had been a part of him for years, but they had assured him that he was wrong. As he grew older, the perception faded, and he came to believe them.

Why had they wanted him to forget the father who had played with him, and loved him? He grew up thinking the man didn't care that he existed, that his father walked away and never looked back. Why had they done that not only to him, but to the loving man who had been his father?

Nausea roiled in his stomach, and once more his vision blurred.

"Hey, Paav! Can't believe you're still around when you've got a woman waiting for you." Homicide Inspector Bo Benson came in carrying a tall cup of coffee. Paavo glanced up at him.

"What's wrong?" Benson asked. "You look like you've just seen a ghost."

"Maybe so," Paavo said. He slid the photo back into the envelope, carefully locked everything away inside a desk drawer, then picked up his jacket and left.

Chapter 19

"Make sure you leave me out of your freaking videos, kid." Cousin Richie punctuated the air with his steak knife.

Angie swiveled her camcorder away from his glistening head and toward unsuspecting diners in the Bella Rosa restaurant. "Why don't you want to be on TV?"

"I got my reasons. Hell, I'm surprised none of these customers punches you out." He took a big bite of his New York steak. Richard Amalfi, the son of her father Sal's older brother, wasn't one for delicate veals and sauces as his main course. At age forty-four, he was speeding toward the age when men fight middle age with a vengeance. He was overweight and the expanding sand trap in the back of his head was beginning to give him a complex. What was left of his hair was shiny blue-black and curly. His hands were thick, with hairy knuckles on short fingers. He wore a Rolex the size of a pancake on his wrist, plus enough gold against his deeply tanned, black-haired chest to fill all the teeth in a small city.

They had already finished a *minèstra* of swiss chard and cannelli beans, rigatoni with mussel and

146

basil sauce, and were into the main course. "So, when you going to tell me why you asked me here?" he asked, taking a long swig of Krug's cabernet sauvignon.

"How suspicious! I wanted to thank you for the house, that's all," Angie said between bites of veal roll stuffed with tomato, anchovy, and parmesan. "We're loving it."

"Yeah, and I didn't say a word to Sal or Serefina, just like you asked." He gave her a wink. "If they ever find out, I'll deny everything."

"Absolutely. Oh, I almost forgot, but since you brought it up, I do have one teensy little favor I wanted to ask of you."

"Uh-huh." He smirked.

"Don't give me that look! This is important. Paavo's been trying to find a guy, an ex–FBI agent named Eldridge Sawyer."

"Eldridge? What the hell kind of name is Eldridge?"

"I have no idea. Anyway, the guy seems to have gone into hiding." She handed him a piece of paper. "Here's his last address. He owned the place and sold it. Paavo tried state records, but there was nothing."

"What do you think I am, some freaking private eye?"

Now it was her turn to smirk. "I think a pack of bloodhounds would have nothing on you, cousin. You're someone who has sources in real estate, who has friends who can see where this guy was when the title documents and other papers were sent long after he left his house, and who can, somehow, track him from place to place after that."

Round, innocent brown eyes gawked at her. "What makes you think realtors keep records like that?"

He was innocent as a retriever in a duck pond. "A lot don't, I'm sure," she said, adding more wine to his glass. "Your friends are special. That's all I know. I don't know anything else. Nothing at all."

He chortled. "That's my girl."

"You'll give it a try, then?"

"It'll cost."

"No problem."

He leaned way back, raising his hip in order to stuff Sawyer's address into his pants pocket. "An ex–special agent trying to hide? It'll be like taking candy from a baby."

A squatty two-story building designed to look like a Spanish hacienda with chipped stucco walls and a row of red tile edging a tar and gravel roof bore the sign CYPRESS MOTEL in neon letters. Below it, the single word VACANCY. The rooms all faced the center parking lot, and the motel office guarded the entrance.

Paavo studied the motel from his car a moment, then walked into the parking lot. It was half-filled. From inside the lot, the motel looked even seedier than from the street. He focused on the door to Room 8, then abruptly turned back toward the office. A small alcove, built between the office and the first rental, caught his eye.

As if against his will, he moved in its direction and stepped inside.

The alcove had an ice machine and several vending machines for soda, candy, cookies, and crackers. The vending machines were new . . . but this alcove . . . right next to the office . . .

"Looking for someone?"

Paavo spun around to see a middle-aged man warily frowning at him. He took out his badge. "I'm checking up on an old case. About thirty years ago a man was shot in this motel. Do you know anything about it?"

"Thirty years ago?" The man scoffed. "You kidding me? I don't give a damn about that. I only bought this flea trap ten years ago. Worst thing I ever did. They was supposed to put a shopping mall 'cross the street. Upgrade the area. Then it fell through. This area's getting worse than ever.

"I had a guy OD last year. A suicide three years ago. But no murder. Not yet, anyhow. Wouldn't surprise me, though. After being in this business, seeing the customers, nothing surprises me no more."

Paavo glanced again at the alcove with the ice machines—*the children were playing with ice*—then at the door to Room 8.

"You being a cop," the motel owner said, hands on hips, "I guess you know what I mean about the public being for shit. That nothing they do surprises you anymore, right?"

"You're right," Paavo replied after a while. "Nothing surprises me much at all anymore."

He left the motel in a fog, his usual dogged clarity blurred and distorted by the past. His life had been nothing but a house of cards, and he was now in a game of fifty-two pickup. He couldn't say he remembered having been at the motel as a child, but an eerie familiarity about it haunted him.

As much as he wanted to see Angie, he needed a little time to digest all he had learned and seen. He drove, not paying attention to the streets.

The motel had brought back the nightmare with Jessica, but what he found was reality—the gunfire, the loss of his father, and soon after, of his mother.

Her loss must have overshadowed everything else for him. That was the only way he could imagine believing Aulis and Jessica's lies about his father. He rubbed his temple. It was all so very fuzzy to him, memories mixed together with lies.

What must have been going through his child's mind back then? And through Jessica's for that matter? She wasn't much older, but old enough to feel the full impact of everything that happened—old enough to understand, but not to have the maturity to handle it. That was probably why she'd been so close to him for so many years, closer than most brothers and sisters. Despite her youth, she'd learned how quickly those you love could be taken away from you.

Was that why she'd been so eager to live life to the hilt? Why she had burned as a bright young flame that died too soon?

Damn, if only she'd told him. If only he'd known the truth. Maybe he could have helped.

Somehow he ended up on his street, in front of his house. The car that continued past him and stopped at the corner barely registered on his consciousness.

Angie told him she'd sent a cleaning service over to haul away destroyed furniture, and pick up mattress feathers and other debris. He'd like to see his home again.

As Paavo got out of the car, he didn't look around him and particularly not to the end of the block. The shooter hadn't expected him to. That was why this parking spot was chosen, along with an M40A1 rifle with a Unertl 9X scope. The car engine remained running as the black-clad sniper dropped behind the fender.

Paavo bounded up the steps to his front door, reaching into his pocket for the key. The scope aligned the back of his head in its crosshairs. He slid the key into the hole, turned, and pushed.

The world exploded.

* * *

As Angie drove away from the restaurant, she noticed the headlights of the car behind her. It stayed back some distance, but made all the same turns as she did, and seemed to speed up whenever another car tried to slip between them.

She made four lefts in a row. The car followed.

Going home was no longer an option. Instead, she headed for the Hall of Justice, unable to lose her tail the entire way.

Parking at the Hall was restricted to employees and people with special passes. Because it was an administrative building, not a police station as such, and fairly quiet at night, she didn't want to park in a nearly empty public lot either.

As she neared, she phoned Paavo to come down and meet her at the entrance. His phone rang, but he wasn't there to answer it.

Now what?

She could call his cell phone, but he could be miles away at some crime scene.

Hell, she had a Ferrari. Why not use it, just like she had when those jokers were outside her apartment? A freeway on-ramp was up ahead. Turning the wheel sharply, she darted through lanes of traffic and swung onto the freeway, flicked her radar-laser detector to high, and punched the accelerator. The car following her sped up as well, cutting off other drivers to reach the freeway entrance. For a while it succeeded in keeping up with her since she had to keep changing lanes to get around drivers paying attention to the speed limit. Once she passed the airport, however, the congestion loosened and her pedal hit the metal.

The car following didn't have a chance. And people asked her why she needed a Ferrari in San Francisco!

She glanced at her silent radar detector. She'd received tickets for going 68 in a 65-mile zone. At one point tonight she'd hit 105, and nary a CHP in sight . . . thank God.

When she finally reached the Filbert Street cottage, she was still pumped from her version of Mr. Toad's Wild Ride. Paavo wasn't there. The answering machine she'd recently hooked up had no message from him, and neither did her cell phone.

Where was he? A homicide must have happened. She wished Yosh would hurry back to work. Having Paavo go off on calls alone made her even more nervous than usual. She held Hercules, scratching him behind the ears as she stood at the window.

She assumed Paavo had caught a bite for dinner while he was out, but a warm, comforting dessert waiting for him when he got home would be a nice treat. She enjoyed cooking. Relaxing yet engrossing, it required a degree of expertise and creativity to do well, much as handcrafters found with needlepoint or crochet. Her Amaretto-pecan bread pudding was a particular favorite of his. She happily mixed enough to fill a nine-by-thirteen-inch-baking dish.

Hours later, the bread pudding had grown cold and he still wasn't home.

At midnight she called Homicide, with no luck, and his cell phone was switched to go straight to messages.

At two-thirty she heard footsteps on the front walk. She sprang from the bed to the window. It was Paavo.

They both reached the front door at the same time.

He grabbed her, his face buried against her neck, and held her tight.

Chapter 20

 "That's the house," Angie said. She and Paavo parked across from the Liberty Street building where Cecily, Aulis, and the Finnish students had lived. "Do you remember it at all?"

"I don't know," he said. "I had a murder case up here about three years ago. A dentist. I don't know if the area feels familiar because of him or some other reason."

"Let's walk around a bit," she suggested.

Walking the quiet street in the sunshine, even though the weather was chilly, gave Angie time to reflect on all that was happening. Last night she'd been frightened and horrified to hear about Paavo's close call. He had paid no attention as the purr of a car engine grew louder behind him, and then a gun fired and the streetlight outside his house exploded in a hail of glass. Instinctively he'd ducked just as a bullet smashed into his front door, right where he'd been standing a split second earlier. More shots were fired at the end of the street, followed by two cars screeching away.

Chasing them in his old Austin Healey wasn't even a consideration. Everyone on the block, ap-

parently, had called the police, because half the
Richmond station's black-and-whites roared to the
scene. The slug found in his house was from a
high-powered rifle, a sniper's weapon. The danger
level of whatever was going on had just been
upped tenfold.

Angie's freeway adventure paled in comparison,
at least to her, although he seemed as worried about
her as she was about him. That neither of them had
any idea of what was happening didn't seem to
matter to the person, or people, behind it.

Paavo had also told her about the homicide files
he'd read, as well as Cecily's. The police had based
their conclusion that Cecily had gone into hiding on
her having brought her children with her, but she
hadn't. Did that mean she was dead?

Angie's head spun. They'd stayed up until dawn
trying to put the pieces together, but nothing fit.

"When you were a boy, what did Aulis say when
you questioned him about your parents and your
name?" Angie asked as they walked.

"He gave me answers that, as a child, I accepted.
He told me what to say when I went to school, and I
did. It was only when I was older that I began to
wonder."

"Such as?"

"I learned that the Child Protective Services
would never have allowed a neighbor to keep a
child whose mother had abandoned him. Aulis told
me that when Mary Smith disappeared, he had
filed a missing person's report, but they never
found her. We moved our things to his apartment,
and simply stayed. I now know that would have
been impossible."

"He had no family of his own, right?" Angie
asked. "No one to question or complain about you
and your sister?"

"He was alone. I always thought he saw us as the children he might have had, had his life worked out differently. He told us about his past many times when we were growing up."

"Oh?" she asked, her voice lifting. He smiled at her obvious curiosity about the tale.

"Aulis left Finland immediately following World War Two," Paavo began. "He was engaged to a woman named Müna, a neighbor. The two of them grew up together, always knowing they would marry. He'd been drafted into the Finnish army to fight the Soviets. After the war, the Soviets moved in. Parts of Finland were ceded to them. People were displaced, their land taken away, their freedoms lost."

"How frightening," she said.

"Aulis decided to leave the country. He told Müna he would send for her. He used to tell harrowing stories to Jessica and me of how he escaped through icy water in a small fishing boat crammed with other men. He landed in Sweden, and found a way to join the refugee groups popping up throughout Europe. After two years, he made it to the United States, and a year later he'd crossed the country to San Francisco."

Angie nodded. After the war, refugees coming to California was a common story.

"Aulis arrived, got settled, and wrote to Müna. He had complete faith she'd waited for him. Instead, she'd gotten married a year after he'd left. She'd assumed he'd been killed."

"How awful," Angie cried.

"He swore he'd tried to forget her, but after so many years of loving just one person, the disappointment seemed to take the heart out of him."

"He's such a nice man. How could other women not have noticed?"

"Maybe they did, and he ignored them," Paavo said. "He used to tell me and Jessie that we reminded him that there was more to the world than his own self-pity."

Hearing those words let Angie understand how much those children must have meant to Aulis—the laughing, devil-may-care Jessica, and the quiet, somber little Paavo. Her hand tightened on his. "I'm glad—for all of you."

When they reached the intersection of Sanchez and Liberty, Paavo gave a long, last look down Liberty Street, then headed toward Angie's Ferrari.

"I just don't remember this area," he stated.

"Let's try one more spot," she suggested.

They drove westward, first to the Lutheran church, which Paavo remembered Aulis taking him to as a boy, and then continued for another mile to a two-story brown-shingle home. "The Eschenbachs live there," Angie said.

Paavo stared at it a long while. He shut his eyes, leaning back against the headrest. "I don't know, Angie. There's something familiar about it—something I don't like about it—but I've covered so many areas as a cop, who knows what it is?"

"The way the wife acted troubles me. She seemed to know something—something that frightened her."

"It's weird—when I look at the house, I think of a lion, which makes no sense."

She gasped. "But it does! The door knocker is shaped like a lion's head. You were here! Aulis must have brought you here. But I wonder why."

He stared at the house. "Whatever it was, I hated it. I wanted to go home ... but I couldn't." He shook his head, and a look of such profound sadness came over him that it tore at her heart.

She was about to suggest that he could go home

now, to *their* little home, when, to her surprise, he got out of the car.

"Let's find out what this is all about," he said, marching straight for the house and its lion-head door knocker.

Mrs. Eschenbach scowled ferociously when she saw Angie, then turned toward Paavo. She gasped, her eyes wide. "Oh, my," she murmured, pressing her fingers to her mouth.

"I do remember you," Paavo said. "From church."

She rested her hand on her bosom as if to calm her heart. "My God, you look so much like your father now, you startled me."

A moment passed. "I'd like to talk to you about him."

She stiffened, casting another angry glance at Angie. "All right."

Angie expected to be led to the back of the house to see the pastor, but Mrs. Eschenbach brought them into the kitchen and gestured for them to sit at the table. "It's such a shock seeing you again, Paavo," she said as she darted about, flustered and nervous, and then poured them each a glass of red wine from a jug. "What do you do for a living now?"

He glanced quickly at Angie. "I'm a homicide inspector."

The elderly woman paused, then slowly nodded. "I'm not surprised," she murmured, and Angie wondered what she meant. She joined them at the table and lifted her wineglass. "Skoal!"

They responded and sipped the heavy burgundy.

"What can you tell me, Mrs. Eschenbach?" Paavo asked. "I'm trying to find out what happened all those years ago."

"All I know is that Aulis brought you and your sister here one day. He asked us to hide you and said no one, no one at all, was to know you were here. I had read about your father's murder in the papers, and the day after you came here, we received word that your mother's car had gone into the ocean. I asked Aulis about her, but he just shook his head. We needed to forget everything we ever knew about her or your father. They were gone, and the only way to keep you children safe was to change everything about who you were and who they were. You stayed here for ten days, then he came and got you. I didn't see you again for almost five years, when Aulis again began to attend our church. We never spoke of those times with him."

"What was he so afraid of?" Paavo asked.

She shook her head. "He never said, and we were afraid to ask. All we knew was that it was very, very bad, and the people involved were completely ruthless." She turned to Angie. "When I heard your questions, the fear we lived with during those days came rushing back to me. Our lives were in danger—Aulis knew it, and so did we—because of the children. That was why I asked you to stay away."

Her wrinkled hand touched Paavo's, and her eyes grew teary. "I'll admit that, right now, I'm glad you didn't listen."

Paavo showed up in Homicide that afternoon to find a message from Tucker Bond's secretary. He answered her call, and was faxed a list of names and phone numbers of people who had worked with Cecily.

They all gave the same responses to his questions—none of them knew her. They remembered that she was a research clerk, but they didn't remember her being in the office, or even where her desk was situated, or what she did. The few times they saw her she was pleasant and likable. They knew she'd worked for Eldridge Sawyer, but nothing more.

Paavo phoned Tucker Bond. "Ah, Inspector," Bond answered. "Did you get the information from my secretary?"

"Yes, thanks. I was calling with a different question about Cecily Campbell," Paavo replied.

"Oh?"

"There's nothing in her file about her second marriage."

"Second marriage? I don't remember anything about that. She must have chosen to keep it from us."

"Why would she?"

"Well, some women believed they'd go further in their career if unmarried. I don't know if that was true in her case—"

"She married a Finn. He was here on a work visa."

"Not an American. Well, that might have bothered us if she were placed in any sensitive areas. But she was just a clerk, Inspector. I'm afraid I don't understand your interest in her at all."

Paavo didn't bother to explain. "Did you know her body was never recovered?"

"Now that you mention it, that does sound vaguely familiar. I'm afraid that detail slipped my memory. There was no question about her death that I was aware of."

"You didn't know the S.F.P.D. asked Sawyer's help, treating her as a missing person?"

"I knew he was asked about her, but he was her boss. That wasn't unusual in a situation that might have been suicide for all anyone knew."

"What can you tell me about Eldridge Sawyer?" Paavo asked.

"Actually, our prior conversation got me to thinking about the old days," Bond said. "Sawyer was mixed up with a lot of strange business back then. I suspect he had Cecily Campbell researching—or whatever—quite a bit of that stuff. If you ask me, find him, and you'll find the answers you're looking for."

"What kind of strange business?" Paavo asked.

"If I knew the answer to that, I might be able to help you myself."

"One last question," Paavo said. "How long after Cecily Campbell's death did Sawyer quit the Bureau?"

"How long?" Bond didn't say anything for a moment. "Well, as I recall, it was almost immediately after. I can't imagine, however, that the two were in any way connected."

Chapter 21

"Maybe there's a better way," Connie moaned, elbows on the bar, head in her hands.

"The better way is to drink tonic without gin in it," Angie scoffed. "You're getting sloshed."

"I'm just doing my part to help find Paavo's mama," Connie said, swirling the toothpick-skewered lime wedge in her drink. She wore a short, sleeveless black dress that fit like a wide band of Spandex. "Anyway, if neither of us drank, for us to come to a bar would look very suspicious."

"If you'd stop making googly-eyes at all the men, they wouldn't be sending over so many drinks." Angie's Versace ice-blue outfit had an equally short, shiny skirt, and sleeveless, V-neck top. The heel of one high, ankle-strapped shoe was hooked on the rail of her stool, while the other foot waggled impatiently.

"I come to bars for one reason—and it's not to quench my thirst," Connie said. "Anyway, I'm not making eyes at anyone. This is just how I look."

"Hah! If you were any more kissy-faced, we'd have to run your lips through a mangle iron to straighten them out."

Connie stopped listening when a blond hunk entered the bar.

Angie took another sip of her virgin piña colada. The entire evening had been a waste of time. They were on Noe Street, in an area of neighborhood shops, bars, and restaurants just a couple of blocks from Liberty.

After learning that Paavo was nearly killed the night before, she wasn't about to sit around tonight nervously pacing and cooking and praying he made it home in one piece. She was determined to do something! To find out exactly what was going on here. Whatever it was, it had drawn in people who'd lived in this neighborhood thirty years ago. And as Bianca had said, people talk. They knew a lot more about what happened in their neighborhoods than the police ever imagined.

She would discover what the police hadn't. Aulis and his Finnish friends had lived here. Most were young men, and except for Mika, bachelors. She didn't know any bachelors who didn't go to neighborhood restaurants at least once in a while, and often to bars as well. The Noe Valley area was filled with friendly neighborhood establishments, and enough singles to make them interesting. The area hadn't changed that much in the past thirty years, from all she'd heard.

She made a list of long-established nightspots and restaurants.

She and Connie began the evening at a listed bar, asking if the owner or anyone else there had lived in the neighborhood some thirty years earlier. No one had. They worked their way through other places, asking about customers, owners, and other establishments as they went. A few "old-timers" remembered some Finns in the neighborhood, but no one remembered their names or what happened to them. At The Golden Spike restaurant, the chatty owner suggested a nearby Swedish smorgasbord. No Finnish restaurants existed in the city, now or thirty years ago, or Angie would have gone there first.

The Swedish restaurant's owner was active in the community, and the Lutheran church, and knew Aulis, but that was as far as it went.

Back to barhopping, they came across some people who'd been students back in the late sixties and who remembered a Finnish guy named Sam. All they remembered was that he had been killed— they thought by another Finn.

Angie doggedly dragged Connie to the one last restaurant and three last bars on her list, tearing her away from a number of gallant men who offered drinks and anything else they wanted.

"We're so close," Angie cried with frustration, shoving her piña colada aside. "But this just isn't panning out. Let's go home."

"Good idea." Connie stood, but was a bit wobbly on her stiletto heels. "I don't even like the guys in this place. We could go back to that second bar, though. Did you notice the Polynesian-looking fellow who kept smiling at me? To die! Or, wait, was he at the third?"

"Forget it, Connie." Angie looped her arm around Connie's and the two of them tottered outside.

As they reached Angie's car, Connie rubbed her stomach. "I don't feel so good."

"You aren't going to be sick, are you?" Angie asked in alarm.

"I don't think so. It must be just a stomach ache. From all that herring at the smorgasbord. I should never eat herring."

"And everyone knows herring doesn't mix with gin and tonic."

"Oh, please!" Connie turned several shades of green.

A small grocery store was at the corner. "Let's get you some Pepto-Bismol. It should help until you get home and lie down."

The grocer took one look at Connie's sickly pallor and tipsy state and pointed Angie in the direction of the medicines.

Connie leaned heavily against the counter, her shoulder against a bread rack. "We're here trying to find anyone who knows Cecily," she said, her words a little slurred. The grocer was a middle-aged Chinese man. He stared silently at Connie, clearly torn between wanting her gone before she squashed the bread, and human curiosity as to how long she could stand upright. "You don't know Cecily, do you? It was a long time ago. No, you're too young to remember her."

"Did she live around here?" he asked.

Connie rubbed her forehead. "She sure did. Right up there on Liberty Street, according to my friend Angie. She was young and pretty—I mean Cecily, not Angie. Angie's single. I was married once, though. A real shithead. My ex, not Cecily's. She was nice. She had a couple of kids, and a Finnish friend. But then she left, or died, or something."

"Oh, *that* Cecily," the grocer said.

Angie walked up with the biggest bottle of Pepto-Bismol she could find. She couldn't believe her ears. "You knew Cecily Turunen?" she asked, and shoved the bottle into Connie's hands.

"I didn't know her personally, but I knew who she was. My father used to own this store, and I worked here after school. She used to come in with her kids. She was a nice lady. Then it seems something or other happened, and they all disappeared—her, her husband, their friends. It was weird. Everyone talked about it for days."

"Oh, my God!" Angie cried, scarcely able to believe her good fortune. "You did know her!"

Connie was fighting with the bottle top. "See, I told you it was a bad idea to go to all those bars and restaurants."

"I didn't *know* her," the grocer said. "Not really. One of my customers was a good friend of hers. Why?"

"We could have simply gone grocery shopping," Connie murmured, whacking the side of the cap on the counter. "But no-o-o-o-o."

"I need to find out more about Cecily," Angie said. "Lots more. Can you tell me how to reach that customer?"

He thought a moment while eyeballing Connie, who had finally gotten the bottle open and was now glugging pink stuff like it was water. He winced and said, "Well, I couldn't do that, but if you want to leave your name and phone number, I'll tell her about you. She'll need to decide if she wants to contact you or not."

Angie quickly wrote down the information and gave it to the grocer. "Thank you so much. Tell her it's very, very important that I speak to her. It'll just take a little while, and I'd be eternally grateful."

"Sure thing. By the way, I think your friend is going to need more than Pepto-Bismol."

Angie had forgotten all about Connie. She swiveled around to find her still standing, but her eyes were shut and her forehead rested on a flattened loaf of Wonder bread.

Chapter 22

On the northern, Mendocino coast, five miles past the fishing town of Gualala, Paavo turned Angie's Ferrari onto a small paved road that snaked uphill into the coast range mountains. Ten minutes later, he reached a gravel-packed private road.

He and Angie were headed toward a home he'd visited a few times as a teenager with Aulis. The area had changed very little, and the route came back to mind with surprising ease.

A large wooden gate stood open in the barbed-wire fence, leading to a wood-framed house. Beyond it, the forest was thick and dark with pines. Joonas Mäki opened the front door and walked toward them.

He greeted Angie, then clutched Paavo's arms and gave him a kiss on the cheek just as he used to when Paavo was a little boy. He was lanky, with a full head of bushy salt-and-pepper hair. His eyebrows were gray, the individual hairs thick, coarse, and corkscrewed, and, as Professor White had remembered, met in the center.

Paavo and Angie followed him into the house Aulis had helped him build. Paavo was about eight or nine years old at the time, and had enjoyed coming to the country to play while the men worked.

Before that, Joonas had also lived in San Francisco.

Memories flooded Paavo's head as he entered the main room, with a potbellied stove in the corner and small double-hung windows. Originally the house was one big room with an outhouse in the back, but when Joonas married, a bathroom was among the new additions.

Joonas's wife waited in the house for them. She'd prepared a hearty brunch and they caught up on old times and Aulis's condition as they ate. Afterward, Angie gave Paavo a nod. She and Hannah took care of the cleanup while Paavo and Joonas put on heavy coats and went outdoors.

They walked to a bluff overlooking highway, beach, and ocean. In a mesmerizing rhythm, waves crashed onto tall boulders standing in the water, sending magnificent white plumes high into the air. The land was lonely and isolated and cold, but it was also incredibly beautiful. Both men took in the vista before them in a moment of mutual awe.

"Did you know that Finland was created by the Water Mother, Paavo?" Joonas's voice smiled.

"No. I've not heard that."

"Water and wood and winter. That's what Finland is all about." He seemed lost in thought.

After a respite, Paavo said, "I've learned a little about my parents, factual things, but not about their character. Some of this present danger, I've come to suspect, goes back to them and their causes, and their deaths. Help me understand, Joonas."

Joonas's gaze fixed on Paavo, sorrowful and wistful. "You are so much like your father, sometimes it makes me think I am still a young man. How could I be this old when I look across the room, and there is Mika, just the way I remember him?"

A sudden anger gnawed at Paavo. "All these years you knew, and you kept it from me. Why?"

"I had to. Aulis made me promise."

He tamped his ire. "Tell me about him."

"There were four of us," Joonas began, hands tucked into pockets, eyes fixed on the sea. "Myself, your father, Sami Vansha, who Americanized his name and called himself Sam Vanse, and a fourth man, Okko Heikkila. The four of us worked to help our people back in Finland."

"You had family there?" Paavo asked.

"Okko and Sami did. Okko's brother was imprisoned by the Soviets and died in the Gulag. Sami had family, too, but where Okko was quiet, Sami was a hothead. Any chance to cause trouble, Sami was right there. I imagine that's what got him and Mika killed."

He fell silent. Paavo waited.

"When I was in Finland, after the war, when the Soviets occupied the lands our government had ceded to them, I will never forget how my father kept a suitcase packed with warm clothes and canned and dried food near the door, ready to grab it and run if necessary. He had been a vocal opponent of the Soviets, and knew he could be arrested at any minute. Although it never happened, he lived only to age fifty-three. My mother said he died because all that happened to his country broke his heart."

Paavo remained quiet as Joonas's thoughts drifted to the past.

"She died not long after helping me get passage to the United States."

"And Mika?" Paavo asked finally.

Joonas hesitated, and then said slowly, "After the Soviets finished fighting against the Germans, Mika and his parents lived in Soviet-occupied territory.

Many people tried to escape the madness of those years, and were killed. Mika's parents were among them."

A chill stabbed through Paavo, and he hunched deeper into the thick fleece coat. He told himself it was the icy ocean wind.

"Mika was just a child," Joonas said. "Other refugees fleeing the country, friends of his father, took him with them. He lived in England until he graduated from school, then came to the U.S. on a student visa. He was the only one in his family to make it to this country, although it had been the dream for all of them. That was one reason, I believe, that he was so passionately against the Soviet Union. He blamed it for his parents' deaths."

Paavo nodded silently. So his father had lost his own parents. At least he had known why. Paavo mentally gave a shake of the head. He was not here to judge or accuse, but to learn the truth. To find out as much as he could about the man who had been his father.

"I saw what an all-too-powerful government could do to the rights of individuals," Joonas continued. "Even after the Soviets returned some of our land, Finland still lived under its shadow. That was why I joined with Mika and the others. That was why we worked together for our homeland, and its freedom."

"Did Mika have any living relatives in Finland? Any here?"

Joonas sighed. "None that he knew of. He left the old country as a child alone. I expect you might have some distant cousins, but I don't know who."

For the second time in this visit, he was shaken. He hadn't thought about having people related to him, not even when he had asked Joonas. He'd asked as a cop, seeking facts, but suddenly the thought of having cousins, however removed, was inexplicably welcome.

"I am sorry I don't know more, Paavo."

He stared out at the water before answering. "Don't be. I never expected to learn who my father was, let alone his background or what he looked like."

"He had your eyes. Very big, very blue. His hair was dark brown, almost black." Joonas paused, then grinned with warm affection. "You have your father's nature. He was always serious, very intense. He had a high idealism as well, one that remained unshaken. As time went on, things began to happen . . . dangerous things, and more and more dangerous people became drawn in, for reasons far different from Mika's and the group's original reasons."

"Who were these people?"

"What can I say? They were in it for the money—money began to be a part of our work. I was not working with them at that point. I got out. I told Mika to do the same."

"But he didn't."

They walked along the windy bluff awhile before Joonas answered. "He felt it was wrong to ignore the sorrows of people back home. Your mother tried to turn him around, but Sami . . . Sami was like a cancer, always eating at him, always reminding him of what had happened at home, and that he needed to take revenge on the Soviets for what they did to Finland, and to his family."

Paavo sucked in his breath, finally reaching the point to ask the question he came here for. "Who killed them, Joonas?"

"Aulis never wanted you to know. He was afraid for you."

"It's time I learned," Paavo said.

"We worked with Russian smugglers—they were criminals, and in time it became clear they belonged to the *Organizatsiya*. There's nothing worse than them. Not the Italian Mafia, none of it. The only thing worse, maybe, was the old KGB. But they're gone, and the *Organizatsiya* continues to this day."

"Who are they?"

"These days we call them the Russian Mafia."

Paavo was staggered. "They killed him? You're sure?"

Joonas's eyes softened, his voice low. "I understand your mother witnessed it."

Paavo's stomach clenched at the horror of it. "Tell me about my mother," he said after a while.

"All I know is that she died. She loved you and your sister very much. That was the part that hurt the most, telling you she was no good, that she had abandoned you and your sister. But it was the only way Aulis believed you would not try to find her— the only way to keep you safe. If he told you she was dead, as you got older, you'd say where is her grave? Where is her death certificate? Her will? How did she die? He knew you might ask a million questions he had no answer for. So he told you your name was Smith, you were illegitimate, and that your mother had walked out. It was the kind of story you wouldn't be inclined to pursue."

He sucked in his breath. Aulis's assumption was accurate. He said, "The police thought she faked her death."

"Did she?" Joonas asked. "Or did the *Organizatsiya*? Or did she truly die there? I don't know. I don't *want* to know. I was scared. I moved up here, bought this land."

Paavo closed his eyes briefly, feeling a sudden sting behind his eyelids. Joonas, more than any document or FBI file, had made these people come alive for him. "I need to find out what happened back then."

Joonas turned world-weary eyes on him. "Okko might know more—he worked with Mika and Sami and was much closer to all they did than I was. He can tell you more about those days. Let us go inside and call him. You two need to meet. He lives high in the Sierras."

Joonas found the number and phoned, but an answering machine came on with a long beep, as if filled with messages. Joonas dialed Okko's close friend and neighbor to ask if he had any idea when Okko would return. The neighbor said he didn't know, but that Okko had left suddenly, and had been gone for over a week.

Chapter 23

"I don't believe this," Angie said as she and her cousin Richie sat by the window in a coffee shop in the town of Gideon. Four hours ago she hadn't even known there was a town called Gideon halfway between Sacramento and Mount Shasta, and now that she'd seen it, all two blocks of it, she didn't *want* to know it existed.

"Eat your banana split, but not too fast, we might be here awhile." Richie adjusted the red bandanna on his neck. "This thing is too damn tight. How do cowboys wear them? Don't they have no Adam's apples?"

Angie studied the street and tried not to laugh. Last night a message from Richie said he'd see her in the morning, that they were going to the country. Since she'd just returned from a journey to Mendocino with Paavo, traveling with her cousin was hardly appealing.

It became even less so when, shortly after Paavo left for work, she heard a knock and found Yosemite Sam in her doorway. Richie announced he wanted to fit in with the locals. Somehow, an overweight, middle-aged, olive-complexioned Italian in a butternut leather vest, blue and white striped Ralph Lauren shirt, red bandanna, starched and creased Calvin Klein denims, beige hand-tooled cowboy boots, and a silver rodeo belt buckle big and bright enough to signal distant planets was not her idea of how to fit in with anyone, anywhere, ever. She gave thanks he wasn't also wearing a white ten-gallon hat and hip-hugging holster.

He swore he knew what he was doing. She felt positively conservative in her twill trousers, turtleneck sweater, boots, and new purple parka.

Things went from bad to worse when she walked out to the street.

A red Ford F350 one-ton long-bed truck with purple and yellow phantom flames, a silver grill guard, and monstrous off-road mud Super Swamper tires awaited them. He practically had to lift her into the extended cab's passenger seat.

"What's going on?" she'd asked, peering out the window to the sidewalk far below. She'd been on lower Ferris wheels.

"You'll see," he'd said with a grin, crawling into the driver's seat. Then they were off. He spent the rest of the trip talking into his cell phone, making deals, buying and selling stocks, betting on horses. . . .

From Gideon's only restaurant, Linda's Eats and Sweets, they had a clear view of the post office. Richie's so-called real estate connections had tracked Eldridge Sawyer to "Edward Sanders" with a post office box in Gideon. It was up to Richie from that point. He began by mailing Sawyer a nine-by-twelve fluorescent pink envelope filled with information on discounted rifle and ammo supplies. He then called the Gideon post office and learned that mail became available around noon each day.

"If he don't show up today," Richie said, "we're going to be stuck here overnight."

"What do you mean by that?" The horror of being stuck anywhere with Richie was more than she wanted to contemplate. "There's a chance he's not here?"

"Well, see, when I was sweet-talking the lil' gal at the post office to find out when the mail would be delivered, I casually mentioned it was for Ed Sanders—something he wanted right away. And she said that was odd because he was away. He'd told them hold his mail. But then she checked the hold and it was over today."

Angie gaped. "You got a postal employee to give you that information?"

He beamed. "Women love me."

She bit her tongue. "I hope she was right. I don't know how much ice cream I can eat before the owner here starts to suspect something. If she doesn't already." Angie again looked askance at her cousin's outfit. At least the diner was empty, so she didn't have to face nearby gawkers.

"Don't worry about it."

She was nibbling on her second banana split, while Richie had eaten two and was now slurping the end of a chocolate malt, when he stiffened, his eyes fixed on the post office. A tall, powerfully built man wearing a camouflage jacket, pants, hat, and jackboots—a real friendly looking guy—stood on the sidewalk, glancing through mail that included a fluorescent pink envelope. He stuffed it inside his jacket and started walking.

"Okay, babe, it's Saturday night!" Richie tossed some money on the table and was out the door, Angie chasing after him. Once on the sidewalk, he grabbed her arm and practically dragged her across the street toward Sawyer's truck. She was too stunned to try to stop him.

Sawyer climbed into the truck and started the ignition just as Richie shoved Angie hard against his back fender. "You bitch!"

With a shriek, she fell to the ground.

"You talk to me like that and you won't say anything for a week!" His face was purple, one hand on the fender as he leaned over her. "Get up!"

He lifted his foot as if he was going to kick her.

"Don't!" she screamed, her arms thrust out protectively. Had he gone crazy?

Suddenly Richie flew about five feet into the air, to land sprawled on his stomach. Sawyer stood over him. "That's no way to treat a lady."

Richie slowly sat up. "Hey, can I say 'that ain't no lady, that's my wife'?" He gave a quivery chuckle.

Sawyer wasn't having it, but turned away from him with contempt. "You all right, lady?" he asked, holding out his hand to help her stand.

Angie nodded. He grasped her wrist and her entire body left the ground as he pulled her to her feet. When she landed, she thanked him and brushed herself off.

"Hey, she don't like my new truck." Richie, also standing, pointed to his flashy long-bed. "I don't have to put up with shit like that!"

Sawyer jabbed a finger into her cousin's chest, his nose nearly touching Richie's forehead. "Listen, rhinestone cowboy, you take your problems somewhere else. Gideon doesn't want your kind around here."

"I want to go home," Angie said, stomping toward the truck.

Richie lifted his hands, stepping back out of Sawyer's way. Sawyer looked from him to Angie in disgust, then got into his truck and drove off.

"What was that all about?" she asked when Richie joined her.

"Slight of hand. Hope I didn't hurt you none. Follow me."

Just around the corner was a ten-year-old black Chevy sedan. He unlocked the doors. "Hurry."

Her head was reeling as she jumped into the passenger seat. Richie flipped a switch on something that looked like a radar detector and headed back to the main road, turning in the direction Sawyer had gone.

The detector beeped.

"Where did you get this car? And what's beeping?" Angie asked.

"It's easy to pay someone to drop off a car for you," he explained, cruising away from the town. "The rest of it, we had to do on our own—you got to be ready to improvise. You were pretty good back there."

She decided not to say she wasn't acting.

He continued. "The beep means we're connected with a little homing device under Sawyer's back fender. Soon we'll know where he lives. After that, it's up to you and your boyfriend. On the way back, let's stop at that restaurant again."

"Not another banana split?"

"No. I saw some tutti-frutti on the menu. I haven't had any of that since I was a kid."

Although it was late when Angie returned to the city, she contacted Paavo and agreed to meet him in Aulis's hospital room. She'd felt bad that a couple of days had gone by since she'd last been there. Cousin Richie dropped her off on the sidewalk, refusing to drive up to the entrance. "Hospitals are bad luck," he said. "I leave them alone, and they do the same for me."

She had just turned onto the corridor with Aulis's room when she saw a little man wearing work pants, a black watch cap, and denim jacket sneak inside. He quietly shut the door behind him.

No guard was present. The city couldn't afford to continue with one full-time, so Paavo's friends on the force stopped by regularly. The stranger must be one of Aulis's friends, she told herself, and he wasn't being sneaky, but careful and quiet, not wanting to disturb a man in a coma . . . ?

Angie teetered in the hallway, torn between going to find a nurse to enter the room with her, or bursting in immediately to find out who the man was. How long would she have to wait before convincing a nurse to join her? If the man meant harm, how much damage could he do while she dickered? She had no choice.

Hitting the door hard, she swung it open. The little man was bending low over Aulis. "Who are you?" she demanded.

At the sound of the door flying open, he turned his head, his eyes startled. Suddenly he bolted toward her. She swung her tote bag, smacking him square in the stomach and knocking him back into the room. All she could think of was to escape—and to yell for help. She spun around and ran smack into a brick wall.

Familiar hands caught her. "Paavo! Quick—that man is trying to hurt Aulis!"

She jumped into the hall before looking back into the room to see the little man clutching the foot of the bed with one hand, the other pressed against his stomach.

"Paavo?" he whispered.

Paavo stepped toward him. "You are?"

"Okko Heikkila."

* * *

They went to a Japanese restaurant with small, individual tatami rooms where they could talk uninterrupted and unobserved by others. Although Heikkila agreed to go with them, it was clear he didn't like it. Since Paavo's car was a two-seater, and Okko drove a pickup, they rode separately to the restaurant. Once they arrived, both Heikkila's and Paavo's demeanors were even more serious, and the two said little as they ordered dinner.

No more than ten words passed between the two men until the cocktail waitress brought a flask of warm sake and small porcelain cups. She poured them each some, then left. Heikkila drank his cupful in one gulp, then poured more rice wine for himself.

Angie hated such silence. She tried to relieve the tension by talking about the beauty of the Sierras where Heikkila lived, asking him about the level of snowfall this year compared to others, and anything else innocuous she could think of. The anxiety level at the table remained high, thickening the air.

The waitress brought miso and replenished the flask of sake. Angie noticed that Heikkila was already beginning to feel the effect of it.

The miso was followed by a platter of sashimi, and then the waitress heated the center hot plate for shabu-shabu, in which the diners dip paper-thin raw meat and vegetables into boiling water, cooking their food and creating a broth as they eat. It's a leisurely, congenial meal, and soon, as Angie had hoped, the food and wine began to loosen the taciturn Okko's tongue.

"What are you doing in San Francisco?" Paavo asked.

"Can't a man take a vacation? I heard Aulis was hurt and came to visit him." He glared at Angie.

"Didn't know I'd be hit by a cannonball-hurling harridan for my trouble."

"Well, you scared me, and then you tried to run," she protested.

"I don't like strangers," he said.

Paavo quickly poured them both more sake. "I'm interested in Omega Computing. How it was working there for you and Mika and Sam."

Heikkila sipped his wine. "I'll tell you. Those days were different. Better. People programmed in Fortran. Computers were monsters kept in refrigerated rooms. We thought IBM's 360/65 was the greatest invention known to man."

Angie suppressed a smile, considering she had a Palm, a cell phone, and an electronic scheduler in her tote bag. She hoped none had been damaged by his stomach.

"Did you and my father know each other before going to work at Omega?" Paavo asked.

"We met at work. Mika and Sam met in college—San Francisco State. Later, Sam was also hired. He was a flaky, impulsive guy, always emotional. See, it made sense he got us mixed up with sympathizers against the Soviet government. You got to remember, it was the sixties. People had causes. Students and American-born Finns held protests, petitions, sit-ins. And meetings. Meetings to stage more meetings. Joonas, Mika, Sam—even Aulis—we hated the Soviets." He swished some beef in the hot broth.

"What were your ideas of support?" Paavo asked, doing the same.

Heikkila smiled wryly. He didn't have to say it, but Paavo heard the sentiment: *smart, like your father.* "While in college, Sam went back to Finland to visit family. He made connections with an underground movement, led and driven by the 'intelligentsia,' as he put it. Being a student with an American work visa drew attention. Sam thought of himself as an intellectual—a radical poet. He would have loved Paris in the twenties—except that he didn't know French and he wasn't a poet. He lived for being a radical and making contacts. That was his thing, contacts. Before long, he recruited others, especially Mika. While Sam played with intrigue and heroics, Mika was all idealism and patriotism. You know, his parents were killed by the Communists—"

"Yes," Paavo said softly, "I've heard that."

Angie watched his face and could see how much Okko's simple words troubled him. Even for herself, listening to Okko made Mika and his parents so alive that she, too, felt the grief of their deaths. And Sam, she could have wrung his neck! Didn't he ever consider what might come of his toying with people's lives and emotions?

"So Sam led the rest of you to the movement against the Soviets?" Angie asked.

"That's right. The dissidents needed communications equipment for their *samizdat* movement. Sam had his contacts—a group of radicals called themselves the Kalevala. The name was from the epic poem that gives the legends, myths, and folklore that make up the soul of the Finnish people. Perhaps Joonas was the old and wise Väinämöinen, a powerful seer with supernatural origins, and I was Ilmarinen, a smith, and forged the 'lids of heaven' when the world was created. Sam was Lemminkäinen, an adventurer-warrior and charmer of women. And Mika was the tragic hero Kullervo, who is forced by fate to be a slave from childhood and avenge his father's death."

Paavo broke into the old man's reverie. "So when

Sam came back with this idea of helping this *samiz-dat* movement, what did all of you do?"

"For a long time, our help was fairly minimal. If we could get our hands on equipment the dissidents needed, they'd give us money to buy it, and then connect us to some Russians who'd smuggle it into the USSR. That all changed after Sam met Harold Partridge."

"Partridge? The big name in computers?" Angie glanced at Paavo, not sure she heard right, but Paavo, too, was staring with surprise at the name Okko had just spoken.

"See, we didn't have personal computers then," Heikkila said. "But Partridge had already started with his business. Before anyone knew what hit it, he swallowed up Omega and all the mainframe programmers switched to PC operating systems. But I'm getting ahead of my story."

Thinking of the pictures she'd seen of the diminutive, bespectacled titan of Silicon Valley and famed philanthropist and collector, Angie said, "It's hard to imagine Harold Partridge being caught up in anything like this."

"He was different then," Heikkila explained. "Young, ambitious, and greedy. Now he lives in Silicon Valley with so much money he doesn't know what to do, other than to worry that someone somewhere might steal it. He came from a wealthy family and spent years traveling around the world looking for something to interest him."

"Did he find it?" Angie asked.

"He found two things—computers and Russian art. Computers because he had enough financial savvy and vision to know they were going to be huge, and Russian art because it was the one thing he couldn't go to a store and buy. He could only get it through devious means. And being devious was what he did best."

At the words *Russian art*, Angie and Paavo caught each other's eyes.

As they continued with the meal, Heikkila explained. "When Sam learned that Partridge was willing to pay good money for Russian art, he realized that if he could get his hands on Russian artwork, statues, and jewelry, he could sell them to Partridge for big bucks and buy whatever the dissidents needed. Maybe even buy from Omega at a discount. He went to his contacts about 'exporting' some artwork to Partridge, keeping Partridge's name a secret from everyone. I only found out by accident, overhearing something. Before long, a man named Gregor Rosinsky showed up."

"Rosinsky?" Paavo couldn't hide his shock, while Angie let out a small gasp. "The jeweler?"

"Yes . . . the dead jeweler." Okko's eyes bored into Paavo. "He was a smuggler! One of those guys who moved goods into and out of Russia for the dissidents. He learned all about Russian artwork and jewelry doing that job, and could tell a genuine piece from a fake at fifty paces. Why not go into business?" Heikkila chuckled wryly.

Angie couldn't believe the stooped, soft-spoken jeweler had once been a smuggler.

Suddenly Heikkila asked, "Do you know who killed him?"

"Not yet," Paavo said. "Nothing was stolen, except perhaps a Russian brooch that belonged to my mother. Angie took it to him for repairs, and it's missing."

The Finn's blue gaze went from Paavo to Angie and back. He put down his chopsticks. "That's disturbing news."

"Another Russian connected with jewelry was recently killed," Paavo added. "This one was a forger."

Heikkila nodded. "I know. Jakob Platnikov. He was also one of the smugglers. We mostly dealt with five of them. Rosinsky, Platnikov, Nikolai Drach, Artur Masaryk, and Leonid Boldin."

"How did you know they were dead?" Angie asked.

Heikkila's gaze shifted from her to Paavo. "It was in the newspapers," he replied innocently.

"Joonas thought the smugglers were part of what became the Russian Mafia. Do you agree?" Paavo asked after a pause. Angie's attention was glued on Okko.

"Absolutely. The *mafiya,* emphasis on the 'ya' as they say it, is the reason I live where I do. I don't want to be anywhere near them. I don't want them to even imagine I can be trouble for them. They're the scariest people I've ever seen. I know a story of someone in the Middle East who captured a Russian businessman and held him for ransom, threatening to kill him if their demands weren't met. They didn't know that the businessman belonged to the *mafiya.* The *mafiya* found out who the kidnappers were and captured some of their relatives. They cut off a finger from one, an ear from another, and mailed them to the kidnappers. They said that for each day the businessman was not released, a package with another body part would be delivered. The Russian was released immediately. That's how the Russian *mafiya* plays."

Angie felt a cold chill.

"Why did they kill Sam and Mika?" Paavo asked.

A weariness came onto Heikkila's lined face, and he said, "The Soviet government rounded up a group of dissidents and smugglers and sent them to the Gulag. The *mafiya* thought we gave the Soviets the names. We swore we didn't, but they said they had proof. Next thing I knew, they killed Sam and Mika. And I ran to the Sierras."

"No one told the police any of this," Paavo said.

Heikkila gazed flatly at him. "Do you think we're crazy?"

"The missing brooch was a cameo of the Tsarina Alexandra," Angie said. "Rosinsky said it was museum quality."

"It sounds like the type of thing we smuggled." Heikkila shook his head with disgust. "But that was thirty years ago! No one could possibly still care about all that old history, no one but me, at any rate. It haunted my dreams for years, but in time, even I began to forget. Only once in a while, like when I saw Aulis in the hospital, does it all come back, and I replay the ideas of revenge I used to have."

"Revenge on the *mafiya*?" Paavo asked.

"Who else? Anyway, it's over now. I stay in the mountains because I've come to love them. There's no more to it than that."

Chapter 24

Paavo reread his notes on Jakob Platnikov's case and now turned again to Rosinsky's murder investigation. Rebecca had worked on telephone records and one annotation jumped out at him. Three days before Rosinsky was killed, he had phoned Harold Partridge's residence. Three days . . . the same day his office was broken into, the same day Angie had brought him her brooch.

Rosinsky would have known of Partridge's interest in Russian jewelry. If Partridge were willing to pay enough to convince Angie to sell, Rosinsky easily could have received a generous finder's fee. That would have been a legitimate reason for the phone record.

Except that Rosinsky was dead . . . and the brooch was missing . . . and Jakob Platnikov was also dead. And both men were suspected of being part of a group with ties to the Russian Mafia. And somehow, Mika's and Sam's murders had included these same characters, as did the break-ins now.

The answer to what was happening had to be right there in front of him, but he just couldn't see it.

One thing he did know was that he needed to

186

learn more about computer magnate Harold Partridge.

He didn't wait for the elevator, but took the stairs up one floor to Room 558, where the Special Investigation Division Gang Task Force was located. Since the infamous Golden Dragon restaurant massacre, most of the task force's work concerned Chinese gangs. Two gangs, Joe's Boys and the Wah Ching, had opened fire on each other in a crowded Chinatown restaurant and innocent customers were caught in the murderous cross fire. Even though the Italian Mafia had never been a real factor in San Francisco, the Golden Dragon carnage had announced that the city wasn't free of crime gangs. To have them in the heart of one of the city's landmark tourist areas stirred the city's government into action.

Paavo knew both Joe's Boys and the Wah Ching had all but ceased to exist, but other gangs had taken their place in Chinatown, and new ethnic gangs were emerging elsewhere in the city. He needed to find out to what extent the Russians were among them, and Partridge's role, if any, in all of it.

Inspector Fogarty, one of the key members of the Gang Task Force, pulled out a file on Harold Partridge and handed it to Paavo. "We don't have Partridge down for doing anything illegal," Fogarty said, "but we have a file on him because his name turned up so many times while investigating the Russian Mafia. Partridge isn't too particular about the company he keeps. He ain't no Partridge in a pear tree."

Paavo groaned. "Bad jokes aside, just how active is the Russian Mafia in the city?" he asked.

"We got some problems. Nothing like the East Coast, luckily. They aren't like most gangs, those that immigrants formed to give themselves some clout or a way to get money after arriving in this country. Those Russian mafiosi were already hardened criminals when they arrived. Their West Coast leader calls himself Koba—'protector of the little people.' "

"And Partridge works with them?"

"There's no doubt in my mind—just no proof he's done anything illegal. We share what we turn up with the FBI. I haven't heard back from them, though. Either they think he's clean or just have other fish to fry."

Paavo sat down to read Partridge's file. While Partridge had a long history of association with reputed members of the Russian Mafia, keeping bad company was no crime, even if the unlikely socializing between a Silicon Valley magnate and Russian crime lords reeked with suspicion.

"Thanks for the information," Paavo said as he handed the file back.

"I just hope you nail the bastard, Paavo. He's dirty. I know he is."

Harold Partridge lived in a massive white stucco house on a bluff overlooking the Silicon Valley.

Silicon Valley was not so much a geographical feature as a state of mind, an exciting state of wild competition, startling innovation, cutthroat deals, and fabulous wealth. In size it was a roughly thirty-by-ten-mile strip in Santa Clara County anchored by Stanford University at the northwest corner and the Stanford Research Park on the southeast.

For Harold Partridge's home to look out over the place that had given him everything he could ever want made sense. The house was quiet as a mausoleum. An elderly butler opened the door and said almost nothing as Paavo showed his badge and asked to speak to Partridge. Silently he led Paavo to the living room, then walked away.

The interior was more of a display center than a home. The floors were a smooth, golden hardwood, the walls bright white, with picture windows facing the hills. In the center of the room were two black leather chairs and a matching sofa. One wall had a display of triptych icons mounted on it; another had shelves filled with collectibles.

Paavo slowly worked his way around the room, first studying the icons with their religious scenes. The shelves displayed candlesticks, cloisonné enamel boxes, miniatures, pen trays, cigarette cases, and a variety of fancy bottles.

When Partridge still didn't appear, Paavo wandered out of the living room into the hallway.

Across the hall was a plain, almost Shaker-like dining room. The room just past it was lined with display cases.

The center case held jewelry. Three necklaces with diamonds and emeralds had center stage. There were also a variety of diamond earrings, brooches made with gold and diamonds, with aquamarine, silver and agate, and rubies, and a number of heavily jeweled boxes, many with portraits of Nicholas or Alexandra or both.

The value of the pieces was beyond his ability to comprehend.

"My, my, a policeman with a nose for art."

Paavo turned at the voice. Partridge was an even smaller man than news photos indicated, with a wiry build, wispy brown hair, and oversized glasses. His left eye twitched nervously.

"I'm Inspector Smith, Homicide, San Francisco," Paavo said, holding out his hand.

Partridge's hand felt soft and squishy, almost like cheese.

"Homicide? I take it you're investigating someone's death?" Partridge's voice quavered, and he tried to laugh it off. "I don't think I know anyone who's died under unusual circumstances, do I?"

"It has to do with the death of Gregor Rosinsky, owner of Rose Jewelry in San Francisco."

Partridge gasped. "Yes, I know that store. As you can see, I collect Russian pieces, and the owner of the shop was an excellent craftsman, an expert. He could tell me if the pieces I was interested in were genuine, and I always went to him to have them cleaned and repaired, if necessary. I'm afraid I haven't spoken to him recently. Not for a couple of years." He took a breath. "You said he died—a homicide? How horrible! What happened to him?"

"He was shot in his store. We're looking for any possible leads and are contacting recent customers. His telephone records show that he called this house three days before his death."

"They do? I never received any such call. I spend a fair amount of time at the Industries complex. If he called me, he didn't leave a message."

"Is there anyone else he might have spoken to?"

"My butler should have told me about any phone calls, although he's getting a little forgetful. Still, after so many years of faithful service, how can I complain? The same is true for my housekeeper. She would definitely have given me a message, unless he didn't leave his name or anything. That's probably it. I can ask her if she remembers such a thing. She's out grocery shopping at the moment, I'm afraid."

"Please do," Paavo said. "But tell me more about Rosinsky."

"I have nothing more to tell. I'm sorry."

"If he found a piece of jewelry that you would be interested in, do you think he'd call?"

"I would imagine so. But my pieces are extremely valuable. I doubt he would come across a piece I'd want. In the early part of this century, when Russia first went under Communism, many people escaped and brought jewels and artwork with them. They had to sell them to live in the West. What a treasure trove that was for collectors like myself! Now that source has dried up. And the few new pieces that emerge are outrageously marked. Everyone's gotten into the act, I'm afraid."

"What about the *samizdat* movement some years ago? I imagine you've heard of it."

"Yes . . . yes, I have." Partridge gave a mousy little smile. "I'm afraid I don't ask the sellers where the art came from originally. They give me assurances I will become the legal owner, and I accept them."

"I see," Paavo replied. Something about Partridge annoyed him. He decided not to ask about the brooch at the moment. "Thank you for your time. Let me know if your housekeeper spoke to Rosinsky. For now, I'll ask your butler."

Partridge's eyes narrowed. "Of course, Inspector. I'll ring for him."

Partridge hovered about as Paavo questioned the butler, but the servant had no memory of a telephone call from Rosinsky.

"They're all closing in." Partridge sniveled into the phone. "Paavo Smith was just here! He doesn't know yet, but it's just a matter of time."

"What do you expect?" the voice bellowed. "You try to kill a cop, and you think they're going to sit back and play tiddledywinks? Keep away from everything and everybody! Too many questions are being asked, too much old shit being stirred up. I'm doing what I can to put a lid on it, *but you have to stay clear!*"

"None of this would have happened if it weren't

for Rosinsky and Platnikov!" Partridge whined. "You're taking too long! You've got to stop him— and, from what I hear, he's got a girlfriend who sticks her nose into as much or more than he does."

"I'll handle them both. Leave everything to me." The connection went dead.

Partridge glared at the phone. *Like hell I will!*

Chapter 25

Angie was glad to stay in the city today. Last night, as she gave Paavo a shortened version of her visit north with cousin Richie, she had visions of him wanting to drive up to Gideon immediately. Luckily, he was too busy with an autopsy and a deposition at the Hall of Justice, plus he'd set up a meeting with a couple of specialists at San Francisco General to discuss Aulis's treatment.

Shortly after he left for work, Angie received a phone call from Irene Billot, the customer the grocer had mentioned. Angie asked if they could meet to discuss Cecily, and she agreed.

Irene lived on a ground-floor apartment on Diamond Street, several blocks away from Liberty. She appeared to be in her sixties, with large, green eyes and beautifully coiffed coppery brown hair, and wore a pants outfit that looked like a Chanel. And she was in a wheelchair.

"The grocer assured me you seemed like a nice—and safe—person to talk to," Mrs. Billot said after they'd introduced themselves. "Can't be too careful anymore! But you're too young to have known Cecily."

"I didn't," Angie said. "I'm a friend of Aulis Kokkonen's. I hope you remember him."

"Mr. Kokkonen? Of course I remember him. He was a quiet man, and so very nice." The woman continued to look quizzically at Angie. "Please come inside."

Angie followed her into a living room filled with photos of children and grandchildren. She had set out cookies and a pitcher of iced tea, and poured them each some.

Angie sat on a yellow armchair facing the woman. "Mr. Kokkonen is the reason I was asking questions in the neighborhood. Cecily's son, you see, is a close friend of mine. Almost a fiancé—once he gets around to asking me." Angie smiled, and to her thanks, the woman did as well. "His name is Paavo. You might remember him?"

"Paavo? Little Paavo? He's all grown up now? Oh, of course he is! My, it was long ago, wasn't it?" Irene smiled from her memories. "Such a cute little boy. He had curly brown hair, so soft and springy I'd love to run my fingers through it, and huge blue eyes. He was always talking and laughing. I used to tell Cecily she was going to have to beat the women off with a stick from that boy."

"Well . . . he's still as handsome as ever," Angie admitted. "Although his hair isn't curly anymore. But I still love running my fingers through it." Then her spirits fell. "He doesn't laugh much, though, and he isn't a very talkative person either."

The woman studied her face. "Please tell me what's wrong."

Angie proceeded to tell her a little about Aulis and Paavo. "So I'm trying to find out something about Cecily from someone who knew her. There's even a question as to whether she's alive or dead. Do you think she might still be alive?"

Irene dropped her gaze and quietly said, "No. At first I had hoped she'd managed to get away, but when she never came back, when she abandoned her children, I realized she must have died."

"What was she like, Mrs. Billot?" Angie asked. "What happened to her? Do you know?"

"Well, Cecily and I were as close as . . . as sisters back then, but in hindsight, I realize there was a side of her that was different from the goody-goody loving wife strangers might have seen her as. She had her secrets."

Angie sat straighter in her chair. "What do you mean?"

"Cecily's first marriage wasn't a happy one."

"Oh?" Angie's voice rose. "I've never heard anything at all about it."

Irene took a sip of her tea. "Well, I'm just guessing here, from a few things she said. It seemed her first husband was a lot older. She, like Mika, had lost both her parents, although she had lost hers to illnesses. Her first husband, if you ask me, was the father she had grieved for. She loved him in a quiet way, and he was good to her, and protective. But then he died from a stroke or something. She had a lot of tragedy in her life. A lot of tragedy. Some people, trouble seems to stalk them, no matter what they do. Cecily was one of those people."

"That's terrible," Angie cried, her heart going out to the woman, despite her vow to never forgive Cecily for her treatment of Paavo and his sister.

"She left D.C. with her young daughter and eventually moved to the apartment on Liberty Street. I lived next door back then. Since we both had daughters, we got along. I was a manager at PG & E, and Cecily was a researcher at a law library."

Angie nodded, remembering that was apparently the story Cecily had used as a cover.

"I didn't know it was a lie at first," Irene said pointedly, to Angie's amazement.

"She told you it was a lie?" she asked.

Irene nodded. "I was the only one she confided in. She worked for the FBI and moved into the building to watch a group of Finns mixed up in anti-Soviet activities, and—"

"Wait," Angie interrupted. "I thought she was a research clerk."

"That was the job she began with, but they quickly moved her into surveillance—undercover work."

Angie was too stunned to say a word.

"At first the Finns did amateur stuff like what everyone was doing," Irene said. "At times Sam or Mika or sometimes one of the others would go off on nightly errands. The last time I saw her, in fact, it was evening. Mika got a call from Sam and left quickly. The next day, he was killed."

"Oh, my!"

"Sometimes Cecily would go off, too, by herself. She'd ask me to look after Paavo and Jessica. She'd be back in less than half an hour, looking stormy and angry."

"Did you ask Cecily where she went or what upset her?"

"I asked. She was having a difficult time with her boss. In fact, she was having problems going through with her work because of Mika. She kept it from him."

Angie wasn't sure she'd heard right. "He didn't know she worked for the FBI?"

"How could she admit to spying on him for the government, even though they were both on the same anti-Soviet side? What she was doing both-ered her a lot. Deep down, she knew she should have quit her job and told Mika everything. But she didn't. Her boss apparently talked her into staying. She never went near the FBI office, but used to meet him every few weeks. He convinced her she could actually watch over Mika and the others by staying with the Bureau—that the whole U.S. government would be looking out for them as they got in deeper and deeper with the Russian Mafia."

"And she believed them?"

"To her eternal regret, I'm sure."

Angie could scarcely believe it. "Was she an activist?"

"Not at all. Cecily wasn't a bohemian, a rebel, or even a government critic. Maybe it was because her parents died early and she had to look after herself. She was a survivor; there was an inner toughness to her that not even Mika saw. Oh, that didn't mean she wasn't nice or that she wasn't innocent in some ways. Back then we were all so innocent, believing we could change the world, believing in the good of man. Trusting and naïve—that was all of us, including Cecily."

Irene's cynicism was startling.

"I apologize," Irene said. "But sometimes I get cranky here in this chair. I know you want to ask— it's muscular dystrophy."

"I'm sorry."

"Don't bother." Irene reached for more tea, and so did Angie.

After a while, Angie drew in her breath, and then said, "I hope you don't mind my saying, but it sounds like you were more than a little exasperated with Cecily."

Irene nodded solemnly. "As I said, all this is in hindsight. She was my truest friend, but I see now that she was too ambitious; she wanted to succeed in the Bureau. She saw a chance to get ahead—there was lots of pressure to recruit women agents. Cecily might have been one of the first. She had the mind, talent, and ambition for it, or so she believed. So did I. On the other hand, she also had a family and a good man. Then, in the end, she had nothing."

"My God," Angie cried, finally realizing the enormity of Cecily's deception. "The minute she married Mika, she should have been pulled from the assignment. How could the Bureau have left her in it? How could she have remained? You don't spy on your own husband!"

"That's right. We talked about it at length. Her boss wanted her to stay on, and her ambitious part agreed with him."

"That's madness. Why would her boss have done that?"

"She gave him information about the Russian smugglers—organized crime, in other words, their activities. The Finns were nothing to them, but an insight to what became the Russian Mafia was important. She didn't understand that back then. She believed in God and country. Had she lived, I'm sure she would have spent the last thirty years asking herself how she had been such a fool. She misread the signs, and kept her secret from Mika, and her ambitions drove her to trust the wrong man."

"Her boss?"

Irene's eyes turned hard as steel. "That's right. She always said he was the one."

"My God!" Angie's stomach churned, and tears of frustration and anger on Paavo's behalf came to her eyes. "It's so hard to believe. What about her children, her responsibility as a parent, if not as a wife? What was the woman thinking?"

"I warned her." Irene's tone was cold, almost clinical. "Cecily believed they were all protected. She was close to delusional, playing her games with all their lives, thinking she was beating the system. She beat no one."

Perversely, Angie felt the need to defend Paavo's mother. "Maybe you don't know the whole story. Sometimes there are circumstances beyond anyone's control. You can't control everyone. You can only be responsible for yourself, and hope you take the right step."

Irene gazed at her a long moment. "You're a good person, Miss Amalfi. Paavo's very lucky to have found you," she said, leaving Angie flustered. "But how can you excuse Cecily for leaving her children? That was the result, no matter how you paint it."

"I don't excuse her at all." Angie tried to explain her complex feelings. "Or Aulis. Or even Jessica for perpetuating the lie. I can't forgive any of them for that, but I would like to think she really did love her children and did what she believed was best. I don't know for sure. Just as I don't know if she would have been a great mother. Those are 'what ifs' and 'might have beens.' I'm not here to judge her. I just want the truth. And I don't want Paavo to be hurt anymore."

Irene looked shocked. "That's all this means to you, Paavo's feelings?"

"Yes! Of course my concern is for him, his feelings and his safety. My God, someone tried to kill him! All the rest is in the past. Mistakes were made, and nothing can be done about them. I want to be sure they aren't perpetuated. I can't imagine what it was like for Paavo to grow up without his parents, but he's a fine man because of what his life experience made him, and what he is inside. Now these past secrets are hurting him, and the danger is much, much too close. I've got to stop it. That's what's important, Irene. That's the only thing that's important."

Irene slowly nodded. "You're right. The past sometimes seems more real to me than the present. Maybe for a reason." She patted her useless legs. "I wish you luck, Miss Amalfi. You and Paavo. I hope you both find what you're seeking."

"I appreciate that," Angie said. After some small talk, Angie made her good-byes and left the apartment.

When all was quiet once more, the woman rose from the wheelchair, folded it, and placed it by the front door. She popped the bug from the telephone receiver, dropped it in her pocket, and, after waiting a few minutes, walked out the door, carrying the chair with her.

Chapter 26

"Inspector Smith, Homicide," Paavo said, showing his badge as he stood at the front door of the home of Craig Weston, the onetime owner of Omega Computing. "I'd like to speak to Mr. Weston."

"Homicide?" The man cocked his head, peering hard at the ID. His skin was dark olive, his head completely bald. Rounded shoulders caused a stooped posture, and the skin around his eyes and mouth hung in loose, rubbery folds. "I'm Craig Weston." His voice was gruff. "What's the problem?"

"There's no problem. I'm investigating a murder case in San Francisco," Paavo said, "the murder of a Russian jeweler. In the course of the investigation something came up that happened many years ago. It doesn't involve you, but I did have questions about some of your former employees."

The man visibly relaxed. The way people became uptight when first contacted by police never ceased to surprise Paavo. They could be perfectly innocent, but you wouldn't know it from the way they looked.

"Come on in," Weston said. The house was a sim-

ple ranch style, the type that carried an affordable,
middle-class price tag almost anywhere but in Palo
Alto, the home of Stanford University and many Silicon Valley executives and managers. Weston
walked straight through it to the backyard. Across a
concrete patio was a clapboard workshop. "We can
talk in here so the wife won't be listening and
butting in every two seconds."

The workshop looked like a junkyard for old
computer parts. A couple of complete systems were
up and running, but most of the room was filled
with miscellaneous pieces, soldering irons, tools,
and electrical equipment. "I'm working on a new
invention. Soon it'll be ready to market."

Paavo nodded. Weston removed a crumb-filled
plate, utensils, and an empty coffee cup from a chair
near the work area, and motioned for Paavo to sit
there.

"What do you want to know?" Weston asked,
easing his bulk into the chair in front of one of the
computers.

"About the Omega Corporation."

"Omega?" Weston leaned back in the chair. "That
was years ago."

"You had some Finns working for you there."

"Yep. Three of my programmers. They'd get to
talking Finnish, I didn't have a clue. They were
good, though. Smart boys. They stayed with the
company after I sold it. I heard a couple of them
died or were killed not too long after that. I suppose
that's why you're asking. I didn't know anything
about it, though. I was long gone by then, thanks to
Partridge."

"Partridge bought Omega, I understand."

"Right." He bent forward, suddenly steely eyed.
"Partridge forced me out. To this day, I'm not sure
how he did it, but he decided he wanted Omega,

and went head to head with us, contacting my customers and undercutting my deals even if he was losing money on them. The customers didn't care as long as they got a better bottom line. After a while I couldn't afford to make my payroll. Guess who showed up to offer to help."

"Partridge."

"You're damned right." Weston reached for a pack of Marlboros and matches on the worktable, shook out some smokes, and offered one to Paavo. Paavo declined. Weston lifted the pack to his mouth and wrapped his lips around one cigarette, pulling it free from the others. "I had no choice, so I borrowed from him. He was a smooth bastard, offering help, saying he understood. What he understood was how to run me out of my own company. Before long, I owed him more than my share of the business."

Weston paused long enough to light the cigarette bobbing up and down between his lips. "He became the owner, and booted me out the door. Made me an offer—not nearly what the place was worth. Back then, the computer industry hadn't yet taken off. We were young, we knew the future, but few of us had the business sense to jump from here to there. Look at Altair or Osborne or Commodore computers—they owned the early days. Where are they now? It was the same with a lot of us. Me included."

Paavo nodded. Weston was simply stating the facts and there was no recrimination or resentment. Even his dislike of Partridge was coldly clinical . . . like a computer.

"What I'll never understand was how Partridge was able to match the technological side of what I was doing. I had programmers, but I also had engineers. In the old days we did everything. Hardware

and software. It was all connected in our minds—
computers. Period. Anyway, we were working on
light-emitting diodes—LED displays. They're what
made little calculators possible. And then"—
Weston's face grew taut, his breathing quickened—
"before we could get ours on the market, Partridge
suddenly had them in use, in his company! It pulled
the rug right out from under us." For the first time
in the interview, Weston's analytical demeanor van-
ished in rage at a betrayal that still ate at him.

Paavo prompted, "How did that happen?"

"Partridge had to have had some outside help—I
mean, outside-the-country help! The Finns that you
mentioned, they were suspicious of that, too. I
remember having a conversation with one of
them—Sam, I think his name was."

"Sam Vanse?"

"Uh, I guess." Weston seemed startled by the
question, as if he meant this to be a monologue.
"Yeah, Sam. That's right." He flicked cigarette ash
into a used plate by his monitor. "Anyway, Sam said
that he had been back home, and he'd heard that
Soviet scientists were working on different digital
display methods for computers and other things,
probably for their space program. The Soviet scientists had the necessary theoretical knowledge, the
math and the science, but they didn't have any
industry. The complete thrust of their technology
was aimed at satellites—the space program—but
they developed the LED display, and suddenly so
did Partridge."

Weston stopped talking and fixated on the tip of
his cigarette as if watching Partridge burning there.

"So you agreed with the Finns that Partridge had
Soviet sources?" Paavo asked.

Before continuing, Weston filled his lungs with

smoke. "At first I didn't believe it, even though that was always Sam's idea. Mike and Oscar agreed."

"You mean Mika and Okko?"

"If you say so—they were Mike and Oscar to me. Anyway, that was their explanation for the way Partridge jumped ahead of the competition the way he did. Then, after he bought Omega, he made it sound as if the LED display technology had originated with us. That was when I really began to get suspicious of his sources. The bastard couldn't tell the difference between computer parts and those of a toaster." Weston gazed at the far wall and shook his head. "The worst part is, I still don't see how he did it. He had to have had the cooperation of the Soviet government . . . or our government. But why? He was just a nerdy computer builder in California. I don't get it."

"Neither do I," Paavo admitted. "But it's a good question. One that bears looking into."

"Good luck, fella. I used to try to wise up folks in the industry—hell, anybody who'd listen—about Harold-The-Shit Partridge. All it got me was a rep as a bitter loser. Everybody loved Harold—and if you didn't, you faced his lawyers or got blackballed in the Valley or both." Weston's face darkened. "I've been watching him . . . waiting. He's going to get his comeuppance. Soon, too."

As if realizing what he'd just said to a cop, he added, "If you think I'm worried telling you this, I'm not. When I act, no one will be able to pin it on me. I was one of the founders of this Valley. Most of what Partridge has is rightly mine. I just need to remind him of that fact, and someday soon, I will."

"Paavo, I'm at the Au Claire restaurant, Union and Grant." Angie spoke quietly into her cell phone.

"Why don't you meet me here? I've got lots of information for you."

"Okay. I'll drop my things off at the house and walk down. I should be there in fifteen, twenty minutes or so."

"Great. Love you!"

"You, too."

She listened to the receiver disconnect, and couldn't help but smile. He still wasn't one to get mushy on the phone. Or ask questions. Cops—they always act as if their phone is being tapped.

She put her phone in her tote bag and took out her camcorder. She wouldn't use this restaurant as one of her review subjects since it was near the house she and Paavo were sharing and she might want to come here fairly often. Still, she couldn't pass up the chance to take a few shots.

As she panned the room, she became aware of someone standing behind her. She stopped filming and glanced over her shoulder. The older man who had been seated at the next table now stood frowning at her. "I'm sorry," she said. "It's just that it's a lovely restaurant."

To her surprise, his frown changed to a smile. He was a big man, in his late sixties or so, with broad shoulders and a thick chest, waist, and hips. His hair was the color of steel, receded quite far at the temples, with a slicked-back center tuft. His eyebrows were gray, and his lashes so pale she could scarcely see them. His brown eyes were thin slits in a fleshy face, almost Boris Yeltsin-like, or maybe she just had Russians on the brain after all Paavo's stories.

"No need to be sorry. I'm the one who should say that! I had to look at your camera—and I didn't want you to break it by getting my ugly mug on film! I'm most intrigued by it." His voice was deep, and his enunciation beautifully precise in a British or even European manner—not at all like an American accent. "It's such a tiny thing."

"It's the latest model." Angie handed it to him. "It's a digital video recorder. I look into the square on the side, and take my videos."

He slid out the chair across from her and sat. "They haven't brought my dinner out yet," he murmured, lost in studying the camera. "This is nice. Quite nice. Can I try it?"

"Sure. Look into the little square, and hold down the button on the side."

"Ah, I see." He focused on Angie, taped her for a moment, then panned the restaurant. "I should tell my son about this. He does photography."

"Then he's probably aware of it. I'm not sure if serious photographers like these much or not. They seem to use mostly old, heavy stuff."

"That's what my son uses. He fills the car with equipment." He chuckled. "I don't know why he does it."

"Is he a professional photographer?"

"Yes. He takes videos at weddings, bar mitzvahs, all that sort of thing. He enjoys it."

"That's great." Angie looked at the small video camera. Maybe she should forget about food-related jobs and become a photographer herself. Making a living going to happy occasions and getting people to smile sounded easy enough. But then she thought of her sister Caterina, and how she tended to scream at photographers for always catching her with the most unflattering expressions. Actually, the photos were quite accurate.

"My name is Nick," the old man said. "I must say, I don't understand your country."

That surprised her. "You don't? Why not?"

"Because—a beautiful young woman like you should not be sitting alone in a restaurant. Back

home, when I was young, you would have been circled by men like roosters around a hen."

A hen? How unflattering. "All pecking at me?"

"Not pecking in a bad sense . . . pecking as in a
kiss."

Her eyebrows rose up, and then she burst out
laughing. "You do have a way with words, Nick."

He chuckled. "That's what the ladies used to say.
Those days were great fun. So, why is someone as
beautiful as you alone?"

"I won't be for long. My boyfriend is going to
meet me here."

"Ah! My bad luck! Well, I won't keep you. I see
they've finally brought out my salad. I'd better
leave—I wouldn't want your boyfriend to get the
wrong idea." He held out his hand. "It's been very
nice talking to you, Miss . . . ?"

"Call me Angie." She reached her hand out to
shake his.

"Angie." He gently revolved her hand, clicked
his heels, bowed forward, and kissed the back of it.
"My pleasure." Then he walked away.

Instead of returning to his table, he continued
toward the back of the restaurant. Going to the
men's room, she supposed. She had to smile. It had
been a long time since she'd met anyone who knew
the proper way to kiss a lady's hand, or, for that
matter, knew any of the old-world mannerisms on
how to treat a lady. Nick. She liked him. Ah, if he
were about thirty years younger, watch out, Paavo.

Since Nick wasn't there to make her feel self-
conscious, she took a few more pictures of the
restaurant. It had a warm charm about it.

The waiter brought out the lobster bisque she'd
ordered, and soon Nick returned to his table. She
returned his smile as he sat and began to eat.

He seemed to forget about her, and she took a few more shots of the restaurant. She had no sooner finished the salad than the waiter brought her crab-stuffed filet of sole. She tried to eat slowly, waiting for Paavo, but he was taking longer than he'd expected. The man seemed to think he had wings, and forgot that annoyances like traffic jams could slow down his progress.

She nibbled at her sole. Had she been able to concentrate on it instead of Paavo's whereabouts, it would have been delicious. Nick sent a bottle of Chalone Vineyard Reserve Chenin Blanc 1996 to her table.

She had the waiter ask him if he'd like to join her.

Quietly, and smoothly, the waiter moved him to her table, and poured them each a glass of the wine. Nick had ordered *frutti di mare* with white beans—*mare i monte*. "I don't know where my friend is," Angie said, as he settled in across from her, "but it seems a shame for both of us to be eating alone."

"You are very kind to an old man. Most young people don't give us a second thought these days," he said.

"You're very kind to send me this wine. It's excellent."

"You seemed to be someone who would know and appreciate a fine vintage."

They talked about wines, and food, and music, and Angie discovered that Nick liked classical as much as she did, and they launched into a discussion of the San Francisco Symphony and Michael Tilson Thomas's conducting. Nick had grown up with classical music, and Angie had come to it because of violin lessons as a child. Later, when her family realized that she wouldn't grow very tall, they had her take ballet lessons. Neither had worked out at all—her musical talent was nonexistent and her dancing ability was even worse—but she came to appreciate the music.

As they talked, she caught a view of a tall man walking along the sidewalk toward the restaurant. "Oh! That's my boyfriend now," she said. She picked up her camcorder, set the viewer to enlarge the picture. She began filming him as he approached.

"You're filming your friend?" Nick asked with amusement.

"Won't he be surprised?" she said.

"I'm sure he—"

"Oh, my God!" she cried.

"What?"

She stood up, still looking through the viewer. "Help! Somebody! He's being attacked!"

"Attacked?" Nick stood as well and looked out the window. The other customers put down their forks and knives and stared at Angie.

"He's fighting with some guy!" she yelled. "Call the police! Waiter! Stop them!"

"I'll call nine-one-one," the waiter said, but instead, he rushed to the window with other customers. No one stepped out the door.

Angie looked up, as if in a daze, to see the people crowded around the window. She grabbed her tote bag, a heavy lethal weapon in itself, and ran outside, determined to swing it at the attacker and send him flying away from Paavo.

As soon as she reached the sidewalk, the attacker fled. Paavo was standing a bit wobbly, his hand pressing his mouth as if to make sure his teeth were all still there.

She grabbed his arm. "Are you all right?"

"I think so," he said.

"There's some blood on your lip," she said. "Let's get you inside the restaurant."

Inside, she led him into the women's room. He hesitated, but she dragged him in and locked the door. She drenched a paper towel with water and dabbed the blood from his lip and chin.

"What was that all about?" she asked.

"I have no idea," he mumbled.

"Did he try to rob you?" She angled his head and patted cold water on his cheekbone where a weal was already building.

"No."

"Did you recognize him at all?" Angie asked, back at his lip.

"Uh-uh."

"Well, for what it's worth, I've got his picture on tape. I was filming you walking toward the restaurant when he attacked."

He pulled the towel out of her hand. "You didn't stop filming?"

"I was too stunned to do anything. I'd set the focus to blow up the picture a lot and I could see better looking though the lens than not. That was why I kept using it."

He looked at her strangely.

"Do you feel up to eating dinner? Or do you just want to go home?"

"Home."

As she led the way to the table to pay the bill, she saw that Nick and his place setting were gone. The waiter was clearing his spot, and setting it again for Paavo until Angie told him they weren't staying. "The elderly gentleman took care of your bill, ma'am," the waiter informed her. "He said to tell you he had a very nice time, and he was sure you'd want to be alone with your young man."

Angie was strangely touched by the message, and the man's generosity. "How very kind. I'd like to thank him. Does he come here often?"

The waiter shook his head. "I've never seen him before."

Chapter 27

Paavo drove them back to the bungalow in Angie's car, taking a circular route to be sure they weren't being followed. After arriving, Angie immediately set up the camcorder with the VCR and she and Paavo sat on the sofa to watch the tape over the television screen. Immediately Angie saw that Paavo hadn't been attacked at all, but the stranger had said something to him and tried to leave. Paavo decided to stop him. That was when the fight broke out.

The lighting was poor, but as the two men struggled, they moved near a storefront that was lit up and the other man's face became clearer. He was enormous, with the physique of a bodybuilder. Finally he pushed Paavo hard and, half stumbling, ran away.

Paavo didn't follow.

"What did he say to you?" Angie asked.

" 'Back off and you won't get killed.' I wanted him to explain himself, but he was feeling shy."

"Hmm. I might be imagining things, but I think I've seen him before." She rewound and played the fight again. "Muscles like that don't show up every day, especially not in this city. They're quite remarkable."

"You've established you like his looks; now, where did you see him?"

"Actually, bubbly muscles like that don't do it for me. I prefer—"

"Angie."

"I've got an idea." She sprang off the sofa to her stack of camcorder tapes. "Let's take a look at some of these restaurant shots." Setting up the tapes, she fast-forwarded through them until she reached the Basque restaurant she'd gone to with her sister. Seated alone at a table was Paavo's studly friend. "Voilà!"

"Damn, I don't get it." Paavo leaned back, arms folded, and glared at the TV. "He had to know you were taking pictures. Why didn't he care? Is it all a game with him, or what?"

"How did he find us tonight? That's what I want to know," Angie said, sitting on the floor and restacking her tapes in chronological order.

"He must be following you," Paavo surmised. "It's the only explanation. He could have been waiting to go into the restaurant, or watching you from the sidewalk—you'd been seated at the window the whole time, right?"

"That could be," she said thoughtfully.

Paavo fingered his swollen lip where his teeth had hit and caused the bleeding. It made him mad all over again. "I'll take your tape to the Hall tomorrow and run a search on Jesse The Body. You'd better stay put in the house. Order out if you don't want to cook, but keep away from restaurants."

"Stay home? No way!" Angie was appalled. "I *should* go out. Now that I know I'm being followed, I'll be extra alert. If the guy shows up again, I'll hurry to a safe place and call you. Then you can arrest him and find out what's going on."

"It's too dangerous," Paavo said.

"But if I stay home, I won't be able to learn things the way I did yesterday with Sawyer . . . and again today."

"Uh-oh," he murmured. "What now?"

"It's what I'd hoped to discuss with you at the restaurant." She excitedly joined him again on the sofa. "Today I visited Irene Billot."

"Who?"

"She was a good friend of your mother's."

He looked at her as if he didn't believe her. Since he hadn't eaten dinner, as she told him about finding Irene—leaving out the bars and restaurants—and then everything she'd learned during her visit, they moved into the kitchen where she put on some lentil soup and he made himself a ham and cheese sandwich.

Paavo was silent for a long while after Angie completed the story. "Jesus," he said finally. "Spying on her own husband. It's crazy."

"But it sounds like she thought she was protecting him," Angie countered.

"Are you sure you could trust this Irene? I don't remember any of that stuff coming out in Mika's investigation. I remember seeing her interviewed, but that's it."

"Why would she lie now? It's more likely she lied thirty years ago—the FBI and the Russian Mafia? Heck, I'd lie, too."

"Damn it!" Paavo slammed down the knife he had used to cut the sandwich in half, and faced her. "That's exactly what this is all about. Lies. Thirty years worth of lies! I'm fed up with the lies and the people making them. Damn them all!"

"Paavo!" She was shocked. He almost never raised his voice.

"Hell, Angie. Think about it. You're caught up in

this, too. You're in danger and can't even go to your own apartment because years ago, people didn't have the balls to level with me. What does that make them? Or me?"

"It's not your fault," she began.

"I'm not talking fault. I'm talking deeper. Who *are* these people? A mother who lies to her husband? A father who goes off on some idealistic mission and gets himself killed?"

She didn't speak, giving him the chance to open up, to vent all he'd been holding in since this began.

"I was better off not knowing," he said grimly. "I don't want to know about them, not like this! I don't want you to be a part of it. And most of all, I wish they hadn't been so goddamn stupid!"

She reached for his hand, but he got up and walked into the living room. She shut off the gas beneath the soup, put his sandwich on a plate, and followed.

"You don't mean any of that," she said.

"I sure as hell do!" He paced. "But I'm not giving up. I'll find out the truth now that I've come this far. It'll tell me who I am."

"What they were has nothing to do with you," she cried, following him back and forth across the living room, the plate still in her hands.

"It has everything to do with me!"

"No. You're wrong!"

"You just don't get it," he yelled, facing her. "You, with a city filled with Amalfis—more cousins than you can count—cannot begin to understand what it means to have no one. No one, Angie. I can't look around and see anyone else with the same features, the same blood. No one with the same background that made me who I am and what I believe. I don't *know* who I am. It's all buried. And now that I'm trying to dig beneath it, it keeps getting worse."

"You're who *you* created," she cried. "And you did a damned fine job, Inspector."

His voice turned as cold as she'd ever heard it. "Don't patronize me, Angie. That's one thing I will not tolerate."

"I'm not patronizing you!" She waved an arm in frustration. "I'm trying to tell you that whatever turns up about your parents, your past, doesn't matter as far as who you are!"

"It does to me. Can't you see that? How can you not understand something so simple, so basic?"

"Oh, I understand, all right. I understand this is an excuse of yours. You skitter away like a feral cat—"

"A *cat*?"

"Whenever I try to talk to you about our future— about getting married!"

He looked like he couldn't believe his ears. "What does getting married have to do with anything?"

"It has everything to do with how you're feeling about yourself. About us! I love you. I don't give a damn about your ancestors. I want to marry you, not them."

His mood was too ugly to listen. "You're obsessed with the subject."

"Obsessed!" The word exploded. "I'm trying to tell you how I feel, to let you know I see that you're hurting, and I understand."

"The only thing you understand is a white dress and wedding veil."

She was literally hopping mad. "You arrogant jackass!"

"My, my. From cat to jackass. Sounds like I'm moving up on the food chain." He folded his arms, looking so smug she picked up half his sandwich and threw it at him. He ducked and it sailed past him to land with a splat on the television screen.

"Hah!" he shouted in triumph just as the second half hit him square on the chin. The sandwich opened up as it flew, and mayonnaise and mustard caused the bread slices to stick a moment before dropping to the floor.

Realizing what she'd just done, Angie covered her mouth as he slowly wiped his face. He looked at his greasy hand, then at her.

She backed up.

He stepped toward her.

She took another step backward. "Now, Paavo."

Suddenly his eyes filled with mirth and, to her surprise, he began to laugh.

And so did she.

Jane Platt awoke with a start. A strong, icy cold hand covered her mouth and nose, smothering her. The child's eyes flew open to see a woman's face looming in front of her.

"Stop struggling!" the woman hissed, pressing Jane's head farther down into the pillow. "Stop struggling and I'll remove my hand. Will you do that?"

Jane tried to nod as tears rolled down her cheeks. She wanted her grandpa. If he were still alive, this woman wouldn't be here scaring her. No one would ever scare her.

The woman eased back a little, and when Jane didn't call out or try to get away, she sat on the edge of the bed.

The bedroom window was wide open, and Jane realized that was how the woman got into her room. She tried hard to stop crying, but it wasn't easy. The foster family she'd been sent to wouldn't like it if they found out that someone broke into the house because of her. They wouldn't want her any-more, she feared, just as her aunt didn't want her.

"Now, Jane," the woman said in a harsh whisper, "we're going to talk about your grandfather, and a cameo brooch. Do you know what a cameo is, Jane?"

Chapter 28

Paavo walked into the crime lab with Angie's videotape first thing in the morning, and talked to his friend Ray Faldo. They ran the video until they found a clear shot of the man Paavo had fought with, froze the frame, and made a print. While Paavo phoned contacts in the FBI and Interpol—he had worked with one of their agents not long ago—and transmitted copies of the photo to them, Faldo put the suspect's characteristics into the database and set up a photo lineup. They found no hits in the state or city mug shots.

The homicide book on Mika's murder was still on Paavo's desk, and he looked up interviews with Irene Billot. The woman had given the homicide inspectors no information beyond being a neighbor and recognizing the family if she passed them on the street. She wasn't mentioned at all in the investigation on Cecily's auto accident, conducted mostly by a different police force due to the jurisdiction of her death.

On a hunch, he decided to see what, if anything, the S.F.P.D. had on Irene Billot. The information that turned up surprised him.

Records of her calls to the Mission Station about Cecily existed—dire warnings, conspiracy theories, fears for her own life—contact after contact, all dismissed as a troubled woman who couldn't cope with her friend's death. The beat cops who talked to Irene weren't given access to the background of Cecily's disappearance. They were simply told her car had plunged off a cliff into the Pacific. Faced with Irene's weird ravings, they half expected her to announce aliens had abducted Cecily. Irene's own words didn't help her case any, and Paavo couldn't reconcile the difference between the alarming, shrill woman the police reported and the calm, collected woman Angie told him about.

He had just finished reading the reports on Mrs. Billot when Interpol contacted him. They had a photo match on Mr. Muscle and faxed him the information.

Leonid Stavrogin: Russian Mafia enforcer. Right-hand man to the leader of the West Coast Mafia, known only as Koba, the Russian Robin Hood "little people's protector" figure the Gang Task Force inspector told him about.

Stavrogin, despite his physical strength, wasn't a man who gave out verbal warnings. He shot people. Why should a man like that warn Paavo?

More distressing than his remark, though, was the knowledge that he'd been watching Angie, and following her.

Angie was a target.

Paavo had to find out why.

Angie and Paavo stood in front of the Diamond Street apartment where Irene Billot lived.

They rang the bell, and when there was no answer, knocked. The door next to Irene's opened and a man came out. He had a pencil-thin mustache and slick, shoe-polish-black hair. "She isn't home," he said.

"Do you know when she'll be back?" Angie asked. "I'm a friend."

"Try April," he announced, looking rather pleased with himself.

"April?" Angie was shocked. "Where has she gone?"

"Arizona. She always goes down there for the winter. Likes the sun, hates the rain."

Angie and Paavo glanced at each other.

"Wasn't she here yesterday?" Paavo asked.

"Yesterday?" The man chuckled. "My goodness, no. I've been taking care of the place for her, watering her plants and all. She's been gone a month already."

"Were you home yesterday?" Angie asked, trying to get to the bottom of this.

"Yes . . . except for while I was at racquetball."

"When was that?"

"In the afternoon. I go every Tuesday and Thursday."

"You are talking about Irene Billot, right?" Paavo asked. "Sixties, in a wheelchair."

Now it was the neighbor's turn to appear shocked. "Well . . . yes and no. I am talking about Irene Billot. She is sixty-something, but she's not in any wheelchair. She's the reason I began exercising—to be in half as good a shape as she is."

"Oh, dear," Angie murmured.

"Has she ever mentioned an old friend named Cecily?" Paavo asked.

The man's eyebrows rose. "As a matter of fact, she has. Several times. Cecily was the reason she moved here. She said she had to get away from her old place because it wasn't safe. Someone killed her friend, and as much as she tried to tell the police about it, they wouldn't listen. As far as she was concerned, they proved their incompetency, and made it clear she would have to take care of herself, because no one else would do it. She took lessons in self-defense, even"—he shuddered—"learned to use a gun."

"Did she say who she was afraid of?"

"It sounded like just about everybody."

Angie felt as if she were walking on air. She was in the television studios of Bay TV. This was her milieu, she decided. Television. It was what she'd been born for, lived for. After all, she was a child of the age of television. She simply had to find herself a job here and all would be well with the career part of her life—she just knew it.

In a way, she was glad they hadn't been able to talk with Irene that afternoon. Paavo returned to work and she didn't have to tell him about the call she'd received that morning from *BayLife Today*. Their scheduled guest canceled and they needed an immediate replacement. Was she available? Her heart was in her mouth, but she managed to croak out, *"Yes!"*

It wasn't a prime-time news show, and it wasn't a major syndicated program. Instead, it was an area "events" show on a local cable channel. As cousin Richie would say, "Hey, a start is a start."

Bended-knee begging and a hefty tip got her an immediate appointment at her hairdresser's, plus a manicurist. Careful not to destroy her hair, she rushed from the beauty parlor to Sissy's of Maiden Lane for a new suit. A peppermint-pink Anne Klein looked properly Diane Sawyerish.

She signed in at the guard station on the ground floor and a casually dressed fellow with dreadlocks greeted her and silently led her up to the studio.

"Which way is makeup?" she asked.

He looked confused. "The women's room is down that hall."

She glanced where he pointed. "Oh?"

"The studio's in there." He gestured toward double swinging doors at the end of a wide hallway filled with computer terminals. No one sat at any of them, though.

The dreadlocks fellow disappeared. Angie gaily bustled into the studio and promptly tripped over a maze of cables on the floor. To avoid stumbling again, she minced toward the brightly lit set.

A woman with hair shorter than Paavo's, wearing a beige smock tied around her much like a butcher's apron, ran up to her. "Miss Amalfi?"

"Oh!" She put her hand to her chest. "You recognize me!"

The woman looked at her strangely. "Well . . . you *are* the only guest on the show tonight. I'll take your restaurant-review tapes to the producer. You can sit over there. You've got a half hour before the live show. Any questions?"

Angie looked at the chair the woman pointed at. It was in a dark corner. "Aren't we going to rehearse?"

"Rehearse? No. We like spontaneity."

"Aren't we at least going to run through my videotape?"

"No need. You know what's on it. You tell us when to run it, and we will. Then you explain to the audience what we're seeing. It's simple." The woman smiled.

Angie had her doubts about how simple it would be. The first inklings of panic began to tickle her. "Where's makeup?"

"Makeup? You're fine." She dashed off and left Angie clutching her makeup case.

She always wore makeup, and wore it with care so that it didn't look like she had it plastered to her face. TV makeup was different, or should have been. She thought it was supposed to look plastered so that when the lights washed out the color, she would look alive rather than ghostly pale.

In the women's room, she darkened her makeup, then returned to the studio to sit and wait. She practiced her opening lines—a clever, witty little speech about who she was and what her video restaurant reviews were all about. She wished she could talk someone into a teensy-tiny rehearsal.

The technicians were running about shouting incomprehensible jargon at one another, and the woman who took her tapes was nowhere to be seen.

Carol Metcalf, the star of *BayLife Today*, suddenly appeared and stepped onto the set, the lights bright on her face. One instant, people dashed in frenzy, and then the next, all fell silent. The program began.

Angie could scarcely breathe. Hers was the third segment. She sat, without moving a single muscle, through the endless television ramblings and bad jokes until she heard the announcer say, "Next, San Francisco's own restaurant reviewer, Angelina Amalfi, will be here to present a *video* restaurant review. We'll see for ourselves the restaurant Angie went to, and hear what she has to say about it! Stay tuned!"

Her legs wobbled as she approached the set and sat beside the star. Carol turned to her. "Now, remember, keep your answers short, and be as outrageous as you wish."

"What?" Angie looked at her blankly.

"No speeches," Carol ordered. "And be controversial."

Angie nodded, taking deep breaths. The opening she'd prepared was a bit lengthy, but surely she could introduce herself. No one would object. Nevertheless, she grew so nervous, she was sure perspiration glistened on her face. She remembered a scene from an old movie in which a guy had spent his entire career thinking he could be a news anchor on TV. When he finally got his chance, he sweat so much, viewers began to call the station thinking he was having a heart attack. She prayed she wouldn't be like that.

When a production assistant called out, "Five seconds!" her mind went absolutely blank. Her only coherent thought was *Get me out of here!*

She was hyperventilating when Carol Metcalf began speaking into the camera. "Angelina Amalfi is, herself, a gourmet cook and frequent restaurant reviewer for *Haute Cuisine* magazine, published here in the Bay Area. Angie, which restaurant did you go to?"

"Thank you, Carol," she said. Her mouth felt like it was filled with uncooked Quaker Oats. "I—" Her voice came out in a high squeak and she just hoped it would drop an octave. Or two. She began her introduction. "I'm here to give a video restaurant review. I—"

"Yes!" Carol interrupted. "I've never seen one before. So you went to an interesting restaurant, I take it?"

"I did." Her eyes caught the camera and all she could think of was all the people in the Bay Area watching her at that very moment. She tried to return to the introduction she'd practiced. "Video restaurant reviews are a new concept."

Carol frowned.

Angie hurried on. "They're something I just dreamed up for this very program. For you. And for your viewer . . . viewers." She was dying inside. She wished she could die on the outside; then at least she'd get sympathy instead of being laughed at.

"How nice, Angie." The woman's jaw was tight. *"Where* did you go?"

Panic set in as she noticed that the veins on Carol Metcalf's neck were beginning to protrude. She threw away her set speech, but nothing filled what now felt like a huge, empty gap where clever bon mots and turns of phrase should have been. "I went to a restaurant that is called"—*Oh, God, what, what, what?*—"Pisces. It is a zodiac that features seafood." She took a deep breath. Time for the videotape. "Here are some scenes from it." *I hope.*

Like magic, her video began to roll.

She tried to think of what Carol had said. Short answers. Controversial. "See how pretty it is. See the waiter. See the customers. See them eat."

Carol Metcalf kicked her.

She was ready to cry.

"Did you like the restaurant, Angie?" Carol asked.

"Yes. I liked it very much. This is my waiter now. He is bringing me steamed lobster with a saffron-tomato broth." Angie racked her brain for something interesting and controversial to say. She definitely wanted to make it big on TV, and she had to make up for her blown introduction. The camera stared at her. "The lobster was a little mushy and a little stronger than lobster should be. Sounds disgusting, doesn't it? And . . ." Her voice rose. "There was too much thyme in the broth. It overwhelmed the saffron. Usually there's not enough thyme for anything . . . ha, ha. Get it? Time . . ." *Oh, Lord!*

Carol looked stricken. "How was the dessert?"

"I had a hazelnut torte à la mode." *Controversial! Be controversial!* "It was, um, um, uh, a little stale. A little like chalk. Here is my waiter bringing me my dessert." He slammed it onto the table—the camcorder had irritated him, Angie recalled—and the ice cream slid from the torte and off the plate onto the tablecloth. He scooped it up, stormed away, and soon was seen bringing her another plate. He made faces at the camera, then left.

"He must have thought this was a *Candid Camera* revival, ha, ha!"

Carol gave her a long, withering stare, then signaled the camera to focus on her. "And now, for our weather report. Here for an *expanded* report is our meteorologist . . ."

Angie stopped listening. All she wanted to do was curl up and die. Thank God she hadn't told Paavo she was going to be on TV tonight. Unfortunately, she did tell her parents, her four sisters, several girlfriends, a number of cousins, the grocer, her hairdresser, the woman who did her nails, and some guy selling newspapers on the corner. When would she ever learn to keep her mouth shut?

Chapter 29

After calling it a day in Homicide, Paavo went to visit Aulis.

His condition hadn't changed any. The doctors were growing increasingly alarmed about his continued inability to wake up.

Fear and frustration flooded through Paavo as he stood in that sterile hospital room and watched over the man who had raised him, now looking so small and shriveled under the white sheets. Usually Paavo didn't notice the lines on Aulis's face or the thinness of his white hair. He still saw Aulis very much as he had appeared when Paavo was growing up: an older but spry man. Now Paavo observed all the changes, and thought about the fact that someday he was going to lose the one who'd been there almost forever for him.

He wondered what Aulis had known all those years about Cecily and Mika, and why in God's name he had kept it hidden.

He sat alone by the bed for about twenty minutes. But then he realized it didn't make any sense for him to just sit there and do nothing. Once Aulis awoke, he'd want to know who had done this to him, and had the assailant been caught? Paavo didn't want to have to answer, "No."

After about five more minutes, he decided it was time to go home.

Home. He wished he didn't get a kick in the gut each time he thought about the cottage. He liked being there more than he ever dreamed he would, and more than he really wanted to admit. He had found a place away from the world's cruelty and losses where there was love and laughter, and he wondered how long he could accept it, or if he would soon want to retreat to his own quiet solitude once more.

In no time, he'd driven across town and parked on Montgomery Street, right in front of a four-story apartment house that looked like a ship, and had been used in an old Bogart and Bacall film, *Dark Passage.* Maybe, someday, he'd rent the movie and see what all the fuss was about.

He fairly ran down the Filbert steps to the little house, and burst into the living room to find Angie sitting on the sofa, Hercules on her lap, staring at the wall. She didn't look at him, didn't say a word.

"What's wrong?" he asked. Angie was not one to sit silently. Usually she greeted him with a hug and a kiss.

"Nothing," she replied.

Sure, and there's no ice in the Arctic.

She sighed heavily and mumbled something about coffee. He followed her into the kitchen. "You can tell me about it," he said as she filled the carafe with water.

She silently measured coffee into the filter. *We're together,* he wanted to say, *so we can talk to each other when we're unhappy or disappointed or just need a shoulder to lean on.* He didn't say that, though. He didn't quite know how. Instead, he waited.

"I blew it," she murmured, and flipped the On switch.

He captured her. "Why don't you start at the beginning?"

She leaned her head against his shoulder. "I was awful."

"Awful? You mean you did something awful?" he asked, confused. "What did you do?"

"I went on television. Oh, God! Why, why, why did I ever dream I could do TV? I'm just not Barbara Walters. Not even Carol Metcalf."

"Who?"

"She's on *BayLife Today*."

"Ah."

She covered her face. "I was so hideous! My mind went blank. I couldn't get the words out. What came out was like listening to a tape that someone had slowed down. I can never show myself in public again! Heck, I don't even want to see me!"

He gathered her closer. "I'm sure you weren't as bad as all that. You're always your own worst critic."

"If I wasn't so bad, why did Carol kick me?"

He had no answer.

She made her hands into fists. "I should have seen it coming, but did I? No! Not until it was too late. Then I saw it. Here I go again, I said to myself. Angie Amalfi, looking foolish. Why do I do it?"

"You aren't foolish, Angie." He stroked her hair.

"I so much want to do interesting things," she said, burrowing against his chest. "I want to be accomplished, an achiever. I want to be a person who is independent and successful, and good at her job—not daddy's privileged little rich girl. Not that that's so tragic. But I'm more than that, aren't I?"

"Of course."

"I'll take that as an enthusiastic yes." She sighed heavily. "I know I try too hard sometimes. Maybe a lot of times. I know I push it. Occasionally I even leap before thinking. It's fun sometimes, but not when I disappoint myself."

He placed his hand under her chin and forced her to look at him. "You never disappoint me, Angie. Promise me you'll never change."

Those were the words she needed to hear. They held each other in the lengthening silence. "Maybe I should just go to bed," she said finally. "This won't look so bleak in the morning."

"Want company?" Paavo offered.

She glanced up at him. He grinned. She couldn't help herself and smiled back. "I'll turn off the coffee."

A loud bang woke them both. Paavo was on his feet while Angie clutched her pillow, probably trying to figure out if she was dreaming or if the roof had just fallen in. She lifted her head and looked at him. "What was that?"

He pulled the bedroom drapes aside to see a strange glow in the sky.

"Call nine-one-one. Tell them it's a fire," he said as he put on trousers and shoes, then grabbed his badge and gun.

As he pulled a heavy sweater over his head, Angie put on her bathrobe and followed him to the door. "Don't go out there," he ordered. "Call."

He ran up the Filbert steps to Montgomery Street, not believing the sight before him.

Angie's Ferrari was a ball of fire, flames stabbing the night sky. Behind him, others emerged, sleepily confused and chattering, a few venturing too close to the burning car. He held up his badge. "Police officer! Stay back! Go back inside!"

The crowd wasn't about to disperse, but they didn't move closer. He walked around the car to its far side.

A man's body lay on the ground. The body must have been close to the car when it exploded, and had been flung aside like a rag doll. The clothes were still burning. Paavo turned away. One look and he knew there was nothing that could be done for the man. His hair was gone, his facial skin black and charred, his eyes dark pits. The smell of burnt flesh hit Paavo's nostrils.

"Oh, my God!"

Paavo spun around at the sound of Angie's voice. She had put on slippers and stood at the top of the stairs. He ran to her and grabbed her arm, not wanting her to see the horror on the far side of the car.

"What happened?" she cried.

"I'll tell you when I find out. Right now, go back inside."

"No. It's my car! My beautiful car!" Then she seemed to notice people's reactions to something on the opposite side of it. Paavo stopped her from approaching.

"Don't," he ordered. "A man's dead. Burned. You don't want to see him."

Shock and horror filled her face. Fire sirens and the shrill sound of police cars could be heard over the crackle of flames and murmurs of the still-gathering crowd. She backed away from the street and waited.

The police and fire trucks arrived at the same time. The firemen immediately began hosing the car with heavy water pressure.

Paavo met the uniformed officer and showed his badge. "The car is, was, my girlfriend's. I can give you the particulars. We were asleep when it happened. I don't recognize the victim."

"Does she?"

"The way he looks right now, I don't think his own sister would recognize him. I haven't asked her to look."

The policeman glanced at the victim, then nodded.

Once the car fire was out, Paavo moved closer to the burned man. A couple of patrol officers joined him. "Looks like a car bomb went off," one of them said. "I wonder if the vic was just passing by and unlucky, or if he'd been trying to rig a bomb up and had slippery fingers."

"Or if something caused an accidental detonation." Paavo pointed to a small hole in one side of the dead man's skull, and a larger hole opposite it. It looked like entry and exit wounds from a large-caliber handgun or rifle.

Instinctively the officer looked over his shoulder. Up Filbert were more steps and, a little beyond that, the circular road to Coit Tower on the very top of Telegraph Hill.

"That's right," Paavo said. "A shooter could have easily stood anywhere up there and found a clear shot. The question is, who was he?"

"There's another question, too," the officer said, looking at the shell of the car. "Who wants your girlfriend dead?"

Chapter 30

"We have a make on the marshmallow," Yosh said to Paavo, hanging up the phone. Yosh had returned from vacation and had quickly been brought up to speed on Paavo's cases, and also on Aulis's condition.

Toshiro Yoshiwara, a second-generation Japanese-American, was Paavo's partner. They'd had an uneasy start when Yosh first joined Homicide and was given the spot that had been held by Paavo's best friend and partner of many years, Matt Kowalski. Matt had been killed while investigating a murder, and Paavo had been reluctant to establish deep ties to a new partner. Since then, Yosh had proven himself to be an outstanding detective, a good partner, and an even better friend. He was a big man, "from the sumo wrestler part of Japan," he liked to say, with close-cropped hair, a thick neck, and powerful chest and arms.

"He was a Russian with ties to organized crime," Yosh said. "His name was Yuri Krakovar."

"Christ! Aulis being targeted was bad enough," Paavo said, "but now it's Angie. If I knew who was behind this, I'd say here I am, come and get me and leave the others alone. But I don't know how to stop it." The crime scene technicians had determined a plastic explosive device that would have been set to the ignition had blown up Angie's car.

"These Russians are scary," Yosh said. "You've got to get Angie out of there before they come back. Better yet, get her out of town."

"I brought her over to her friend Connie's house this morning. We need to figure out what to do. I don't want her family or friends mixed up in this."

"Any idea how the Russians found her?"

"She was on live TV yesterday evening. Apparently they were running promos about the show all day long. Someone who knew they were interested in Angie might have heard about her appearance. I'm guessing it was just a lucky break for them—not for Angie, though."

"She was on TV?"

"She did a restaurant review. Someone could have had her followed when she left the studio and went home. Or"—he thought of the photos she'd taken of Stavrogin sitting in restaurants where she'd been—"they've been watching her all along and for some reason decided to take action last night."

"This is weird, pal. First someone shoots at you, then a Russian enforcer warns you off, and the next thing, another Russian's trying to blow up Angie's car. I thought the Cold War was over. What the hell is this all about? Why would anyone go after Angie?"

"She's been asking questions about this case, about the past. Maybe she's getting closer than we realized."

"Don't worry, pal," Yosh said. "We'll find out who's targeted her."

"That's half of the million-dollar question," Paavo said.

"Half? What's the other half?"

"A bullet killed the bomber before he rigged it up to the car. Who pulled the trigger?"

Yosh nodded. "That's right. Whoever did had to have been a good shot."

"They found the slug—identified it as a Federal Premium hollow-point. It's high-powered rifle stuff—a sniper's weapon. Just like the slug that ended up in my front door."

"You don't see many people walking around San Francisco with one of those."

"That's what I would have thought, but all of a sudden we seem to be holding a convention for them, starting with Leonid Stavrogin."

"Why would Stavrogin try to take out his own man?"

"He wouldn't, unless there's been a falling out within the mob."

"Shoot," Yosh said, rubbing his temple. "With friends like that, who needs enemies? I don't want to have a war going on in the middle of this city between those guys."

"A cat-and-mouse game with the Russian Mafia is too dangerous to play. And I won't have Angie being the goddamn mouse. I've got to get her out of the way, then go after them directly. I want a piece of those bastards!"

"Whoa, Paavo. You're making this personal." Yosh eyed his partner steadily. "We know personal gets cops killed. Watch yourself."

"Yosh, it *is* personal."

"I don't want to do this, Paavo," Angie insisted. "Filbert Street is home now."

He didn't like it either. He had come to love the cottage and the garden-filled Filbert steps that led to it. But it was known that Angie lived there, and he couldn't take any chances.

"And I don't want you dead." He hustled her and her luggage into the enormous red, gold, and marble lobby of the Fairmont. He chose a big hotel where they could enter from a number of entrances and not be noticed. A place in which she could simply get lost among the crowds of tourists.

Angie had called ahead from Connie's for a reservation, then registered as Mrs. Nancy Yoshiwara, using one of Yosh's wife's credit cards. The desk clerk looked questioningly from her to Paavo, but didn't say a word.

"I don't want to stay here," Angie repeated quietly while the clerk stepped away to process the registration. "I want to be with you!"

Paavo didn't answer as the clerk returned with the key-card for the room.

They headed toward the tower elevators. "You can leave as soon as I know it's safe," Paavo said. "In the meantime, keep out of sight. I don't want you in any more danger."

They stepped onto the elevator. Angie pushed floor eight.

"It'll be hard for me to travel very far anyway, with no car," she said moodily.

"Good!"

They stopped talking as others got on. On the eighth floor, Angie had a question the minute they got off. "Will you come back tonight?" she asked.

"I'll try, but if I don't make it, be ready to leave early tomorrow to pay a visit to Eldridge Sawyer."

She frowned. "What about Aulis? Can I go see him?"

Paavo found the room and unlocked the door. He went in first. "They know you'll be wanting to go there," he said as he checked closets and the bathroom. "They'll be watching his room. I don't want them following you the way they did when you were on TV."

"You don't know that's what they did."

"I don't for sure, but it's a good guess. Keep away from Aulis. He's in a coma and won't know if you're there or not. If he wakes up and you still can't see him, I'll explain why not. He'll understand."

Angie sat on the bed. The hotel room was lovely, but it wasn't her apartment, or Paavo's house, and not even the bungalow they'd shared. "I don't like this, Paavo. I feel lost here."

He put his hands on her shoulders. "It's better you feel lost than I lose you."

She gazed up at him. "Be careful."

"I will."

"I love you."

"I love you, too," he said. "That's why I want you here and safe."

He kissed her, then left the hotel room. She put the dead bolt on the door, and turned around to face the tiny room alone.

If Paavo thought she was going to cower in some hotel room, he still didn't know her very well. She spent a while thinking through her plan, stopped in the Fairmont gift shop for an I LEFT MY HEART IN SAN FRANCISCO hooded sweatshirt, and headed for the hotel entrance where taxis flocked like hungry vultures.

As she rode across the city she kept glancing through the back window. She quit looking when the cabbie started staring at her in his rearview mirror. Judging from his smirk, he must have thought she was completely paranoid.

When the cab stopped outside Aulis's apartment, she paid the fare, pulled the sweatshirt hood up, and ran indoors.

Aulis had hidden Cecily's letter in a Ford mailer. Other important clues could be lying all around, waiting for someone to find them.

She began with the drawer filled with important papers. An hour later, she'd gone through every envelope, then continued on to the rest of the bureau, checking under clothes and even pulling out drawers to look under and behind them. She found nothing.

In the living room Aulis had a small desk where he kept bills and such. Going through each item there met with the same result.

Several cabinets lined the kitchen walls, but the house contained only one large closet. She headed for the bedroom.

Two boxes leaned against the back wall of the closet. Christmas decorations filled the first one. The next held yearbooks, report cards, and class projects from Paavo and Jessica's school years. Angie was awestruck as she went through them, the latest on top to the earlier ones farther down, glimpsing this part of Paavo's childhood. He was so skinny during early adolescence, she wondered that he didn't stab himself with his elbows. His haircut was probably cool at the time, but it made her laugh now. She had to force herself to stop reading school papers or she'd never get through this.

At the bottom of the box was a large paper bag. When she opened it, her heart lurched. She lifted out a little boy's blue and white striped T-shirt and jeans. They had a slightly gummy feel to them as she unfolded them and smoothed them over her lap.

Next she took out a pale yellow T-shirt, larger than the blue and white one, but not big enough for an adult. Girl's jeans, light blue tie-dyes, were under the T-shirt.

She checked the sizes, ten for the girl's clothes and six for the boy's. Didn't lots of boys wear that size when they were about four years old? The significance of the clothes—of the age—hit her.

"Oh, my!" A little brown stuffed bear, only about six inches tall, lay in the bag, right next to a half-dressed, scraggly-haired Barbie doll. She picked up the bear. One black-button eye was loose, and the red ribbon he wore around his neck was limp and bedraggled. He looked like an often-played-with little bear. Angie's chest tightened. He must have been a well-loved bear besides.

She smoothed his bow and felt tears form in her eyes. Could these have been the toys, the clothes, the children brought when they came to Aulis? Or an extra set Cecily sent with them? Was that how they ended up forgotten in this box?

Angie gazed at the spotless clothes. The memory came to her of how Paavo once described his childhood. That he was the boy in school whose clothes were too big or too small, who wore sneakers with holes, and socks that didn't match. He said he was the boy who other kids stayed away from. How different his life would have been had his mother lived—or stayed with him.

She put her hands in the pockets of the little boy's jeans. A Bazooka bubble gum was in it, plus a shiny black rock. Her hand tightened on them.

In the girl's jeans pocket was a pink plastic wallet with 101 Dalmatians on it. She found herself smiling as she looked inside. A picture of Paavo and Jessica was covered in clear plastic, in the spot where "big people" would put a driver's license. It was an adorable photo—Paavo, about age three, sat on a carousel pony, Jessica behind him, her arms around him, holding him in place. She leaned forward, cheek to cheek with him. They were both smiling broadly.

She searched the other compartments in the wallet, but all she found were three movie-stub halves, one adult and two child tickets, with the letters LOVE S before the tear, and BHT plus a string of numbers along the other edge of each.

What movie could the children have gone to back then with that title? *Love Story?* An odd choice for kids, but maybe Cecily had wanted to see it, and brought them along. Jessica probably appointed herself the keeper of the tickets. Angie had liked to be similarly "in charge" when she was a child.

She tried to remove the photo from the wallet, but it stuck to the plastic cover. In the kitchen she found a sandwich-sized Ziploc bag, put Paavo's pocket treasures in it, then placed it and the wallet in her tote bag. She picked up the bear and put it in as well. Paavo should see these things again. It wasn't all misery and sadness in his childhood. Happiness existed, too, and he shouldn't dismiss it so readily.

And it just might be good for Paavo to know his mother had a romantic streak and saw movies like *Love Story*. This wasn't the time to talk to him about love and romance, or to think much about them, but day by day in the little cottage, she could see the word *marriageable* appearing on his forehead with more and more clarity—no matter how much he outwardly dismissed it.

From Aulis's house, she took a taxi to the hospital.

She firmly believed that even though Aulis was in a coma, he had awareness, at some level, of what was happening around him. The idea that this man could be lying there feeling frightened and abandoned was more than she could handle.

The moment she realized she was going to go

against Paavo's wishes and leave the hotel room, she decided to visit Aulis as well. For the sake of his recovery, calming his fears and letting him know how much he was loved and cared for was important.

When she reached the hospital, the knowledge that she'd been followed in the past caused her to pull up the sweatshirt hood and draw the strings tight around her face. On the main floor, she slipped into the women's room near the cafeteria and removed the sweatshirt, black chinos, and running shoes she'd been wearing, and changed to a jersey jumpsuit and heels. She put the running shoes into her tote bag, and the other clothes, rolled up, under her arm. She hoped to have a chance to speak with Aulis's doctors. Although in the great scheme of things, it didn't matter how she dressed to meet with them, for whatever reason, it did to her.

She left the bathroom and rode the elevator to Aulis's floor.

In his room, she put her tote bag and clothes on a chair in the back, then walked to the side of his bed and took his hand. He looked thin and terribly frail, yet the way his eyes were closed and the peaceful look on his face made it seem he was simply asleep.

"Hello, Mr. Kokkonen," she said. "It's Angie. I know it must seem like it's been a while since I was here last. Believe me, I came back as soon as I could. Your doctors are wonderful. They keep Paavo and me informed of how well you're doing. You're going to be fine very soon. They've assured us of that. You know how Paavo is. He wouldn't let the doctors get away with anything less than your full recovery. It will take a few more days, though. You have to be patient. We all do. We're so much looking forward to you coming home once more. I'm sure you are looking forward to it as well."

She bent over and kissed his cheek. The doctors weren't nearly as upbeat as she had just said, but it would do Aulis no good to hear the truth. What he needed now was hope, and it was her job to give it to him.

"I love you, Mr. Kokkonen, and so does Paavo." She had to wait a moment to control her voice. "He loves you very much, so please be strong for him. Fight this. Come back to us. We want to talk to you and laugh with you. We're here waiting. Please come back to us."

She waited, but as always, saw no reaction whatsoever. She let go of his hand and turned around. To her surprise, the nun was standing in the back of the room beside the chair she usually sat in. Angie's things remained on the seat.

"Hello," Sister Ignatius said, stepping toward the bed. "I didn't want to disturb you, but I also didn't want to leave without Aulis knowing I'd been here."

"Please stay. I'll move my belongings from the chair."

Angie hurried to her tote, but mistakenly only grabbed one strap. As the nun was saying, "Don't bother, I have some other patients to visit," the bag tipped over and dumped the contents onto the floor.

Lipstick rolled, the electronic planner case flew open, the cell phone took a wicked bounce, Paavo's bear tumbled, Jessica's wallet opened and rotated end over end, the coin section of Angie's wallet unclasped and loose change scattered, and little pieces of paper fluttered and skittered around the room like snow in an updraft.

"Oh, my God!" Angie cried, running about, gathering up pieces of her belongings. She shook the Palm Pilot—luckily, nothing rattled.

"Let me help you," Sister Ignatius said, as she picked up the bear and gently smoothed the bow, and then picked up Jessica's wallet. She studied the photo silently.

"My boyfriend and his older sister," Angie explained.

"What lovely children they were," the elderly nun said softly.

Together they quickly dumped everything back into the tote bag. "Thank you, Sister," Angie said. Then she glanced at Aulis and again her face fell.

"Somehow this will all work out," Sister Ignatius said. "Have faith, Angie."

They both smiled at that, and the nun said good evening.

Angie stayed a short while longer, then went in search of his doctor.

Afterward she returned to the women's room near the cafeteria. Once again she changed into her black pants, sweatshirt, and sneakers, and walked out of the cafeteria with the hood covering her head.

Chapter 31

It was all Paavo could do to stand in Bond's waiting room while his secretary announced his visit. Visit—hah! He wanted to punch the guy's lights out—but Bond was a SAC. Paavo wouldn't be doing any investigating at all if he was locked up in a federal prison.

The secretary told him he could enter. Bond glared at him as he marched into the room. "What's this about? My secretary said you *insisted* on seeing me. That isn't how I operate, Inspector Smith."

"Your memory isn't what it should be, Special Agent Bond," Paavo said coldly.

Bond stiffened.

"You seemed to have forgotten not only that Cecily Campbell Turunen was married, but that she spied on her husband and his associates and he ended up killed by the Russian Mafia."

Bond took a nail clipper out of his top drawer and began to trim his nails and cuticles. "I have no idea what you're talking about, Inspector Smith. *Turunen?* Are you getting this information from Eldridge Sawyer?"

"No."

Only the click-click of Bond's manicure could be heard. "Have you found Sawyer?"

"I haven't found anyone," Paavo said truthfully.

Bond put the clippers away. "I think someone's been telling you outrageous tales, Inspector. We don't use research clerks to spy on anyone. My understanding is that she was a research clerk, and nothing more."

"You're wrong, Bond. What I've said is the only explanation for what's going on now. For people like Leonid Stavrogin accosting me and following my girlfriend. Or didn't you know about that either?"

Bond's face went white with restrained fury. "We keep an eye on men like him. If he confronted you, it was a warning, or you'd be dead. You've gotten too close to something. He could have simply put a bullet in you and ended any threats you might pose that way." Bond rubbed his fingers across his mouth. "Stavrogin had to know you'd recognize him as soon as you looked at some mug shots."

"I did."

"Damn! What are they thinking!" He ground his fist against his palm. "You understand this changes everything. The S.F.P.D. isn't equipped to handle the Russian Mafia. Few local law enforcements are. Since they're a part of this, we'll have to take over from here."

"I don't think so," Paavo replied coldly. "This—now—is about me, my stepfather, and my girlfriend. I'm not backing off."

"You have no choice." Bond's eyes narrowed. "The Russian Mafia is FBI jurisdiction."

"Just like Cecily Campbell Turunen's death? The FBI was called in to help find her, and apparently scarcely bothered to look."

"I don't know what you're talking about."

"You should. You're the one in charge. Eldridge Sawyer was the S.F.P.D.'s contact."

"Sawyer." Bond paled. He stood up then, his hands in his pockets, and walked to the window peering out onto Polk Street before he turned and spoke. "None of that matters, Inspector. It's ancient history. Stavrogin is now. He's a killer. A sniper. He got his training in Afghanistan, fighting on the Reds' side. He nearly took down a whole squad single-handed over there before the CIA and the Muhajadeen busted his base camp and he had to move. The guy's too dangerous for the S.F.P.D."

"No way I'm pulling out of this," Paavo said, bristling at the man's high-handedness. "I intend to find out what's really coming down and stop it. With the FBI's help or without it."

Bond folded his arms. "It could be Washington's choice. A few well-placed phone calls. Do you really think the chief of police will argue? Do you think the mayor will? They're political creatures. They'll tell you to keep your mouth shut and your nose clean, and you know it."

"Call whoever you want!" Paavo stood up and headed for the front door.

Bond stepped toward him as Paavo opened it. "The authority of the FBI—"

Paavo didn't bother to glance back as he walked out the door. "I don't give a damn about your authority."

Paavo was still struggling to control his anger when he walked into Angie's hotel room that same evening. "Paavo, what's wrong?" she asked, alarmed and also afraid to know.

"Bond—that FBI agent. Damn him! I'm sure he knows more than he's telling. If he'd just come clean, this would be so much . . ." His eyes caught hers. "You've got an odd expression. What is it?"

"Sit down."

His face went from anger to stark fear. Suddenly she realized what he must have been thinking. "It's not Aulis. He's the same." She saw his immediate relief. "I know you asked me to stay here, but I just made a quick run to Aulis's house." She reached into her tote bag. "I found this."

She took out the little bear and held it toward him.

Paavo stared at it without expression.

Had she been wrong? She had nearly cried over the stuffed animal and he had no reaction. "He isn't yours?"

His hand reached out. The toy seemed dwarfed in it. "He's mine." He fiddled with the dangling eye and smoothed the rumpled fur. "I used to sleep with him."

She knelt down on the floor near his feet, her hand on his knee as she watched a panoply of emotions flicker across his face.

"I'm amazed I remember him. I'd forgotten what my own father looked like, but I remember a crummy toy." He stared hard at it, as if waiting for it to talk to him, to tell him about the past.

"He's a very cute little bear," Angie said. "I know it sounds silly, but a part of me kept hoping you'd be glad to have him back."

Long moments passed. "I am glad," he murmured. "It's a silly connection, this child's toy, yet it brings me back." He struggled with the words. "As if I've gone in a full circle."

"And then?" she asked.

He rubbed the bear's ear. "Found *me*, all over again." He lifted agonized eyes to her. "I'm not making sense." He put the bear down on the table, but Angie noticed that he kept glancing at it, and every so often would fiddle with the ribbon or brush a minuscule speck of lint from it, even if only he could see it.

"I understand what you mean. And I'm glad," she said softly.

He drew in a deep breath. "Aulis didn't keep any other surprises like this, did he?"

"Wait until you see what I found in your pocket!" She gave a small laugh to lighten the mood.

He grinned back, curious. "My pocket?"

"A set of your clothes was there, along with your sister's." She quickly turned away and reached into her tote bag for the Ziploc bag. "One rock and a petrified piece of bubble gum. I wonder which is harder."

He took out the rock and rubbed it. She could imagine him doing that as a boy.

"And look here. Your sister's wallet. It's got a great picture of you both, and wait until you see the movie you went to! I have evidence, Inspector."

"What's this?" He took the wallet from her and studied the picture. Sadness tinged his eyes, even as he smiled.

"Look at the movie tickets," she said, wanting to give him something to laugh about. "In the money compartment."

He opened the section where cash would be kept. "It's empty."

"What? I'm sure they were there," she cried. "I can't have lost them! Oh, I'll bet when my tote bag tipped over at the hospital, they fell out." She went over to the tote and began pulling things out of it.

"What do you mean, at the hospital?"

Her hands stilled. "Well . . ."

He waited.

She left her tote bag and returned to his side. Confession time. "All right. After Aulis's apartment, I went to the hospital. Don't worry. I was very careful."

His shoulders slumped. "I can't believe . . ." He cut himself off. "You're sure no one followed you?"

"I'm sure. I can't tell you what I put the cab driver through."

"I can imagine, Angie." Unexpectedly he asked, "What movie did I go to?"

"Of all things, the ticket stubs were for *Love Story*."

"*Love Story?*"

"A weepy about a woman who dies," Angie said. "The great emotional wallow of its time. I never saw it."

"I've heard of it. And all the girls named Jennifer. It's nothing I'd want to see."

She grinned. "I think you already have."

Putt-putting along in Paavo's ancient, minuscule Austin Healey was a far cry from roaring over back roads in her dearly departed Ferrari. Angie had ridden in faster bumper cars. Every so often they had to stop, open the hood, and feed the mice.

Eventually they reached the beautiful—hah!— town of Gideon. Just looking at the restaurant made her stomach rebel. She had done a considerable amount of talking to convince Paavo that he would never find Sawyer's compound without her, and she didn't use the term *compound* lightly, even though he seemed to live there alone.

Past Gideon, the road wound higher into the hills, through a heavy pine forest. Angie had to watch carefully for the turnoff, and even at that, she nearly missed it. She felt as if they were looking for the Phantom of the Forest. Someone singing "The

Music of the Night" wouldn't astound her any more
than she already was by all this.

After another mile, a log house became visible
through the foliage. They got out of the car and
were approaching the house when the cocking of a
shotgun shattered the bucolic silence.

Chapter 32

Paavo raised one arm over his head, while the other grabbed Angie's shoulder, stopping her from going another step. He didn't need to. She was shaking too furiously to move.

"Take it easy," Paavo shouted. "I just want to ask some questions about a woman you worked with years ago in the FBI."

"You've got the wrong man," the voice hollered from somewhere behind them.

"Don't play games, Sawyer. I don't like it, and you don't either," Paavo said. "I just want to talk, then we'll be on our way and forget we ever spoke to you."

"How did you find me?"

"Let her turn around and you'll know." Paavo gestured toward Angie.

"All right."

Angie turned, and despite the weirdness, even despite the danger, she called out, "Hello! You were such a hero the other day, I can't believe you'd shoot me now."

Paavo turned too, but Sawyer remained hidden.

"Where's the other guy? The flashy one?" Sawyer asked.

"He's my cousin," Angie said. "He's back in San Francisco."

"Good place for him." Sawyer moved forward, and for the first time, Angie fully understood why his garb was called camouflage. "Okay, you two, you got more balls than brains coming here like this. What's it about?"

"I talk better if I'm not looking down the barrel of a double-gauge shotgun," Paavo said.

"And I don't want to talk to you at all," Sawyer responded.

"It's about Cecily Campbell. I know a little about her. I want to know more. I understand she worked for you."

"What of it?"

Paavo hesitated, then replied, "She was my mother."

Sawyer stared at them both a long while, then turned the shotgun so it rested across his chest even as his finger stayed on the trigger. "Let me see some ID."

Using two fingers, Paavo eased his badge from his jacket pocket. Sawyer motioned for him to toss it, and he did. Sawyer looked at the name and his eyes darted quickly to Paavo's face. "I still don't see why I should tell you a thing," he said, throwing the badge back to Paavo.

"You ordered her to take actions that eventually cost her her life. I want to know why," Paavo said. "The whole story."

"Me? You're wrong. I rarely saw her. I wasn't important enough for the likes of her."

"You were her boss."

"Only on paper."

"What do you mean, you weren't important enough?"

"I mean she was a conniving, scheming bitch. She

slept her way to everything she got, and then it blew up in her face."

Angie gasped and watched Paavo's reaction.

"Who was she sleeping with?" he asked coldly.

Sawyer's mouth twisted. "Tucker Bond is one. He was as ambitious as she was."

"Bond acts as if he scarcely remembers her," Paavo said.

"Scum rises, Smith. So do con men and liars."

"No one else said anything like that about Cecily," Angie added, unable to keep out of this any longer.

Sawyer's heavy legs were in a wide stance, his chin high. "Maybe they didn't know her well enough. Or maybe it's not something most people would tell a son. But hell, you two asked. It was all a long time ago. A lot of things happened back then that I didn't like."

"That's why you left, live up here like this?" Paavo asked.

"It might be a common story, Smith," Sawyer said, his tone sneering, "but there was nothing common in what went on there."

"The old-boy network in full force?"

"More than that."

Angie watched the strange male dance continue, both men establishing what they were about.

Paavo turned their discussion to Cecily's spying on Mika and his murder. "I understand the Russian Mafia was a part of it—and now they're back, after us."

"If that's so, it can't be because of what happened thirty years ago," Sawyer said. "The Russians couldn't care less. They aren't that way."

"Somebody does, and I agree, the danger is now, but its roots are old. There are too many coincidences to deny it."

"What happened back then is nobody's business

but mine. I'll tell you one thing and one thing only because you should know it. After Cecily saw the Russians kill her husband, she was going to go into the Witness Protection Program. But something scared her. She came to me for a *different* set of fake documents—different from the ones the Bureau was making for her. She was all broken up—said she was betrayed. Her lover didn't come through, I guess. She wouldn't give particulars. I helped her. I'm not even sure why, except that she'd been used and was paying big time for it. No one had ever trained her, taught her the way an agent would have been taught. She was thrown to the wolves and ended up being shredded by them. So I gave her a driver's license and birth certificates for her and her kids showing the name Smith—Mary, Jessica, and Paavo Smith."

Angie felt a chill all the way to her toes.

"She nailed the bastards that killed her husband," Sawyer continued. "Did you know that?"

Paavo stared without speaking a long while. "I had no idea."

"Yeah. Two of the smugglers. Then she disappeared—or died. Either way, after offing those Russians, she was dead."

I'm a dead woman. Angie remembered the chilling opening words of Cecily's letter to Aulis.

"So you don't know, either, what happened to her?" Paavo asked.

Sawyer paused, then said, "My guess is, she's dead."

"Killed by the Russians?"

Sawyer looked evasive. "Who knows?"

"What scared her about the Witness Protection Program?"

"Look, Smith, you're like a bad penny showing

up here after all these years. I've said all I'm going to. I don't want to hear from you—or anyone else—again."

"You know where to find me, Sawyer," Paavo said as he motioned to Angie and the two got into his car. "Think about it."

As they rode back to the city in Paavo's Radio Flyer, they tried to put together the pieces they'd learned.

"I don't believe Cecily was having an affair with anyone," Angie said. "I don't know how much I believe any of Sawyer's story. Maybe it was a mistake to come here."

"It wasn't. It's another piece of the puzzle. An important piece. Mika was killed, Cecily retaliated against the Russians, and somehow she ended up with the brooch. She must have pinned it on Jessica—that's got to be how she ended up with it, and probably why she never wore it again."

"Then I brought the brooch back to someone who worked with the Russian mob years ago, and he recognized it," Angie said.

"And called Harold Partridge," Paavo added. "Then the jeweler was killed, and a forger, and our homes ransacked. Partridge is a collector. He surely wanted the brooch, but he wouldn't have to kill for it. He could easily afford it. What am I missing?"

"Who owned the brooch thirty years ago?" she asked. "Let's assume it was brought to this country to be sold to raise money for the dissidents. Your father and his friends did that. Then the Russians killed Mika—believing he betrayed them. And in the course of it, the brooch went to Cecily."

"If we assume Partridge owned it or wanted it

thirty years ago, the timing of Rosinsky's call to him and the events that followed make sense."

"Sounds like you need to visit Mr. Partridge again soon," Angie said.

Paavo agreed.

Chapter 33

Donald Porter, the former museum curator, called Angie's cell phone the next afternoon. He'd found a peculiar story in a Russian newspaper about her brooch. A radical group of dissidents had removed it from the Hermitage, and while it was being smuggled out of the country, the smugglers were caught. They and the dissidents were arrested. The article did not say, however, what had become of the beautiful cameo of the Tsarina. The assumption was that it had been returned to the museum, but since Angie had it, obviously that wasn't true.

"That's an amazing story." She thanked Porter and hung up.

After relaying this information to Paavo's answering machine—he was never around when she called, it seemed—she did something she'd wanted to for some time. She caught a taxi for the trip across town to the Cypress Motel.

An up-close-and-personal view of the seedy area, however, made her question the wisdom of leaving the cab.

"Drive around a bit," she requested. "I'd like to take a look at this part of town."

"You get a kick out of slumming, lady?"

She didn't bother to answer.

Cecily and Mika's apartment was not anywhere near this area. While Angie could understand the family going into hiding after Sam was killed, what had made them come to this part of town?

The driver circled around several busy streets, knowing how to increase a fare. In the middle of a block stood a barren theater, its lobby boarded, and the outdoor ticket booth a poster board for graffiti and cheap, homemade flyers. "Stop!" she yelled.

The words Bernal Heights Theater stretched along the top of the now empty marquee. BHT.

Why would Cecily have brought her children this far from home to a movie? There were plenty of theaters in her area, much nicer ones, too. This area hadn't deteriorated in the last thirty years. It was always bad.

"Let's go back to that motel," she said, deep in thought. "And I'd like you to wait for me."

The cab pulled into the parking lot. Her chest tightened at the sight of the places Paavo had mentioned—Room 8 and the vending area.

"You looking for a room?" A rumpled, middle-aged man stood in the office doorway. As he observed the quality of her Jil Sander pants suit and Gucci boots, he openly ogled her.

"Hi." Her cheerful greeting sounded forced as she introduced herself and handed him a business card. "I'm writing a book on places of some notoriety in San Francisco—exciting spots that people will want to come and visit for a few days."

"I've never heard of notoriety being a drawing card." He frowned, as if she could make his business even worse.

"Oh, but it is. Think of all the people who drove by O.J.'s place on Rockingham Way," she said.

"But would they want to sleep there?"

"Trust me." She followed him into an office furnished in rattan with threadbare cushions in need of fumigation. He stepped behind the counter and swiveled his reservation book toward her. Hope springs eternal, she supposed. "I heard a famous murder happened right here thirty years ago—guns blazing, a Mafia hit, Al Pacino barking orders."

"You're the second person who's asked about that this week." He stroked his chin.

"There you go!" she cried. "Instant fame." She bent close, lowering her voice conspiratorially. "What can you tell me?"

"Nothing. I don't know nothing about it. I'll try to find out for you, though. Fifty bucks for tonight, special rate. I'll give you my best room. Tomorrow I might know something."

She straightened. "No way."

"Yeah, well . . ." He shrugged as if to say it didn't hurt to ask.

"Tell me," she said. "Do you know people you can ask about what happened years back?"

"Not really. It was strange, though, this place." He shut the reservation book and shoved it in the corner. "When I first bought the motel, there were a lot of weird people hanging around it."

"Oh? What kind?"

"You know." He bent forward, elbows on the countertop.

"No, I don't." She casually leaned a hip against it.

"Guys with guns."

Her knees went weak. "Criminals? Gangs?"

"No, no. Not that kind. Suits."

She could scarcely believe her ears. "Suits? You mean government types? G-men?"

"Yeah. You know, they all looked like Efrem Zim-

balist, Jr. They soon stopped coming after I took
over, but for a long time I'd always wondered if this
might have been used as one of those, uh, what do
you call it . . . ?"

She braced her palms on the counter. "A safe
house?"

"Yeah! That's it!"

Harold Partridge sat in the glow of the lamplight in
his big, empty house, a black lacquered Russian
jewelry box nestled in his hands. It was just a little
thing, with a design on its lid of a colorful, fairy-tale
village. For some reason, he loved this symbol of
the natural, peasantlike life he'd never had, of a
warm, happy home, of love and laughter.

Not like his own home, with two ex-wives and
three kids who hated him. At times, guilt and sorrow over the way he'd treated them nearly caused
him to apologize, but then, they didn't behave so
well toward him either. They didn't understand the
pressures he was under. The pressures of business,
and all he'd had to do to make it a success.

It wasn't really his fault. None of it was.

He heard a sound and nearly jumped out of his
skin. Leaping from the chair, his hand on his heart,
he peered into the darkness, trying hard to see. A
secret drawer in the lamp table held a gun, if he
could only reach it.

"Who's there?" he whispered. The gun caught
the light, but the face was in shadow. "Do you want
money? How much? Name your price, and go."

All was silent.

"What do you want of me?" he pleaded.

The last sound he ever heard was a gunshot.

That night, Paavo went to visit Aulis. A night lamp
beside the bed cast a dim yellow glow into the

room. In a dark corner, a nun sat quietly saying the rosary. He'd met her briefly once before.

"Oh my," she said, startled to see him. She jumped to her feet. "I'll be leaving. I don't mean to disturb you."

"You aren't, Sister. Please stay. I'll only be here a minute." He reached for Aulis's hand and held it as he greeted the old man. As ever, Aulis didn't stir in the slightest.

With a heavy sigh, Paavo sat down in a chair beside the bed and bowed his head, still holding Aulis's hand. He had spoken to the doctor on the phone and knew there was nothing that could be done but to wait, and hope.

"It gets to be almost too much, doesn't it?" Sister Ignatius asked, sitting down again.

"It does," he admitted. "It's maddening that I can't get through to him. Can't make him better."

"Sometimes it helps to talk, even if it's only to a sorry old nun who spends her days sitting in hospital rooms."

Her gentle voice warmed him. How could he trust her, though? Nun or not, he found it hard to open up to anyone, to tell others his inner thoughts and feelings. Yet when he gazed at her, something told him he had no reason not to trust this woman. He sensed he could confide in her as a person, not because she was a nun. It was disconcerting. He was a cop, not a psychic. Yet was there really so much difference? Sometimes he thought his most valuable cop's tool was his discernment. To his surprise, he wanted to talk.

"There's not much to tell," he said finally, sitting straighter. He kept his eyes on Aulis.

"You love Angie very much, it seems." The nun's voice came to him from the shadows in which she sat.

Her words surprised him, but then he realized the two women probably had talked at some length. Girl talk, as it were. Angie was that way—very open and easy to converse with. "I do," he admitted.

"Are you planning to marry?"

He kept his eyes on Aulis, and Angie's description of Catholic confessionals came to mind. "I'd like that. She thinks she would."

"You sound doubtful."

"At times."

"Why?"

The soft yellow night-light caught his attention. "Marriage means responsibilities, and to Angie, it means children. With my job, my background, I worry about doing right by them."

"Your background?"

"I have almost no experience with families and how they work. I consider Aulis my father, but I lost my real parents when I was very young."

"Don't you remember them at all?"

He paused, and the silence of the night hospital descended over the room. "I didn't think I remembered my father. Recently I saw a picture of him, and I discovered that I do."

"That . . . that's good." She sounded somewhat puzzled by his words.

"Only a few things, general things, a sense of him, if not the man himself."

"How old were you when he died?"

"Four."

"It's not surprising, then, that you don't have a clear memory." Her voice softened. "And your mother?"

He thought a moment. "I remember missing her." His reply was spoken as quietly as her question. "I remember telling Aulis at times I was going to run away and look for her."

"She . . . isn't dead, then?"

"I don't know."

"You never tried to find out?"

"No. I'll admit I thought about it. But as a child, Aulis taught me to forget about her. He said she was a heavy drinker, and hinted at a lot worse. When I asked Jessica—she was my older sister—she'd get upset, but in the end, she agreed."

The nun fell silent, and Paavo stared a long while at the night-light. "I spent a lot of time questioning, and wondering, about my mother. Wondering about the responsibilities of a parent, and if she had any idea how her kids felt being dumped on some neighbor's doorstep."

The nun's voice was gentle and soothing. "She must have known. Her going left a terrible void in your life—and in hers, too, I would imagine."

"I tried hard to blame her—and to hate her. It never quite worked."

He bowed his head.

"What about your sister?" the nun asked. "Did she remember your mother? Did she ever talk about her, or say she missed her?"

"We didn't talk much about her. When we did, Jessie would grow sad. She remembered her well. The way Jessie used to talk, she made me think mothers were some magical creatures who knew how to make everything better in your life. She said our mom—Jessie used to call her 'Mom'—would know when something was wrong even without us telling her, and she could make us feel better if we were sad. Jessie never gave up hope that Mom would come back. And then Jessie had no more time left to wait for her."

"I'm so sorry," the nun whispered.

The room fell absolutely still.

"If your mother is alive," she said, "I would

imagine she never gave up hoping to come back to you. Whether or not she succeeded was in God's hands. I think that if you were to believe, in your heart, that she wanted to return, you wouldn't be far off, and it would be a comfort to you."

He nodded.

She stood and gathered her things. "Gracious, I didn't realize how late it is. Sister Agnes must be having fits. I'm always Sister Slowpoke. I'm glad we had a chance to talk, Inspector Smith."

"Yes, so am I," he said, feeling the empathy in her eyes.

"Good night, Sister."

She nodded, and he heard the soft swish of her skirt as she left the room.

Chapter 34

Angie awoke late in the day. Paavo had called her last night, but he hadn't come to see her. She suspected he'd spent the night at Filbert Street, puzzling over the gunplay and danger around them, and possibly waiting for someone to approach the bungalow. The five A.M. news came on the radio before exhaustion overtook her worry and racing thoughts and she'd been able to fall asleep.

Before that, she'd spent a lot of time thinking. One question kept returning to her—why had Cecily brought her children to the Bernal Heights Theater? Irene had said she'd been worried about her boss, and Eldridge Sawyer would be plenty to worry about. Irene had also said she'd been visiting Cecily that last night when Sam called Mika and he left in a hurry. It made no sense that Cecily would suddenly decide to take the children to a movie, yet why else would the movie stubs from that particular theater have ended up in Jessica's wallet? Somehow it had to be connected.

As dawn lit the sky, Angie came up with a plan that seemed like a good one. Now, in the harsh light of day, she wondered if she dared try it.

* * *

Paavo turned onto Harold Partridge's driveway and immediately stopped. The large circular path was filled with blue and white cars from the Santa Clara County sheriff's office.

Paavo got out of his car and showed his badge. "What's going on?"

"Harold Partridge was killed. His housekeeper found the body this morning."

"Killed? How?"

"From what I've been told, a single shot, middle of his forehead."

Paavo left Partridge's home as soon as possible after talking to the investigator assigned to the case. The fellow looked stricken. Not only were there few murders in Santa Clara County's jurisdiction, no victims had been as famous as Harold Partridge.

Fortune 500 moguls getting assassinated in their homes tended to create lots of questions, even in the minds of green investigators, and Paavo answered as many as he could, keeping information about the Russian brooch out of the story. He explained his presence by saying that he was investigating Gregor Rosinsky's murder, and that the jeweler had phoned Partridge three days before he'd been killed.

He emphasized that he was unaware of any connection between Partridge and Rosinsky's murder, and that he was merely getting background information on the jeweler. He convinced the county investigator to let him leave before the press got wind that a San Francisco cop was there. They would have a field day speculating on any statement he might give them—including a "No comment." The last thing Paavo wanted was any publicity.

The investigator agreed, and Paavo left, uneasy

about his evasiveness and lack of candor. It nagged at him as he drove back to San Francisco and the Hall of Justice.

Back at his desk, he dialed Bradley's home number. It was already evening on the East Coast. When the special agent came on the line, Paavo asked him for all the background files, paperwork, or reports having to do with the FBI's attempt to place Cecily and her family into the Witness Protection Program.

"First, little if anything is put in writing in cases like that, and second, I can't do it, Paavo." Bradley's voice was subdued. "There are too many questions being asked about these files already. Someone noticed that they've been moving. It sent up a red flag. Any more requests and they'll want to know why. What you're doing isn't department business, and you're getting classified information. There's got to be a reason for it."

"There is a reason. Harold Partridge was murdered this morning."

"I heard. Hell, the whole country heard. You saying he had a hand in this?"

"That's right."

"Holy shit."

"Exactly. He was tied in, somehow, with what went down thirty years ago, and I need to find out what that was."

"Damn, Paavo, I can't do it. You know the penalty for unauthorized use of these files. It could mean my job, and if Partridge was a player as well . . ."

"A lot more than a job is at stake, Bradley. I've got to stop it. I think I've just skimmed the surface. The answer might be in those files."

"Look, I don't have those records anyway. They're in San Francisco. Background reports like you're talking about are in local files, probably microfiche, not anything we'd put in our database. And probably nothing exists, anyway! I can't help you."

"You can get me access to the files," Paavo demanded.

"I can't. They're there; I'm here."

"Fax me an authorization."

"I'm not high enough to authorize shit! I'm sorry, buddy, but you're on your own in this one."

Paavo hung up. Maybe he should try Bond again, see if he could get the guy to level with him. Bond clearly knew a lot more than he was saying, but until finding Sawyer, Paavo had no way to prove it. If he hurried, he'd get to the FBI before the office closed, although he expected Bond and many agents stayed around after hours, much like S.F.P.D. inspectors did.

He went down to the parking lot, to the city-issue car he was using. As he walked toward it, he heard footsteps behind him.

He turned to see Eldridge Sawyer approach. "Let's go for a ride."

"What's this about?" Paavo asked. Sawyer was wearing a suit, carrying a thin brown briefcase, and looked like the quintessential FBI agent.

"I've got some answers for you, but not here." Only the tough, wide-legged stance, the darting steel-gray eyes, resembled the survivalist Paavo had met earlier.

Paavo nodded and unlocked the unmarked Ford. Sawyer got into the passenger seat. "Head toward the Embarcadero," Sawyer said, looking from side to side and back to make sure they weren't being followed.

Once they passed the congestion of the downtown area, Sawyer seemed to relax.

"Any time you're ready to talk," Paavo said, "I'm listening."

"I thought a lot about what you were saying—and the fact that you found me. First, I'm moving on. Gideon's history. But I came across some files I thought you ought to see. They're about your mother."

"Files? Where did you get them?"

"There was a lot of shit going down when I was at the Bureau. I found out too much, and I didn't want to end up dead like Cecily and your old man. I would have been next."

"You worked a lot more closely with her than you wanted me to believe," Paavo said.

"What makes you think that?"

"If you hadn't, you wouldn't have known enough to be worried about. What was your role? Was she ever a research clerk, or did you know from the beginning that she'd be doing a lot more?"

"Take a right up there, then left at the next corner." Sawyer stared straight ahead as Paavo turned as directed. "You knew those times. We were suspicious of everything and everybody, especially those connected to so-called student movements. The groups behind them were no more students than I was."

"And if you could turn up some information no one else knew about, it would have made your career, wouldn't it? You called Cecily ambitious and deceitful—you were the same, right?"

"In the middle of the next block, pull over and park."

Again Paavo did as Sawyer said. They were in an industrial area near the water, the Bay Bridge directly overhead. Sawyer removed a folder from the briefcase and handed it to Paavo. "I never meant for it to end up this way." With that, he got out of the car and ran across four lanes of traffic to a white Chevrolet. The car started up and turned immediately onto the bridge approach.

Paavo could have made a U-turn and followed, but he saw no reason to. Whatever wrong or misplaced ideas Sawyer might have had in the past, he wasn't the one behind all that was going on now. All Sawyer wanted was to hide from those same people—a desire Angie and her cousin had disrupted. That, and an obvious sense of guilt, had brought him here today.

Paavo opened the file. It was filled with photocopies of Cecily's reports, Sawyer's reports, and notes about recruiting her for undercover work—having her befriend a female history professor as a way into the anti-Soviet movement.

Sawyer did a good job sanitizing the file, but still, his own cowardice came through loud and clear.

The investigative report at the end of the file stopped Paavo cold. It wasn't an FBI report at all, but an incident report, prepared by the Federal Building's own security staff in case of escalating trouble, of Cecily Campbell's attack on Tucker Bond.

As he read the eyewitness reports by Filomena Almazol and Roberta King from the typing pool, a clerk named Randy Fineman, and finally Eldridge Sawyer, a startling picture emerged.

Cecily had approached Bond in the building's parking garage as he arrived at work early on the morning of October 8, five days after Mika's death. As soon as he stepped out of his car, she ran up to him and began screaming at him.

All heard her accuse Bond of betrayal—that they'd met Thursday night, she'd told him "everything," and he had used and betrayed her. Bond tried to get her to calm down, but she didn't. She was crying, and said it suddenly had all come together for her. Looking at the words used, Paavo could see Sawyer's conclusion that the two had been lovers.

Bond protested that he'd done nothing, and she ran off, saying she'd get even with him—she'd make him pay.

When the security staffer interviewed Bond about the incident, he said he didn't know what Cecily was talking about, that he'd never met with her anywhere. In fact, on the night she'd alleged they'd met, he'd been out with a friend, and had proof.

Paavo went to the next page on-screen to see Bond's alibi. As he looked at it, he suddenly understood exactly what had happened.

Angie would have liked to give Paavo a call, but she didn't dare dig into her tote bag and try to steer this behemoth at the same time. The fellow at the Mercedes dealership had sworn driving an SUV was as effortless as any automobile when she'd asked to test-drive the ML55 AMG. But she felt like she was navigating a Muni bus, and everyone knew how often they got into accidents in this city. While she liked being up high, she had no idea what was happening along the sides or back of the SUV. Once she'd tried to change lanes, and nearly sideswiped a Honda Civic. She was just starting to get a feel for the side-view mirrors. On top of that, the car had so many dials and gizmos, she was afraid she'd jettison herself if she pushed the wrong button.

She needed a car for a number of reasons, like going to a grocery to stock the Filbert Street bungalow with TV dinners for Paavo, visiting Connie for some clear-eyed, not-caught-in-the-middle perspective on all this, and even going car-shopping at different dealerships. Trying to do all that in taxis was inconvenient and time-consuming. Besides, her hotel room was quickly resembling a prison cell.

The first stop on her itinerary was the most important. Last night she'd thought of someone who might possibly have a good idea of what Cecily had been up to the night Sam was killed.

Up ahead, the building loomed.

Street parking was all filled, as were nearby parking lots. An empty, yellow-painted loading zone took up most of the sidewalk. Heck, as far as she was concerned, the SUV was big enough to be a truck, and it was probably too late for deliveries anyway. She stopped the Mercedes at one end of the zone, locked the doors, and hurried across the street into the building.

As she rode up on the elevator, she checked her cell phone and set it to go straight to the message center so that it wouldn't ring and disturb her meeting. Immediately on reaching her floor, she turned away from the reception area and walked down the hallway, reading nameplates on doors for the person she wanted to speak with. She found the right one and knocked.

"Excuse me, miss." The receptionist stepped out of the public office and called to her. "You need to check in first."

"But this is the person I want to talk to," Angie said.

Just then, a tall, hawklike man opened the door. He looked down at Angie, then at the receptionist. "It's all right," he said. "I'll see her." He meticulously rubbed a speck of dirt off the doorframe, and then held the door wide for Angie to enter.

"Thank you so much," she said. "It'll only take a minute of your time. I wanted to talk to you about a movie-ticket stub I recently found."

Chapter 35

Paavo thought about Bond's alibi—a movie-ticket stub with LOVE ST right before the tear.

One edge of the ticket had a number on it, BHT00243. He knew many theaters used to number the tickets sequentially to account for box office receipts on a daily basis. If he could get hold of the ticket stubs for *Love Story* Angie had found in Jessica's wallet, the numbers would indicate if Bond and Cecily had attended on the same day—or possibly together. The ticket could substantiate Cecily's story, that she *had* met Bond that night . . . and that Bond might well have betrayed Mika and caused his death.

Paavo rubbed his temples, needing to think this through.

Cecily had been an undercover operative. It made sense that her contacts with her handler—Bond— would be covert. What better place than in a darkened theater? What better place to tell Bond that she, Mika, and the children were going into hiding?

Mika had been killed at the motel. In the attack it was apparent that the killers were also seeking Cecily—and possibly her children as well. Why else would the killers have unleashed firepower into every possible hiding place in the motel room after already slaying Mika? Only pure, dumb luck had saved Cecily, Jessica, and him.

After Mika's death, Cecily must have recontacted Bond. He offered to put her and the children into the Witness Protection Program. Having them under wraps would allow him time to plan his next move. Was it unconscious suspicion of Bond that had kept her from revealing where she and the children were hiding after Mika's murder?

Cecily must have been distraught, frightened for herself and her children. But in the days she waited as the WPP machinery moved to create new identities and a new safe place to live, she had time to think. Clearly. Coldly.

And what she came up with was chilling: Bond the agent; Bond the handler; Bond the betrayer.

Paavo could imagine just how desperate and alone Cecily must have felt as she pieced together Bond's pattern of betrayal. Paavo finally understood why she had decided to act as she had, as she realized that neither she or her children dared to be placed under Bond's control. Worse, she had recognized that if Bond gained possession of her children, he would have a weapon against her to force her to his will—and probably to her death. Cecily also must have feared for her children themselves, particularly Jessica, who was old enough to remember too much.

Paavo saw how his mother had analyzed her situation. From what he knew, he could all but envision just how she must have planned, and how she had set her plan in motion. First she'd killed the Russians who'd fired the weapons that murdered Mika, and then with both the Russians and the FBI after her, she'd staged her own death, leaving Jessica with an all-important envelope for Aulis with their forged birth certificates and Cecily's letters. Her task completed, she disappeared.

But why was all this coming out now?

And what was the role of the brooch in it?

Paavo had to talk to Angie and have her read out the numbers on the movie tickets she had. They were the proof he needed to confront Bond.

He called Angie's room at the Fairmont on his cell phone. The phone rang until a message service came on. He called her cell phone, and again received no answer.

He called Connie, and then Angie's sisters, but none of them had heard from her. His nerve endings crackled. Where could she be? She'd sworn she wasn't going anywhere.

Just then, Yosh called. "Has Angie reached you yet?" he asked.

"No. Did you talk to her?" Paavo asked.

"About an hour ago. She said she was going out—had a few errands, and that she had a serious question about something of Jessica's from Aulis's apartment. I hope you understand what she was talking about, because I sure didn't."

Paavo was beginning to feel a little panicky. "Unfortunately, I do understand."

He hung up, and began to drive. If Angie was concerned about something of Jessica's, she had to be talking about the movie-ticket stubs. He, too, had questions about those stubs.

It was time to get some answers.

Up ahead, the building loomed.

Street parking was all filled, as were nearby parking lots. An empty yellow-painted loading zone took up most of the sidewalk. It was too late for deliveries now. He stopped the car at one end of the zone, locked the doors, and hurried across the street into the building.

He rode up on the elevator, and immediately on reaching his floor, turned away from the reception area and headed directly toward the office of the person he wanted to speak with. He found the right one and knocked.

"Excuse me, sir." A security guard stepped out of the public office and called to him. "The offices are closed for the day."

He pulled out his badge. "Inspector Smith. I'd like to speak with Mr. Bond."

"I'm sorry, sir, but I believe he already left."

The woman watched the cop park his car in the loading zone. She slowly drove past, then pulled into a bus stop. A man waiting for the bus marched up to protest, but after one look at her cold, deadly eyes, then at the Glock on the passenger seat, he blanched and backed away, his lips sealed.

Within minutes, the cop raced from the building to his car. She waited until he drove by, and then pulled into traffic and followed a couple of cars behind him.

"Will you stop fiddling with those dials and drive!" Bond demanded.

"There's something wrong with the car," Angie said, making her voice as high, whining, and ditzy as she could manage. "I told you I can feel it straining." So far, she'd turned on the windshield wipers, hazard lights, headlights to high beam, seat warmers, and global positioning system. The car had a hands-free cell phone, and if she could keep punching enough buttons to slip in Paavo's cell phone number and then hit Send, she would. So far, even holding a gun on her, Bond had managed to undo most of what she'd done.

"Maybe we should stop at a gas station and have a mechanic take a look," she said.

"Drive!"

She did. Where was he taking her? They were going around in circles, and the sky was rapidly growing quite dark. She didn't like this one bit.

"Keeping me here is a stupid, ignorant, and foolish thing to do!" she cried. She hit the windshield lever again and the wipers screeched across the dry glass.

"Enough!" the man ordered, smacking the lever back to Off.

"You can't treat me like this!" She was shrill and nearly hysterical. "I'm an innocent person."

"Guess what." His voice turned low, lethal. "I don't care."

She tried pleading. "Let me go and I'll forget all about this. I promise I won't press charges."

"You've got to be joking."

"Who do you think you are?" she yelled.

"I think I'm someone who managed to pull together more wealth than you could imagine. Someone who won't let a twit like you stand in my way. Your friend Aulis Kokkonen is only alive because the sudden noise from a neighbor apparently made my man's shot go wide. Who would have imagined the old fool could hold on this long?" He moved his gun close to her side. "Believe me, no such distractions are here now!"

He had just pronounced her death sentence. Her hands tightened on the steering wheel, her voice meek as she said, "Oh."

Paavo swung into the parking lot at SF General and practically ran through the hospital to Aulis's room. Angie wasn't in it.

He went in search of a nurse and found one at the central station. "I'm trying to find out if my girl-friend, Angie, came by this afternoon to visit Aulis Kokkonen," he said. "I'm worried about her. She's about five two, a hundred fifteen or so—she swears she's one-ten, but I don't think so. Also, she wears these high, chunky shoes that add three or four inches, easy. She's pretty—beautiful actually—with short brown hair and big brown eyes, a classy dresser—"

"Stop." The nurse smiled. "I know Angie. I haven't seen her, but I've only been on duty since four."

"What about Sister Ignatius? Is she here? Maybe she's seen her."

"It's strange you should ask. Sister Agnes was talking to me about her. I'd assumed they were from the same convent, but they aren't. She hasn't been here all day either."

"The air outside will be chilly. I do hope you'll be warm enough in that jacket." Bond spoke as calmly as if they were headed for a sidewalk café. His voice was more chilling than the weather.

"I won't be," Angie said, now certain he'd sim-ply been stalling for night to fall and the streets to empty. They were far from downtown, driving in a residential area near the ocean. Cheerful lights shone through windows of homes, and she could feel the warmth emanating from them, making her colder and lonelier than ever. "And I'm not a part of this, either. I really, really want to go home."

The older man laughed. "Don't be naïve."

For some time she had noticed a car that seemed to be following her. Although it stayed far behind, whenever she turned, so did the black car with tinted glass. She would have liked it to be the police, but they didn't drive BMWs.

"Is this about the brooch?" she asked after a while.

"It's far beyond the brooch," he said. "Partridge cared about it, not me. He was a nervous, simpering fool."

Angie was confused. "Then why are you doing this?"

"Why? Because I have to do everything myself, that's why! Those Russians are inept."

"But I thought Partridge was the one behind it all."

"Partridge—yes, and Sawyer was the one who brought him in to work with us."

She was even more confused. "Are you doing this to help Partridge? If so, you're too late. It's been all over the news today that Partridge is dead. Someone killed him!"

Bond laughed.

Paavo's cell phone began to ring. Relief flooded him as he reached into his breast pocket to retrieve it. It had to be Angie. He'd left messages all over for her to call. The number calling wasn't one he recognized, but who knew where she was?

"Smith," he answered.

"Inspector Smith?" The sound of a man's voice was disappointing.

"Yes?"

"My name is Jim Emory from MBC Motors. I'm calling about Miss Angie Amalfi," the man said.

He tensed. "What is it?"

"She took one of our SUVs out for a test drive about three hours ago, and still hasn't returned it. You were shown as a reference, Inspector. We're hoping you can convince her to bring it back soon."

"I'm afraid I don't know where she is. I've been trying to reach her."

"Oh, that's no problem. She has a GPS and tracking device—that's a satellite positioning system. She turned it on and hit the emergency button, so we know where she is. Don't worry—we know it's not an emergency because she kept driving. Just a new driver trying all the bells and whistles. Happens all the time. Drives our emergency operators crazy, but that's part of the cost of business—"

"Where is she?" Paavo asked.

"I'm really sorry to bother you with something like this, Inspector. I hope you understand. She was driving around most of the evening, but now that she's stopped, we'd like our car back. Do you know how expensive ML55 AMGs are? They're beautiful, the fastest SUVs—"

"Hold it!" Paavo said, then spoke slowly and emphatically. "Tell me where she is."

Angie didn't like it here. To be in a dark, isolated, and spooky place with a madman holding a gun on her was not her idea of a good time.

"Now, Miss Amalfi," Bond said. "Let's begin with you giving me the ticket stubs, then we'll talk about who else knows about them."

From his reaction when she first mentioned the movie tickets, she should have realized her mistake. He wanted to photocopy them, he'd said, and when she told him they were in her tote bag in the car, he went with her to pick them up. Once she unlocked the SUV, he pulled a gun and told her to start driving.

She didn't dare tell him no one else knew about the tickets. He'd kill her and that would be that. But she also didn't want him to set a trap for Paavo.

"They're inside." She pointed at her tote.

"Find them."

Slowly she lifted one item at a time from the bag and placed it on the concrete floor. She had never been in this place before, and hadn't even known such a spot existed. The area was completely hidden from the roadway, and even that was little traveled. Still, they were in a city filled with people. Surely someone would come by in time, perhaps for a moonlit tryst. Or so she prayed.

"Hurry up!" he ordered.

The surf pounded in the distance. He could kill her and drop her body into the water—just like Paavo's mother. She, too, would be missing, and never found again. Is that what Bond did to Cecily? According to Irene, she'd feared her boss. Angie had assumed she was talking about Sawyer, but she'd been talking about Bond.

Angie slowed down more than ever. "Everything got dumped onto the floor not long ago. I don't usually carry so much, but I've been living in a hotel and haven't had time to sort things out."

"Just find them!"

"They're here someplace, but I can't see without some light. We need to go someplace with better lighting than the moon. Let's leave this place. Once I find them, you can take the tickets and go. You go your way, I'll go mine—"

"Shut up!" Bond yanked the bag from her, and pulled out a makeup bag, Palm Pilot, checkbook, camcorder, camcorder tapes, notebooks, pens, mechanical pencils, and a handful of small pieces of paper. He stuffed the papers back inside. Gusts of wind hit the area, and he didn't want to chance the tickets blowing away. "They've got to be here." Bond swore. "How can you collect so much junk? You and your idiot boyfriend are causing me nothing but trouble. He was gullible—just like his mother."

"His mother wasn't gullible."

"No? Could have fooled me! Damn, what are all these scraps of paper?"

"It's always necessary to have receipts for the IRS—for when I start to make a lot of money with my video restaurant review business. I need write-offs, you know. You work for the government. You know how it is."

"The IRS?" He looked at her as if she'd gone mad. "Who cares about them?"

"I do!"

"Lady, you know what they say about death and taxes? Well, guess what—you don't have to worry about taxes anymore."

The woman watched the cop leave the hospital and get into his car. She smiled grimly as she started the engine and followed.

"They aren't here!" Bond was furious.

"They are! You just missed them. Let me look." She grabbed the papers he'd already gone through, shoved them back into her tote bag, and pulled it toward her.

"What the hell are you doing?" Bond yanked one handle from her grasp and tugged it back. "You've just made it worse. Let go!"

"Worse?" She pulled the tote toward herself again. "I don't think so! Everyone knows about these ticket stubs, and everyone knows I have them, so if anything happens to me, they'll come looking for you."

"And I'll deny it." He tugged back, being careful not to let the bag spill. He wouldn't want the wind to catch the ticket stubs—he wanted them safely in hand so he could burn them.

"There's proof out there, and you know it or you

wouldn't care." Angie spat the words at him. "Who has the proof, Bond? Is it Sawyer? Did he know you killed Mika and Cecily? Is that why he's been hiding? We found him, you know. I spoke with him."

"I don't believe you!" Bond gave a hard yank and pulled the tote from her hands.

"Steel-gray eyes, six three, stocky, his hair was probably sandy brown when you two worked together."

"Damn you and your mouth! I'll shoot you right now!"

Chapter 36

Paavo found the silver SUV off-road in a remote area of the Presidio. Angie wasn't in it, and as he scanned the too-quiet landscape, his skin turned icy. Here were fifteen hundred acres of cypress, eucalyptus, and pine forests along the Pacific to the Golden Gate, filled with empty officer housing, barracks, and other structures brought about by the end of over two hundred years of military occupation. Countless possibilities existed to hide a person—or to bury a body.

His heart dropped. What was she doing here? She couldn't have come here on her own—someone brought her to this remote place. Who? Why? He feared whoever did it had but one purpose in mind, to kill her. Paavo couldn't imagine him waiting. He would shoot, then dump her body.

He remembered the guard saying Bond had left with a young woman who fit Angie's description. There were hundreds of young women Bond could have left with—no reason to think Angie had gone to see him, was there? She didn't know Bond . . . did she? But if she had questions about the movie tickets . . . and had used logic . . .

286

Whoever brought her here might want to use the SUV for his own getaway. So there was some chance that whoever came with her was still nearby. That she was still alive. That he could find her in time.

He had never been to this part of the Presidio before, and wasn't sure which way to go. Instinctively he walked away from the road and toward the ocean.

The lights of the roadway quickly dimmed, but up ahead the full moon lit an old gun battlement like a ghostly theater. Built along the edge of a bluff, it was about one and a half stories tall, a massive concrete structure upon which, at one time, heavy guns had been mounted to defend the coast against battleship and cruiser attack. Concrete stairs were built into it, and at the top of each staircase was a gun mount. Protecting the guns on the ocean, left, and right sides were tall, wide concrete platforms. Metal ladders led to the tops of the platforms where artillerymen stood with a clear view of the ocean to direct and service the guns. At the lower levels were small rooms where men worked and for gunpowder and artillery storage. Long ago the guns had been dismounted, and now the battlement stood like haunted monuments to a bygone era.

Moonlight on the salt-air-weathered concrete gave the structure an eerie, whitish glow.

He walked up a hill to get a better view of the battlement before him, and when he did, he could have shouted his despair.

Snaking along the edge of the coast, hidden from view of the road, were more and more of the concrete structures, with steps going up two stories to the gun mounts, and little rooms and tunnels tucked throughout.

How was he going to find Angie in there? And if he found her, would she still be alive?

* * *

In a fit, Bond threw her cell phone, Palm, address book, electronic planner, tapes, and even her camcorder over the edge. Angie had no idea what the structure was, only that they had walked up narrow staircases and tunnels and ladders to the top, and now sat face-to-face near the precipice, pieces of her tote bag and belongings spread all around Tucker Bond. As his frustration grew, so did his anger.

She heard her belongings crack and bounce on the rocks as they plunged toward the water. The thought that she might be next was the only thing that kept her focused on keeping Bond talking, keeping him distracted and interested in her and her questions. At this point she truly had no idea where the ticket stubs were, and gave thanks that Bond kept searching for them. The gun was at Bond's side, and she knew there was no way she could stand up and run before he'd pull the trigger and roll her off the ledge to follow her Palm. One way or the other, she'd end up dead.

"I still don't understand your role in this," she said, trying to ease herself away from him. She knew she was on the Presidio—maybe some MP patrols might come by, unless they, too, had been decommissioned. If she could hold out, someone would help her. She had to believe that. "Did you work for Partridge?"

"*Me* work for him? Hah!" His hands shook as he shredded her leather-bound pocket notebook, fastidiously ripping out gold-edged page after gold-edged page. "I was one of the few with the insight, the prescience, to see the promise in Silicon Valley, the future wealth there. He just needed a little help, that's all. The Finns approached him with the idea of swapping computer technology for Russian artwork. He had everything—and was too stupid to see it."

She remembered Paavo's description of his meeting with Weston. "You were the one who realized the possibility of combining some of the innovations of Soviet technology with Partridge's company, right?" His expression told her she was on the right track. "But the Soviet government controlled the technology. To get the Soviets to work with you and Partridge, you had to give them something in return, didn't you?"

"Think, Miss Amalfi! Where are the tickets?" He ripped the pages, his hands fisting around each sheet, his hysteria building.

"The Soviets wanted more than anything to stop the dissidents in their country," Angie said, guessing, trying to come up with some scenario to capture Bond's interest. "That was where Cecily came in. She could give you the names of dissidents in Russia and Finland with West Coast ties. She was young, innocent, and stupid enough to supply you with what you needed."

"She wasn't stupid—she was smart and ambitious," Bond said. "She could have become a special agent, or grown rich working with me and Partridge."

"Was that where the brooch came in?" Angie asked.

"Exactly," Bond said. "I was going along, just doing my boring, low-pay job, and then one day Partridge told me about the Tsarina cameo. Suddenly the whole idea came to me, full-blown. I knew Partridge wanted the cameo, but he *needed* Soviet technology to get a jump on his competitors, to become a power in Silicon Valley with me as his very silent partner. I also knew the Soviets hadn't been able to infiltrate the particular cadre of dissidents and smugglers working with the Finns, and Partridge and I could help them find those men. So we each had something the other desperately wanted."

"I was told the cameo had been used to capture a bunch of dissidents and smugglers," Angie said. "But I don't see how."

Bond snorted. "It was easy. Since the brooch was distinctive and extraordinarily valuable, and since Partridge was working with the Finns to buy valuable pieces for his collection, he asked for them to get it for him. He offered two hundred thousand dollars—which was worth at least five times that in today's money. Sam Vanse jumped at the chance, and moved heaven and earth setting his contacts in motion.

"At the same time, I went to the Soviets and offered them the people they wanted in exchange for the technology Partridge needed. The Soviets agreed. They then watched and waited, and when the time was right, moved in and rounded up all the dissidents and smugglers who took part in one fell swoop."

"So that was why the Finns got the blame," Angie said. "The Russian smugglers thought one of them leaked the information to the Soviet government. Or"—she was aghast—"you planted the story that the Finns betrayed them."

Bond smirked. "Now you do understand."

"But the brooch ended up in this country . . . ," Angie said, trying to piece together this last twist.

"Go on, Miss Amalfi," Bond said with a sneer. "Since you're so smart, then what?"

Paavo eased himself through the rugged land to the east of the battlements. He looked for light or movement, listened hard for any sound while staying within the shadows of the trees and brush, hoping against hope that he hadn't misread the situation.

Quietly he called Yosh on his cell phone. He needed backup, but not anyone charging in, setting Angie's kidnapper off, possibly hurting Angie if, in fact, she was here somewhere . . . and she was still alive. . . .

"When Partridge called you and said the brooch had reappeared," Angie said, racking her brain, "he was afraid the story might come out—that you and he were the ones who betrayed the Russians, not the Finns. I'm still missing something, though. I don't see how the brooch ended up in this country. . . ." She thought back to the information the museum curator had given her.

"Partridge was in a panic," Bond said. "He was always a skittish fool."

"Did Rosinsky try to blackmail Partridge? Was that it? I suspect he was going to have Jakob Platnikov make a fake to give me, so I'd be happy and not make waves. Did Partridge call you, Bond, telling you about Rosinsky's phone call? Did you kill Rosinsky and Platnikov to keep them quiet? You knew Paavo and I didn't have the brooch. Did you go after Aulis, thinking he had it?"

"I'm tired. You ask too many questions." Bond's eyes were wild.

"He's just a sweet old man." Her throat tightened. "Why did you try to kill him? He couldn't hurt you."

"He might have, if he told the cop what he knew." Bond sounded bitter and disgusted, and Angie realized the coma might have been Aulis's salvation.

He kicked the tote. "Enough of this!"

The woman silently crawled over the battlements, hidden in the dark by her black clothes. She knew this area well. It was a place she'd come years ago, a good spot to meet in secret. She didn't know where the cop was now. He'd taken a look at it and turned away.

She wasn't about to turn. She could smell her prey. She'd find him now. The weapon in her hand directed the way. For the first time in years she felt a frisson of excitement. Of triumph.

"You worked with one of the Soviets to sell the brooch ultimately to Partridge. Perhaps a corrupt official who caused the brooch to vanish while the smugglers were being arrested?" Angie stared at Bond as, horrified, she didn't have to guess any longer, but saw the steps, one after the other, that led to the tragedy. Fear left her and rooted; she gave him her vision.

Bond, equally fixated, listened with growing fury.

"Sam found out," she said, her voice hushed. "Sure—Sam, with all his contacts. They put their information together and must have realized it was an inside job. And when the brooch disappeared, Sam probably thought he knew where it was, with the man who wanted it, the one who put the whole mess into play—Partridge. Is that what happened?"

"Sam talked to Partridge by phone, and Partridge called me, terrified that Sam had figured it all out. Sam showed up at Partridge's home with a gun, demanding the brooch, believing it would be proof that the Finns hadn't betrayed the Russian smugglers. He took it and as he was leaving, Partridge shot him."

"Partridge did?" Angie asked. "But Mika would have recognized him, he owned Omega Corporation where Mika worked." The death report Paavo had relayed was making more sense. "Sam had a superficial wound to his arm—that was from Partridge, wasn't it? And since Mika didn't recognize Sam's killer, it couldn't have been Partridge. It was you, wasn't it, Bond? You went there after getting Partridge's phone call, and hid, waiting to see what happened. And ended up murdering Sam. I bet you never told Partridge, but let him think he was the killer. Was that part of the hold you had over him?"

"You're raving!" Bond cried.

Angie's eyes never left his. "Mika tried to get Sam to the hospital. He gave Mika the brooch, but didn't live to tell him its significance. You must have gone half-crazy trying to find the brooch. Searching crime scenes—probably even the evidence from Mika and Sam's murder. Did you finally assume it ended up on the bottom of the ocean with Cecily?

"She knew about a safe house." Angie could scarcely go on as the full force of Bond's evil turned her stomach. "She told Mika to go to the Cypress Motel while she met with you in secret, her children in the loges or elsewhere in the theater. She trusted you, Bond, told you about Sam and Mika, and the result was, her husband died."

The quiet roll of the surf could be heard in the distance.

"You killed them both, didn't you?" Angie asked, heartsick.

"Partridge called me in sheer terror, ready to crack." His voice was emotionless. "I assured him I would take care of it. After all, the Finns were mostly here on student and work visas; a word from the FBI ought to send them back to Finland where the mob would have a hard time finding them."

Angie stared at Bond. "But something went wrong."

Bond snorted. "That asshole shot Vanse. I was outside when it happened. Vanse came out of the house, wounded, and I knew then it wouldn't be possible to convince him to keep his mouth shut. I had to save Partridge's ass. So I followed him."

Angie cringed at the visions Bond's words conjured, feeling them as body blows. "You shot Sam in a spurt of anger—and Mika saw you!"

Bond smiled mirthlessly as he picked up the gun at his side. "I didn't know he was there. Partridge thought Vanse was alone. Up to that night, Vanse apparently hadn't told anyone Partridge was his contact in this. I was caught off-guard, and had to get away. But then I found Turunen. I had no choice, you see. Just like now."

A cold voice came out of the darkness. "All those years. I never knew why you killed them."

Bond's face went white, his eyes dilated as they searched the darkness. With a half sob, half laugh, he lunged at Angie and, as she screamed, whirled her around, pulling her to her feet in a stranglehold, her arm twisted and her spine tight against his chest.

Chapter 37

Paavo's blood froze at the sound of a cry, a woman's cry. It echoed through the walls, the tunnels, the myriad chambers of the battlements. Where was she? What was happening to her?

"Drop your gun, Bond," the voice said.

"No!" He searched the darkness in vain, then pressed the gun to Angie's head. "Leave here or I'll kill her."

A woman stepped out of the shadows. She was tall and thin, dressed in a black flak jacket, black slacks, and boots. She ripped the black cap from her short, gray-streaked hair. As she moved closer, in the moonlight, Angie could see her cold, green eyes; stern, narrow face; and the large automatic pistol she pointed at Bond.

Bond spoke, not in recognition, but a curse. "You!" He gulped air, tightening his grip on Angie, causing her to press closer to him. "I suspected it was you who ran over the Russian, and shot the other one when he was trying to put the bomb in the bitch's car. Even you who stopped Partridge's hired sniper from killing the cop."

The woman's smile was wolflike. "Nice fire-works, weren't they?"

Bond backed up, clutching Angie in front of him like a shield.

The woman followed, her footsteps soundless. "All these years of waiting. Of needing to know the truth. Why you killed Mika. Why! And all because of Partridge. You see, Mika didn't know about the cameo, what it signified. But you, after you shot Sam, you must have recognized Mika from my sur-veillance photos."

Bond chuckled viciously. "So you finally put it all together, Cecily."

Cecily. Angie's heart thudded. Paavo's mother. The resemblance came as a jolt, but once she saw it, she wondered how she had missed it before. She could blame the disguises, she thought with a twinge of the same hysteria she knew Bond was feeling. Colored contact lens, wigs, clothes, padding, all clever disguises, so clever she never recognized that Irene Billot and the nun—the nun who watched over Aulis and kept him safe from this killer—were the same woman, were this woman. But the resemblance that Angie should have caught went beyond disguises. They were there in the height and breadth of the brow, in the firm set of the mouth, even the quiet, pantherlike way she and her son moved.

Bitterness and hatred filled Cecily's eyes. "It was all a setup from the meeting in the theater. Mika was terrified on the phone. I told you that, didn't I? He'd seen Sam die in the drive to the hospital, but he thought you were part of the mob. He never knew that you were my boss. You sent us to the safe house to be killed by your Russian goons."

"It's too bad they missed you and your brats. We found the kids, by the way. About two years after you disappeared. Using the name Smith! How prosaic. But I admit, you had me fooled. When you didn't deign to show up at your own daughter's funeral, even I figured you were dead. Such a good mother!"

There were no tears, only an icy, brittle hardness and implacability in her. "I knew there were others involved besides you. But nothing I did in the past ever told me who or why. Not until this time. Not until I followed Paavo and his woman, followed the clues to Partridge. He was your weak link. And you killed him." She trained her gun on Bond. "And now I'm going to kill you."

Both Angie and Bond spoke at the same time.

"Drop the gun, Cecily, or I'll kill the little bitch!" Bond yelled.

"No! Wait!" Angie cried. "We can prove he's guilty."

Paavo recognized Angie's voice, and felt a relief so profound that tears came to his eyes. He heard Bond's voice. And another voice. A woman's. Eerily familiar.

"I don't play games, Cecily," Bond shouted. "Drop it now or I'll put a bullet in your son's girlfriend."

"No!" Angie was frantic, trying to wriggle free, but Bond's lock hold on her arm and neck only tightened.

Cecily didn't flinch, and the bitter realization that the woman didn't care hit Angie with a paralyzing force. Suddenly she was more afraid of Cecily than Bond. Bond needed her, but Cecily . . .

"Listen," she cried. "We've got Jessica's ticket stubs! That has to mean something or why is he so desperate to get them from me? With them, along with whatever we find in Partridge's records—and

we've found Sawyer, too; he knows a lot about all
this—together we'll be able to convict Bond. He'll
go to jail. He'll pay!"

Cecily didn't even look at her, but kept malignant
eyes boring into Bond. Her voice was inexorable as
death. "I didn't come back to put him in jail. I
needed to know why he killed Mika. The whole
truth, everyone who took part. I waited for the truth
so I could kill him."

A rush filled Angie's ears. Cecily was going to
shoot. She was going to kill Bond, and he, in turn,
would fire.

"Put down the gun . . . Mother." Paavo stepped
out of the shadows.

"Paavo!" Angie struggled harder, but Bond's
hold cut off her air and nearly tore her arm from its
socket. *No,* she wanted to cry, straining to breathe.
She saw Paavo's gun trained on his mother. *Not this
way, please God,* she whispered.

"Yes, Cecily, do as your son says," echoed Bond.
"Do it or I swear I'll kill her."

Cecily didn't avert her eyes. "Stay back, Paavo.
Don't get in my way."

Paavo stared at the woman in front of him, at the
gun she pointed at Bond.

She was quite different from the photos he'd
seen, not only in age, but much harder, much more
world-weary. He had always wondered what color
her eyes were. Now she was close enough that he
could see they were a light grayish-green color, and
that her once-auburn hair was almost completely
gray. But the shape of her face was the same as in
the photos, as was her nose, her mouth. He should
have noticed them earlier, even with the wimple.
He should have realized why the sound of her voice
in the hospital had such a strange effect on him. He
should have known immediately—rather than

merely suspected much later on—who the nun really was.

This woman was alien and familiar at once to him. He saw traces of himself in her, and memories washed over him, overwhelmed him with a child's joy, a grown man's sorrow, and a cop's futility.

All these weeks of confusion, anger, and longing, epitomized in this one moment. And this was all there ever was.

"Don't do it, Cecily," he said again. Not Mother, but Cecily now—actress, fugitive, killer. The grief that pierced him was sharper than any knife.

Cecily's face, her voice, were terrible. "I betrayed Mika! I loved him more than life, but I gave him to this bastard, and I never knew why."

Angie couldn't stop her tears. "No, you didn't! You couldn't have known. You didn't know he was working with Partridge. It wasn't your fault." She wept for the family broken apart by one man's heinous mistake and another's callous indifference, for the innocent lives lost, for the lies and deceit.

Bond sneered. "How touching! So you didn't come back for your precious son, Cecily. How does that make you feel, Inspector? I hate to break up this reunion, but Miss Amalfi and I are going to walk out of here now. If anyone makes a move, I'll kill her."

"You aren't leaving, Bond!" Cecily said. "Do you really think I can miss at this range? I've learned a lot these past years. I've worked in 'security'—I've learned how to kill. And you taught me all about being ruthless."

Angie saw the unyielding determination in Cecily's eyes and knew she would do as she said. Kill Bond. And she, too, would die. She didn't want the last sight of her life to be the barrel of a gun, and cast her gaze on Paavo, giving him all the love she felt. In her peripheral vision she saw Cecily's arm adjust to a firing position. She held her breath.

"No!" Paavo said with a passion that shook his voice. "Don't you do it! You, Aulis, Jessica, this gutless bastard—all of you deprived me of my parents a long time ago. Don't you take Angie from me, too! Don't you make me live alone for the rest of my life, regretting every minute of every day what happened here. Regretting the trust I gave. I can't, I won't live without her!"

Something flickered across Cecily's face, but Angie's eyes were too filled with tears to see clearly.

A loud report shattered the night.

Angie felt the gun barrel knock hard against her temple, felt shock waves blast through her body. She fell to her knees, her eyes squeezed tight. Not until she heard a thud and metallic clatter did she open them again.

Her gaze flew to Paavo. He stood staring at her, pale as death, without moving, without breathing. Then, when their eyes met, he was suddenly holding her, lifting, moving her away from the open area, his arms wonderfully tight about her, his heart pounding so hard his body shook from it. In a darkly shadowed area, he had her curl up as he hunched low over her, shielding her with his body. Gun raised, he peered into the darkness.

Cecily's gun was also raised, but toward the foliage beyond the battlement, her eyes searching it as she crouched and stepped slowly backwards toward them.

Angie didn't understand what had happened. She lifted her head and found Bond. Shock pulsated through her at the open, unseeing eyes, at the blood-soaked mass where the entire side of his head had been blown away.

"Hold your fire. We aren't after you," a heavy

voice called out. A man came up the stairwell and walked toward them, four others behind him.

As he neared, Angie saw it was the old man she had once met in a restaurant, the flirtatious Nick.

"What's he doing here?" she whispered to Paavo, sitting up.

"You know him?" Paavo asked.

"Nikolai," Cecily said. She stepped forward. Gun in hand, Paavo moved to her side, keeping Angie tucked behind him. She grabbed the back of his jacket just to have something secure—Paavo—to hold on to.

"We meet again, Cecily," Nikolai said. He glanced at Angie peeking around Paavo's shoulder. "And my *devuchka*, hello to you. My men saw Tucker Bond get into your car. They followed and called me, but unfortunately, lost you for a while in this infernal complex. I'm sorry."

Angie was stunned. Even more so when she saw, moving to his side, Stavrogin, holding a rifle. Her fingers gripped Paavo's jacket even tighter.

"Who are you?" Paavo asked.

"You probably know me as Koba," the Russian replied.

Cecily placed her hand atop Paavo's gun and pressed downward. Paavo lowered his arm. Angie realized why. Their weapons were of no use to confront this man. Koba—Nikolai—had a small army to protect him.

"I thought you were a better man than to work with a piece of shit like Tucker Bond," Cecily said to Nikolai, her chin jutting arrogantly.

He gave a loud laugh. "Perhaps now, older and hopefully wiser, I am." Then his eyes turned sorrowful. "We were all so young then, my Cilochka. Some terrible things happened. We made a mistake with the Finns, with your husband. I'm sorry for that."

She continued to glare at him with disgust.

"It was because of the Soviets," he continued. "How I hated them! After they imprisoned our people, we couldn't think straight. When Bond told us where to find Mika, we went and killed him."

"I knew it," she whispered.

"I didn't learn until later, after other things happened, how we had been deceived. Bond was a whore. He'd work with anyone he could use—the Soviet government, the *mafiya*, Partridge. And for us, it was helpful to have an FBI insider on our payroll."

"Yet you killed him?" Cecily couldn't hide her confusion.

"He was out of control and needed to be stopped. We couldn't afford Bond standing trial." Nikolai shrugged. "Such is life."

Cecily drew herself up tall. "So it is." She faced him squarely. "I suspect you want to shoot me, too, now. It doesn't matter, Nikolai. I've lived too long, anyway. But you said you regret what happened in the past. I have a way to ease that regret—let my son and his friend go. They aren't a part of this."

He turned the thin slits of his eyes toward Paavo and Angie.

"Just me, that's enough," Cecily said.

"Don't," Paavo said to her softly. She refused to look at him. All her attention was on Nikolai, her expression uncompromising.

"Let them go," she said.

"Your son is very stubborn, Cecily. I had Stavrogin warn him to back off, but he wouldn't listen. And he's a cop." Nikolai gazed at Paavo, then a long moment at Angie. "All right. He can go—and the young lady, too."

Cecily shut her eyes, but only for an instant.

Nikolai looked from mother to son. Then his gaze

met Cecily's and his expression hardened. "We will not meet again, Mrs. Turunen. The scorecard is even between us. I think I've grown far too old and fat and sentimental for all this. I will let you go as well, even though you know too much about my operation, and you've killed too many of my men. It's true Bond sent them after your son and his friend, but some of my associates do not take kindly to having our men . . . intercepted, shall we say?" He smiled at Cecily's silence, one professional to another. "Exactly. I will hold them off for forty-eight hours. Enough time, I'm sure, for you to disappear again. And my present to Miss Amalfi for the fright we caused her today."

With that, he turned and left.

In the distance came the sound of police sirens.

Cecily faced Paavo then, without a word. Her large green eyes seemed to soften, and he knew he'd never forget the way she looked at him at that moment. He understood that too much had happened, too much death and murder, and she had no choice but to leave now, just as she had so many years ago.

Emotions so strong, so unexpected and turbulent, filled him. She had walked out on him when he was a boy, and hadn't been there all the times he had felt sad and lonely and needed her so much it seemed the center of his being was nothing but a huge, empty hole. She had grown old without him, just as he had lost his youth without her, but now he understood why she'd done it, and that made all the difference.

A moment passed, and then she straightened her spine and raised her chin. He saw that she kept herself under even tighter rein than he, that she had learned the hard way to be self-contained, and that if she was to survive, she had to continue to be stronger and tougher and more alone than he could imagine. Her look said everything and his heart filled with feelings long denied, filled until he thought it would burst. She nodded—once—then turned and walked away.

His arms closed around Angie, gathering her to him, needing her, her love, her warmth, her essence, kissing her and touching her as if to make sure she was really there and all in one piece. He tasted her tears, felt them against his face, and they cut through all his defenses. He shattered inside and tears stung his eyes.

She returned his kisses and caresses, trying to soothe him. His voice was broken and tear filled. "I was so scared. . . . I can't, I don't know if I could have stopped her. . . . God, Angie, I don't know . . . I don't think I could have shot—"

"Hush, Paavo." She placed her fingers against his lips, stopping such words, words no son should ever have to say. "You couldn't have hurt her, Paavo. You couldn't have. She's your mother."

Blue eyes seemed to study her and found her understanding, her acceptance, and her love. He sagged against her. With both a smile and also tears in his voice, he whispered, "Yes, she is my mother."

Angie held him close and kissed him lightly and sweetly at first, until the fire between them ignited, and her kiss grew into a tongue-touching, body-pressing, rapture-building, heart-filling kind of kiss, one that went on and on and showed him fully how happy she was to be alive, happy to be with him, and euphoric over his words about her, about the two of them together. That was what mattered. That was everything.

Forty-eight hours, Nikolai had said. She and Paavo would clean off the sweat and smell of death at the hotel, check out of it, and then she would go with him back to the little house on Filbert Street. Cecily knew where it was, and it was in a safe, secluded location. She and Paavo would wait there. They had forty-eight hours. *She'll come,* Angie told herself. *I'm sure she'll come. . . .*

Chapter 38

A week later, Paavo sat on the edge of Aulis's hospital bed, Angie on a chair at his side. Two days earlier, the old man had come out of his twilight sleep, and with each passing hour had grown stronger and more lucid. His vital signs were excellent, and the prognosis was for a full recovery.

Propped up with pillows, Aulis was eager to hear what had happened since he'd lost consciousness. The doctors had finally given Paavo and Angie the okay to relate the whole story. What they told him, though, was a simple, sanitized version, leaving out most of the dangerous parts.

But Paavo did tell him he had learned about his past.

"I'm glad you finally know the truth," Aulis said. "So many times I wanted to tell you, but I was afraid for you, and of what you might want to do if you learned. I think Cecily's way of handling this was right. If the people who were involved were still so dangerous thirty years later, her instincts to save her children were good ones. I'm glad she got to see what a fine man you turned out to be. You do Mika proud. It's like having him back again."

"Thank you," Paavo said, touched by the words about his father.

"The irony of it all," Angie added, "is that we had to make Tucker Bond a hero by saying he'd died trying to rescue me from kidnappers. His shooting has now been added to the long list of Koba's crimes. To blame the Russian Mafia was, unfortunately, the simplest explanation for his murder, and Partridge's, and all the earlier gunplay."

"I suppose it doesn't do much good for anyone to point out what really happened," Aulis said.

"None at all," Paavo replied.

"It's grim." Aulis shook his head, and they all silently thought about the strangeness that had transpired.

"What isn't grim is that Angie has a new business," Paavo said, trying to make the mood upbeat again. "She's on television!"

"Really?" Aulis smiled. "Well, she's pretty enough, that's for sure. She could be Vanna White if she wanted to."

"She's doing even better." Paavo gave her hand a quick squeeze. "Video restaurant reviews."

Angie felt a little sick inside. It was a subject she'd carefully avoided, and had hoped Paavo had forgotten about. No such luck.

"Ah! I've never heard of anything like that." Aulis's voice was so filled with enthusiasm, she would have gladly crawled under the bed.

"That's the idea," Paavo said. "Angie came up with it all by herself. It's a winner."

"Paavo . . ." She looked from one man to the other. "I'm afraid that idea didn't work out. I'm going to have to drop it."

"You are? Why?"

"Well . . ." How could she tell him? She drew in her breath. "After I did my first review on TV, I was hit with four lawsuits. One was brought by the restaurant owner, who claimed I had no right to show the interior of his business on television." Her throat became dry. "Another was from the cook, saying I had slandered him." Beads of perspiration broke out on her forehead. "Another came from the waiter. He said he should have been paid standard actor's rates because he's a member of some actors' guild waiting for a big break. And the last"—the room began to spin—"the last plaintiff is a customer, who's suing for alienation of affection because my camcorder caught him at the restaurant with a woman who wasn't his wife. Now his wife wants a divorce, and he says it's all my fault!"

Paavo sucked in his breath.

As Angie drank some water to compose herself, the old man chuckled. "Well, at least, child," he said to Angie, "you did get back your Christmas present, didn't you?"

"Well, yes and no," she said, feeling a little better. "Paavo realized that the brooch must have gone to the forger, Jakob Platnikov. Platnikov had a granddaughter who liked it and had put it in her backpack to show a girlfriend in school, knowing her grandfather usually didn't work on jewelry until evening. But when she came home he was dead. Paavo explained to the girl that the brooch was very valuable and had to go back to its owner. Even though she'd kept it hidden from others who asked about it, she gave it to him."

"So you do have it?" Aulis asked.

"No. Its rightful owner, we learned, was the Hermitage in Saint Petersburg. A friend, a retired museum curator, helped us send it back to them with a letter saying it was being returned compliments of Mika Turunen and Sami Vansha."

"Ah, that's good. Very good." Aulis shut his eyes

as she spoke, and now, even though he commented and wore a smile on his face, she could see how tired he had grown. Soon his breathing deepened, and he was asleep.

Paavo caught Angie's eye and motioned toward the door. She nodded, stood, and moved quietly toward it. Paavo stopped in the doorway and took her hand. At the same time, he gazed back at Aulis. He loved these two, and felt their love for him. And for the first time in his adult life, he was able to accept the love they had to give. It was such a cliché, he wanted to laugh at himself, and yet, knowing who his parents were and why they had left him meant more to him than he could ever have imagined.

He felt as if he had needed to get over that hurdle before he could know where his heart was. And now he knew. It was with the people who mattered more than anything else in his life—with Angie, with Aulis, and with the mother who loved him, wherever she might be . . .

From the kitchen of Angelina Amalfia

ANGIE'S PASTA WITH PROSCIUTTO AND SUN-DRIED TOMATOES

This is one of Paavo's favorite dishes. The mincing and chopping take a little time, but the actual cooking goes very fast.

1/4 cup butter or margarine
1/4 cup olive oil
4 garlic cloves, minced
1/2 tsp. crushed red pepper
1/4 lb. thinly sliced prosciutto, cut into thin strips
1/2 cup drained sun-dried tomatoes, chopped
1/4 cup fresh basil, chopped
1/4 cup fresh Italian parsley, chopped
1 spring onion, chopped
1 lb. angel-hair pasta
Parmesan cheese

Cook angel-hair pasta (about 7 minutes) and drain thoroughly.

Put butter and oil in a large skillet, and melt them over a medium-low heat. Add the garlic and red pepper and cook until the garlic is golden (1–2 minutes), stirring frequently. Next add the prosciutto, tomatoes, basil, parsley, and onion. Heat thoroughly (4–5 minutes).

Place pasta in a large serving dish. Pour sauce over pasta and toss, mixing sauce throughout.

Serve with Parmesan cheese.

ANGIE'S AMARETTO-PECAN BREAD PUDDING

This is another of boyfriend Paavo's favorites. It's not traditional bread pudding, but is similar to Mexican-style *capirotada*, with a hint of Italy. It's one of Angie's specialties.

12 slices French bread, crusts removed
2 teaspoons butter
1¹/₂ cups sugar
1¹/₂ cups water
1 cup apple juice
2 tablespoons butter
¹/₂ cup raisins
1 teaspoon vanilla
1¹/₂ teaspoons Amaretto (or omit Amaretto and use an extra ¹/₂ tsp. vanilla here)
6 oz. soft cream cheese
³/₄ cup pecan pieces
1 teaspoon cinnamon
Whipped cream or nondairy (Cool Whip–type) topping

Preheat oven to 350 degrees. Butter a 9-by-13-inch baking dish (use the 2 tsp. of butter here). Tear bread into bite-sized pieces and place it in the buttered baking dish. Toast in the oven for ten minutes.

While bread is toasting, put the sugar in a large saucepan. Over medium high heat, stir the sugar continuously while it melts. When it is melted (it will turn a light caramel color), stand back from the saucepan as much as possible and add the water and apple juice to the sugar. Watch out—when the cold liquid hits the melted sugar, the caramel will splatter, bubble up, and most of it will solidify. Keep it on the heat and soon the caramel will liquefy again. Keep stirring. Add the butter and raisins. When the caramel is completely liquefied, remove the saucepan from the heat. Stir in the vanilla and Amaretto.

Pour the mixture over the bread pieces in the baking dish. Be sure to saturate all the bread with liquid. Drop dollops of cream cheese throughout the bread. Sprinkle the top with pecans and cinnamon. Bake at 350 degrees for 20 to 25 minutes.

Serve the pudding warm, topped with whipped cream or nondairy topping. Serves 6 to 8.

Murder Is on the Menu
at the Hillside Manor Inn
Bed-and-Breakfast Mysteries by
MARY DAHEIM
featuring Judith McMonigle Flynn